"I won't marry you!"

Halfway across the churchyard, Mattie heard Jared calling her name. She didn't stop until she heard his footsteps behind her. She turned to find him towering over her.

"Listen to me, Mattie. We're going back into that church and we're—"

"No!"

"You can't raise this baby by yourself!"

"Yes, I can!" She looked up into his face and saw that Jared was as angry as she.

"Listen to me—"

"No, you listen to me," she told him. "I have a home and a business. I have friends to help me. I'm perfectly capable of raising this baby myself. And that's exactly what I'm going to do."

"You don't know what you're saying. You don't know what you're up against."

Mattie reined in her temper. "This doesn't concern you. Everyone thinks this baby is my husband's, and that suits me fine."

"Well, it doesn't suit me at all!"

* * *

The Widow's Little Secret
Harlequin Historical #571—August 2001

Praise for Judith Stacy's recent works

The Blushing Bride
"…lovable characters that grab your heartstrings…
a fun read all the way."
—*Rendezvous*

The Dreammaker
"…a delightful story of the triumph of love."
—*Rendezvous*

The Heart of a Hero
"Judith Stacy is a fine writer with both polished
style and heartwarming sensitivity."
—Bestselling author Pamela Morsi

JUDITH STACY

THE WIDOW'S LITTLE SECRET

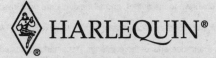

HARLEQUIN®

TORONTO • NEW YORK • LONDON
AMSTERDAM • PARIS • SYDNEY • HAMBURG
STOCKHOLM • ATHENS • TOKYO • MILAN • MADRID
PRAGUE • WARSAW • BUDAPEST • AUCKLAND

ISBN 0-373-29171-X

THE WIDOW'S LITTLE SECRET

Copyright © 2001 by Dorothy Howell

This edition published by arrangement with Harlequin Books S.A.

® and TM are trademarks of the publisher. Trademarks indicated with ® are registered in the United States Patent and Trademark Office, the Canadian Trade Marks Office and in other countries.

Visit us at www.eHarlequin.com

Printed in U.S.A.

Available from Harlequin Historicals and
JUDITH STACY

Please address questions and book requests to:
Harlequin Reader Service
U.S.: 3010 Walden Ave., P.O. Box 1325, Buffalo, NY 14269
Canadian: P.O. Box 609, Fort Erie, Ont. L2A 5X3

To David, Judy and Stacy—the greatest family

Chapter One

Nevada, 1887

It just wasn't right, being envious of a dead man. Still, that's how Jared McQuaid felt sitting on the hotel porch, watching the funeral procession roll by.

He glanced down at the *Stanford Gazette* on his lap. The headline announced the untimely death of Del Ingram, and the front page article extolled the man's many virtues.

A knot formed in Jared's stomach. What were the chances? He'd showed up in this town just today and read the obituary of a man he'd grown up with miles and miles from here. A man he hadn't thought of in years.

According to the newspaper, Ingram had died from a fall. Jared had figured ol' Del was more likely to have been killed by a jealous husband, an irate wife or a poker player with an eye for cheaters.

Not so, according to the newspaper. Del had made something of himself here in Stanford. Owner of a restaurant, a solid citizen with a sterling reputation, he'd had a life any man would envy.

Jared touched his hand to the U.S. Marshal's badge pinned to his vest beneath his coat. Seemed he and his boyhood friend had taken very different roads when they'd parted company some fifteen years ago. This wasn't the man Jared remembered. But maybe Del had changed.

Jared sure as hell had.

The rocker creaked as Jared leaned back and watched from beneath the brim of his black Stetson as the funeral procession passed by. Matched sorrels pulled the wagon bearing the coffin, their hoofs stirring up little swirls of dust. Two dozen mourners followed, all dressed in black, their somber faces flushed red from the raw March wind.

Jared glanced west. Charcoal clouds hung over the Sierra Nevadas, blocking out what was left of the day's sunlight. He had nothing to do, no place to go, no one to talk to until morning when he would relieve Stanford's sheriff of his two prisoners and head to Carson City. Jared may as well pay his respects to Del Ingram, even though he'd never especially liked him.

A few people glanced at Jared as he fell into step behind the mourners. One woman eyed the Colt .45 strapped to his hip and the badge on his chest when the wind whipped open his coat. She chanced a look at his face, then turned away, wondering, he was sure, who he was and why he was here.

Jared found himself on the receiving end of a hundred such looks nearly every time he came to a town like this. Not that he blamed anyone, of course. He'd arrive one day, eat supper alone in some restaurant, sleep in a nameless hotel, then take custody of his prisoners the following morning and disappear.

And those were his good days. Most of the time he was on the trail, sleeping in the saddle, eating jerky and cold beans, hunting down some rabble-rouser who'd broken the law.

He was used to both—the life and the looks he got. Jared had been a marshal for nearly ten years now.

At the cemetery on the edge of town, six men unloaded the coffin from the wagon. Del Ingram's final resting place was deep; freshly turned earth lay beside it.

Reverend Harris stepped to the foot of the grave, yanked his black, wide-brimmed hat over the tufts of his gray hair and struggled to hold open the fluttering pages of his Bible. The townsfolk gathered in a close knot, straining to hear the reverend's words. Jared moved off to one side, uncomfortable among the mourners.

As was his custom, Jared's gaze moved from face to face, sizing up each person assembled there. He was good at it. It had saved his life a time or two.

From all appearances, everyone who was anyone in the town of Stanford was assembled to mourn Del's passing. They all looked prosperous, in dress and in manner. Jared spotted the mayor and his wife; he'd met the man earlier in the sheriff's office. Sheriff Hickert wasn't present, but Jared hadn't expected him to be. He was nursing a nasty leg wound from the shoot-out that had garnered the two prisoners Jared was transporting tomorrow.

The gathering shifted as Reverend Harris reached for the woman standing in front of him. Jared's stomach bottomed out.

"Damn..."

The widow. Del's widow. Jared felt like he'd been sucker-punched in the gut.

He didn't know how Ingram had acquired a prosperous business, a good home, a sterling reputation—and he sure as hell couldn't imagine how he'd found himself such a fine-looking wife.

Even in her mourning dress she looked fit and shapely. She'd draped a black lace scarf over her head, but tendrils of her brown hair escaped in the wind and blew across her pale cheeks. She stood stiff and straight, her full lips pressed tightly together as she gazed past the reverend to some point on the distant horizon.

Jared thought she looked brave, determined not to break down. He wondered if she'd fully accepted the sudden loss of her husband, dead not quite two days now. He'd seen that happen before, where a long time passed before reality set in—and only then did loved ones fall to pieces.

Who would be there to hold Mrs. Del Ingram when that happened? Jared wondered. He wondered, too, why the thought bothered him so much.

He recalled the newspaper article he'd read, and remembered no mention of Ingram having any children. Indeed, no little ones hung on Mrs. Ingram's skirt, sniffling, reaching up to her. Jared found that troubling. The widow was truly alone now, it seemed, without even a child to comfort her.

"Let us pray," Reverend Harris called.

As heads bowed, Jared pulled out the newspaper, which he'd crammed into his pocket, and searched for the widow's name. Matilda. "Mattie," the mayor's wife had called her in a quote.

He turned to her again. His breath caught. Mattie Ingram hadn't bowed her head for the prayer. She was looking straight at him.

Their gazes met and held. She didn't blink, didn't falter, didn't hesitate, just looked at him long and hard, with the biggest, brownest eyes he'd ever seen.

Heat flared in Jared's belly, spreading outward, weakening his knees and making his heart thump harder in his chest.

"Amen," the reverend intoned.

"Amen," the gathering echoed.

Only then did Mattie turn away. Flushed, Jared pushed back his coat to welcome the chilly wind.

He watched her, silently willing her to turn toward him again. But she didn't. Rigid, restrained, Mattie accepted condolences, then headed back toward town, with the other mourners crowded around her.

Standing beside the mound of dirt at Ingram's grave, Jared followed her with his gaze, the bustle under her dark dress swaying, the vision of her deep brown eyes still boring into him. Finally, she disappeared from sight. Jared headed for the closest saloon.

Almost nobody was inside the Lady Luck when Jared passed through the bat-wing doors. Two men stood at the bar; the gaming tables were empty.

"Pretty quiet in here," Jared said to the bartender.

"Everybody's paying their respects," he said, and nodded outside, "down at Mrs. Ingram's place."

Jared should have known that. The mourners would gather at the widow's house, eat the food they'd brought, and talk one final time about the departed.

Jared leaned his elbow on the bar. Had he been on the trail so long he'd forgotten how civilized people acted?

Over the next few hours the saloon filled with men, drinks flowed and the noise level rose. Everybody who came in had something to say about Del Ingram. Jared stood at the bar sipping his drink, trying to block it out. By the time he'd finished his fourth beer he'd heard all the tributes he could stand to hear about the man he remembered to be a first-rate scalawag, the man these townsfolk admired so much.

Outside, the cold wind whipped around Jared as he headed down the boardwalk toward the hotel. It was dark now. The town had closed up for the night.

But when he reached the hotel, Jared kept walking. He didn't stop until he got to the edge of town, to the sturdy house with the picket fence he'd read about in the newspaper. The Ingram home.

And a fine home it was. Neat, clean, well built. A house fit for one of Stanford's most prosperous citizens.

The front door opened and a woman stepped onto the porch, outlined by the glowing lamplight behind her. Jared's heart lurched. Was it her? Was it Mattie?

The woman pulled two small children out of the house behind her and shut the door. Disappointment caused Jared's shoulders to sag a little. He nodded politely to the woman when she passed him on her way back to town.

Minutes dragged by while Jared stood at the end of the boardwalk, looking at the Ingram home. He didn't want to go inside and hear anyone else talk about what a fine man Del was; Jared had had his fill of that already.

He muttered a little curse directed at himself. What kind of man was he, thinking ill of the dead? Had he forgotten all the good manners he'd once prided himself on?

Slowly, he nodded in the darkness. His solitary life on the trail, hunting down criminals, hauling them in for trial, had taken its toll.

The decent thing to do was go pay his respects to the widow of the man he'd grown up with. Del made something of his life and he deserved all the things being said about him. Jared would go into that house and say something nice about him. It was the right thing to do.

And he'd get to see Mattie Ingram again.

Jared crossed the road, passed through the little gate outside the house and stepped up onto the porch. He paused for a moment before he knocked and brushed off his trousers, then took off his hat and smoothed down his dark hair, glad he'd taken a bath and gotten a haircut this afternoon.

He rapped his knuckles against the door, then waited, waited and waited some more before it opened. He'd expected to find the reverend's wife greeting mourners, but instead Jared found himself face-to-face with the widow herself. A long moment dragged by while he just looked at her. When Jared finally came to his senses, he clasped his hat against his chest and tried to think of something to say.

"Mrs. Ingram? My name is Jared McQuaid. I'm— I'm real sorry about your husband."

She stepped back without really looking at him, and opened the door wider. "Won't you come in?"

He followed her down the little hallway, past a neat parlor, to the kitchen at the rear of the house. The room was warm and comfortable. A cookstove and cupboards were at one end, a sideboard and a table and chairs at the other. All manner of food—or what was left of it—covered the table. Jared's steps slowed. No one else was in the house. Had he intruded, when he'd intended to comfort?

"Is it too late to come calling?" he asked.

"No," she said simply, and turned toward the cupboard. "I'll get you something to eat."

Jared watched her skirt swirl, and glimpsed her white ruffled petticoat, then studied her backside as she stretched up and retrieved a plate from the top shelf of the cupboard.

He muttered a silent curse at himself for admiring Del's widow.

"Your husband and I grew up together," Jared said, as he shrugged out of his coat and laid his hat aside.

Mattie didn't answer, just turned again and began filling the plate from the dishes on the table.

"We went to school together," Jared said, feeling the need to say something. He took a step closer. "I'm a U.S. Marshal, just in town for today. I'm leaving in the morning. I read about Del in the newspaper."

Silence filled the house as Mattie heaped food on the plate, and Jared pulled on the back of his neck.

"So, while I was here I wanted to tell you how sorry I am that Del's passed on," he said. "He was a good man. Everybody in town speaks highly of him."

Though Jared didn't understand it, it was true. And regardless of what he thought about Del Ingram, this was his wife, the woman who loved him. She'd married him, lain with him, walked through life with him. The least Jared could do was think of something nice to say.

"Fact is," Jared said, "I never heard so many kind things said about one man before. I was down at the

Lady Luck just now and Del was all anybody talked about.''

A little gasp echoed in the kitchen, and Jared saw Mattie press a hand against her lips. Damn it, what was he thinking, mentioning that he'd been at the saloon? That wasn't what women liked to hear from strangers in their home.

Jared pushed his fingers through his hair. "The mayor…the mayor had nice things to say, too."

She dropped the plate she'd been preparing and leaned forward, bracing her hand on the table. Little sniffles filled the room.

Good Lord, he'd made her cry. Jared stared at her slumping shoulders as she tried bravely to stand upright. He wanted to go to her, take her in his arms, comfort her. But should he? He didn't even know her.

He wasn't sure what to do but keep talking.

"The newspaper article about Del was just about the most glowing report I'd ever read. And that eulogy, that was something, all right."

A sob tore from her lips and her whole body quivered. Jared stepped closer until he stood mere inches away.

He wanted to hold her. Oh, he wanted to hold her like he'd never wanted to hold another thing in his life. She looked so frail and helpless; her sobs sounded so pitiful. He wanted to press her against his chest and let her cry, keep her in his arms until her tears stopped.

"Your husband was a good man. He was well respected, and honest, and hardworking,'' Jared said softly. ''You've every right to be upset, Mrs. Ingram.''

''Don't call me that!''

Mattie swung around, hot anger boiling inside her. She drew back her fist and struck Jared in the chest.

''Don't ever call me by that name again!'' she screamed. ''He was a bastard! A lying, conniving bastard!''

Mattie braced one hand against the table to keep herself up, unable to hold the words inside any longer. She'd done that for nearly two days now, and she couldn't contain them another minute.

''I've had to pretend since he died—pretend that he was a good man, pretend that everything said about him was the truth.'' A sob tore from her lips. ''But none of it is true. None of it!''

''Mrs. Ingram—Mattie—maybe you should—''

She batted away Jared's hand when he reached for her. ''It was all a lie. Right from the beginning. Del never loved me.''

Jared eased closer. ''Things might seem that way now because you're upset, but—''

''He told me! Just before he died!'' Another wave of tears poured down Mattie's cheeks.

Jared frowned. ''He told you he never loved you?''

Mattie nodded, the hurt and humiliation throbbing in her chest. ''He fell off the roof and was injured badly. He knew he was going to die. So he told me. He told me everything. How he followed another woman here to Stanford because he was in love with her. How he couldn't have her because she was marrying someone else. How he married me because I had a restaurant, a good home, a good reputation, money.''

"Son of a..."

Mattie gulped, her strength draining away. She latched on to Jared's arms, gazing up at him. "He just used me," she whispered.

Mattie fell against him, sobbing, the pain too great to bear alone. She felt big arms close around her. She snuggled deeper against his hard chest.

With a sharp, ragged breath she lifted her head and gazed up at Jared. "I went by the bank today. My account was nearly empty. He'd taken my money, gambled it away, most likely. Lord knows he never worked a day since I married him. I had to use the last dollar I have in this world to bury him!"

She fell into racking sobs again and slumped against Jared's chest. Gently, he stroked his fingers down her back, fearing Mattie was on the verge of all-out hysteria.

"You need the doctor," he said. "He can—"

"No!" Mattie pulled away. "No, don't get the doctor. Don't get *anyone*. I don't want people to know how stupid I was, how I let myself be swept off my feet by a man I hardly knew. Everyone said I shouldn't marry him, but I wouldn't listen. I believed that he loved me. I don't want the whole town to know what a fool I was.''

Jared shook his head. "Mattie, you're too upset. You need—"

"—to forget," she said, wiping away her tears with the back of her hand. "I need to forget."

Jared froze as she gazed up at him. The look on her face sent a warm tremor through him.

"Make me forget," she whispered.

Mattie came fully against him and rose on her toes, pressing her lips to his throat. "Please...make me forget."

"Now, just a minute." Jared caught her arms and tried to ease her away. "You're not thinking clear."

"I don't want to think clear. I don't want to think at all," she said, and slid her palm across his chest.

He backed up, but she moved with him. "You don't mean that."

She meant it. With all her heart and soul she meant it. She ached deep inside. She wanted it to go away. She wanted to feel something different.

And who better to do that with than this stranger, who'd be gone in the morning?

Mattie circled her arms around his neck and pressed her lips to his. He pulled away.

"We were married for nearly a year, but he hadn't touched me in months—months!" she said. "Please, I can't lie alone in that bed tonight. I just can't."

Jared hesitated, studying her in the dim light.

"You can do it, can't you?" she asked. "You can make me forget?"

"Damn right I can," he said. "But that's not the point."

"What's wrong with it?" she asked. "I'm not a married woman...not anymore."

"I know, but—"

"I want this," she whispered. "Don't make me plead with you."

"But..."

Mattie stepped away and held out her hand to him. "Please, just make me forget."

He didn't move, not for a long minute. Then, finally, Jared reached for her hand.

Chapter Two

Morning sunlight filtered through the window, illuminating what had to be the dressing table of the widow Mattie Ingram.

Jared, his eyes just opened, studied it as he lay curled on his side at the edge of the soft feather bed. Lace, doilies, fancy bottles, all belonging to the woman who at this very moment slept behind him...

He relaxed against the pillow, his body spent but humming with the contentment only a night with a woman can bring.

Make her forget, she'd said. He'd obliged her numerous times during the night, the last just before dawn. Now, still, he wanted to take her in his arms, do it all again—which didn't make Jared feel particularly proud of himself.

Last night had been different. Standing in the kitchen, Mattie had looked alone and vulnerable. She'd needed somebody—him.

Jared had thought he could just hold her in his arms

and comfort her, and she'd fall asleep. Once in her bedroom, though, Mattie had made it clear that wasn't what she wanted from him.

True, he could have told her, flat out, "No." But she was already feeling bad enough. Spurning her seemed cruel, making her beg intolerable.

Still, he'd tried to convince her otherwise, but she would have no part of it. Del might not have touched her in months, but Mattie knew what she was doing, and Jared had been on the trail too long to resist her considerable charms.

So he'd accommodated her. Given the widow what she'd asked for at her most vulnerable moment.

Why did that leave his gut churning this morning?

Jared didn't rise from the bed, though he thought he should. Instead, he lay still, recalling the last time he'd awakened in bed with a respectable woman. His thoughts swept back, and when the memory came he played it over in his mind a few times, something he'd forbidden himself to do in years past. Surprisingly enough, it didn't hurt so bad. Not now, not this morning.

Not with Mattie in the bed behind him.

In that instant, it all seemed surreal. Jared didn't move, didn't stir on the mattress, didn't roll over to curl against her. If he did, would it all shatter? Would last night and this moment prove to be a dream? The dream that had crept into his sleep so often lately?

He remained where he was for a while longer, on the linens that smelled like Mattie, gazing at as much of her room as he could see—the lace, the figurines, the pictures on the walls. Their clothes scattered across the floor.

No, it hadn't been a dream, he decided. None of it. Jared rolled over, anxious to have her in his arms again.

But the sheets were cold and the bed was empty.

Mattie was gone.

A dozen things needed doing—no, a hundred things.

Mattie darted to the cupboard in the kitchen of the restaurant she owned on Main Street and pulled down a serving platter. The room was silent except for the crackling fire she'd just laid in the cookstove, struggling now to take the morning chill out of the air.

No one else was in the restaurant—not Mrs. Nance, who did the cooking, or the Spencer girls, who served the guests, or Billy, who washed the dishes. None of them had probably even considered that Mattie would open for business today.

She gripped the platter tightly. None of them knew how desperately she needed to open the restaurant today.

And no one would ever know.

Another wave of humiliation washed over Mattie, bearing down on her painfully, bringing the memory of her husband into her mind. How could she have been so stupid?

When Del Ingram had arrived in Stanford a year

ago, he'd taken one look at her and sworn he'd fallen desperately in love. And Mattie had believed him. He'd been so convincing, how could she not? He'd been kind and thoughtful. He'd brought her gifts, praised her every move. He'd been mannerly, well dressed, wise and worldly. He seemed like a godsend.

Mattie had been lonely since both her parents had died the year before Del's arrival. She'd stayed in the house they built and taken over the restaurant they started, and she'd done well for herself. In fact, the restaurant had improved considerably under her ownership.

It helped that her mother was no longer around to do the cooking. Mama, bless her heart, wasn't the best of cooks. Mattie had hired Mrs. Nance and business really picked up.

With pride, Mattie gazed around the kitchen, through the door to the dining room. She'd made other changes as well. Blue checkered linens on the tables, vases with fresh flowers from Mrs. Donovan's garden. She improved the menu to offer heartier meals.

As a result, the restaurant looked so inviting and the food tasted so delicious diners appeared often and regularly, including the mayor and the reverend with their wives and children, out-of-town guests and dignitaries. The town's businessmen had made the Cottonwood Café their spot for breakfast almost every morning. She sent a wagon over to the train depot to bring in diners during their layover. Almost no one commented on the modest price increase she'd made.

All of her changes had paid off handsomely. Everything was going wonderfully. And still seemed to be when Del arrived in town.

Mattie sighed in the empty kitchen remembering how lonely she'd been back then. Even with the restaurant keeping her busy day and night, she'd led a solitary life.

She'd longed for family, wished for her house to come alive with voices and laughter as it had when her parents were alive. She'd caught herself watching enviously as women in town strolled the streets with new babies in their arms. After all, she was twenty-one years old, certainly of sufficient age to have a family of her own.

Del had come along, seemingly just the sort of man she'd prayed for. Then, everything had changed.

After their marriage, which many in town had cautioned her against simply because no one really knew him at the time, another side of her husband emerged. Lazy, shiftless, domineering. He'd insisted on taking over her finances. He'd shouted at her when she questioned what he was doing with her money. He began to spend more and more time away from home. Some nights he hadn't come home at all.

Mattie sagged against the worktable, holding the serving platter against her stomach. She'd never known where she'd gone wrong as a wife. She'd lain awake nights wondering what to do. She hadn't wanted anyone to know the state of her marriage, or how she was treated by her husband—a man the town admired because he was so good at deceiving everyone, as he'd deceived her. She couldn't admit how wrong she'd been in marrying him.

Mattie pinched the bridge of her nose, her mind spinning. It seemed that now, this morning, she could hardly stand up under the weight of it.

If only she could forget.

She bolted upright. Oh, heavens. Last night.

The kitchen door burst open with a gust of cold wind, and a man filled the doorway, his hat pulled low, his long coat whipping around him.

The serving platter slipped from Mattie's hand and shattered on the floor.

Oh, heavens. Last night.

He slammed the door and crossed the kitchen, his gaze sharp and penetrating beneath the brim of his hat. Mattie gulped and backed up a step.

Stopping in front of her, the shattered platter on the floor between them, he gave her a long, grim look.

"I woke up and you were gone," he said, and his tone told her he was none too happy about it.

"I had to leave," she said.

"Why?" His gaze hardened. "Because you were done with me?"

Heat bloomed across Mattie's face, reddening her cheeks as a deeper wave of humiliation swept through her. She'd thrown herself at him—a perfect stranger. She'd asked him to make love to her—practically begged him to do it.

How could she have done such a thing? Never in

her life had she even imagined doing such a reckless thing.

Mattie turned away, unable to look him in the eye. "Last night...last night was a mistake, Mr...." She glanced back at him. "I'm sorry, what did you say your name was?"

"McQuaid," he growled. "Jared McQuaid."

Mattie gulped, trying to force down her embarrassment. "Oh, well, yes of course. I remember." She cleared her throat. "As I said, Mr. McQuaid, last night was a mistake."

"You didn't seem to think so just before dawn."

She winced, remembering what they'd been doing at that particular moment, and her cheeks burned anew. "Well, no, I suppose I didn't. But still, it shouldn't have happened."

"Why not?" he asked. "Seemed to me you needed it."

She moaned with humiliation and squeezed her eyes closed for a moment, clasping her hand to her chest.

"Why wouldn't you?" he asked. "Your husband hadn't made love to you in months."

She gasped and spun to face him again. "How did you know that?"

"You told me."

"I told you that?" she wheezed.

"Yeah. You said it somewhere between 'make me forget' and 'don't stop now.'" Jared leaned closer. "Sound familiar?"

"Oh, heavens..." Mattie spun away, unable to tolerate the heat of his gaze, or the heat burning inside her.

She stalked to the cupboard at the rear of the kitchen and pulled out the broom and dustpan, desperate for something to do. But when she started sweeping up the broken serving platter she felt even more conspicuous with Jared scrutinizing her every move.

Her skin tingled where his gaze touched her. Memories of last night sprang into her mind. She'd never experienced such a night—never imagined it was possible to do some of the things they'd done. Even on his best night, Del, her own husband, had been woefully lacking in comparison.

Mattie cast a furtive glance at the man towering over her, then focused her gaze on her chore. Jared McQuaid was ruggedly handsome. Well over six feet tall; she remembered brushing her legs against his longer ones during the night.

He had big shoulders and arms; he'd rolled her around the bed with considerable ease. A hard chest; her fingers had raked over it a good portion of the night. Thick, black hair; she'd yanked on it more than once.

Now, this morning in the light, she saw that his eyes were blue. The very last secret the man held.

Thanks to her wanton behavior last night.

Mattie cringed, a deeper heat crackling inside her.

But he'd made her forget, just as he'd boasted he could. She'd forgotten all her troubles. And how welcome that had been, even for those few hours.

His strength went beyond the physical. In her kitchen last night she'd seen it. Jared McQuaid could carry the weight of his own troubles, plus hers and dozens more.

Another shudder passed through Mattie and her cheeks heated again. Embarrassment. Humiliation.

What else could it be?

Mattie made tiny strokes with the broom, trying to make the chore last as long as possible. If he saw she was busy maybe he would simply go away.

She wanted him to go away. Good gracious, how she wanted him to leave. She never wanted to lay eyes on this Jared McQuaid again, or to be reminded of last night.

She'd propositioned a stranger. Wrestled him like a wild bear. And liked it.

A little whimper slipped through Mattie's lips at the thought. She dashed to the trash bin with the dustpan full of broken china, and took her time emptying it.

Closing her eyes for a moment, she said a silent prayer that when she turned around, Jared McQuaid would be gone.

"Why are you here today?" she heard him ask.

With a sigh she turned and saw him wave his big hand around the kitchen.

"Nobody expects you to be open for business," he said. "Not today."

Mattie stuffed the broom and dustpan into the cupboard, a little peeved that he wouldn't take the hint, do the decent thing and leave her alone with her humiliation.

"Since you're brimming over with my personal information, and have such an excellent memory of everything I said last night, perhaps you'll recall that my husband left me penniless? I have to open for business today."

"No, you don't," he said softly. "What you've been through isn't easy to bear. You need some time."

"I hope you won't think I'm rude, Mr. McQuaid, when I point out that this is none of your business."

"You made it my business," he told her. "Last night."

She faltered and touched her hand to her throat. "I know you feel...used...under the circumstances."

He raised an eyebrow. "Circumstances?"

"Yes." Mattie tried to look at him, but failed. "The circumstances in which I...used you."

She felt his gaze burn hotter against her skin, and Mattie wished with all her heart that she could simply disappear in a puff of smoke. It was too much. All of it. Everything she'd been through in the past three days was simply too much to bear.

Seeing Del fall from the roof, one of the very few times he'd done something useful at the house.

Realizing that her husband was dying before her eyes.

Hearing his confession.

Knowing what a fool she'd been.

Thinking how disappointed her parents would have been in her.

Imagining what everyone would say about her, if they found out.

Pretending, in front of the whole town.

And now *this*.

A lump rose in Mattie's throat, closing it off, bringing a mist of tears to her eyes. She looked up at Jared and knew she owed him an apology. But somehow, she couldn't bring herself to say she was sorry.

"Mr. McQuaid—" Her voice broke. Mattie gulped down the knot of emotion and tried again. "Mr. McQuaid, I realize you owe me nothing and I have no right to ask anything else of you, but I would appreciate it if you would leave."

He didn't leave. Instead, he studied her for a long moment, then eased closer until she could feel the heat of his body.

"You're going to have to figure out a way to deal with your husband's betrayal, Mattie," he said. "But don't be sorry you reached out for help last night. Don't be sorry you needed somebody."

He touched her chin and brought her face around.

"Don't be sorry it was me," he whispered.

And with that, Jared McQuaid walked out the kitchen door of the Cottonwood Café.

As he stalked down the boardwalk, people got out of his way. Jared strode into the newspaper office, then went to the jail. The sheriff was there, limping on his makeshift crutch, cursing the pain of his gunshot wound.

Jared signed the paperwork, took custody of the prisoners and marched them to the train station at gunpoint. He loaded them into the baggage car, chained their leg irons to the floor and went back out to the platform.

The wind snapped his coat around his knees as he stared down Main Street. Prosperous businesses, likable people; this was a good town.

His gaze landed on the Cottonwood Café, the sign barely visible at the other end of town.

Mattie Ingram.

Yeah, he'd made her forget, all right.

Now, how was *he* going to manage it?

Chapter Three

"Two months? Two months gone by since you were here the last time?" Mayor Rayburn asked.

"Almost three," Jared said.

"Well, if that don't beat all..."

Standing with the mayor inside the sheriff's office, Jared could hardly believe how quickly the time had passed since his first visit to Stanford.

Or how much had happened.

"Where does the time go?" the mayor lamented, stroking his gray side whiskers. "Anyway, take it from me and the town council, we're plum tickled to have you here in Stanford, to stay this time."

Jared looked down at the mayor, dressed in his cravat and the rumpled suit that hung loosely on his thin frame. "Too bad about Sheriff Hickert."

"Yep. A damn shame, all right. Tricky thing about them gunshot wounds. Don't heal right, sometimes. He tried to handle his duties, but just couldn't manage anymore." The mayor clasped Jared's arm. "But I know you're going to do us a fine job in his place. Stanford is a good town, full of good people. We want to keep it that way.''

The mayor and the men of the town council had said those exact words to Jared shortly after he'd arrived on the train this morning, when they'd sworn him in to office at the mayor's house. In fact, Jared had heard those words three times now.

"You can count on it," he declared.

"Just what I like to hear." The mayor rubbed his palms together. "Let me know if there's anything you're needing."

"I'll do that," Jared said, and followed him outside.

"Me and the missus will have you over for supper some night," Mayor Rayburn said, and headed off across the street.

Jared stood on the boardwalk watching the horses, wagons and buggies move along Main Street. Miners, women and children, gentlemen in suits and cowboys wearing guns went about their business.

Jared's chest swelled a little.

Stanford. *His* town.

He glanced down his vest. Gone was the U.S. Marshal's badge he'd worn for nearly ten years. In its place was the tin star declaring him Stanford's sheriff.

When last here, he'd signed up for a subscription to the *Stanford Gazette* on his way out of town. Despite the sporadic mail service and the duties that had kept him on the trail, he'd actually received a few issues. Enough for him to follow the story of Sheriff Hickert, who'd never fully recovered from his gunshot wound. Enough to learn that Stanford needed a new lawman. Jared had telegrammed, asking for the job, and within a few weeks got the answer he'd hoped for.

It hadn't taken much for Jared to make the life-changing decision. Hunkered down by a feeble campfire one cold night, with the wind biting his ears, Jared had thought about why he'd been so envious of Del Ingram, a dead man.

Ingram had everything Jared didn't have—a town, a home, a family, the respect of decent people. In that moment, Jared had realized that's what he wanted for himself.

True, he'd had no desire for any of those things for a long time, for a lot of reasons. But that was behind him now. Jared knew where his future lay.

So here he was.

Jared rested his thumbs in his gun belt and scanned Main Street one final time before going into the sheriff's office. *His* office.

Not only did he have an office, he had a deputy who, at this very minute, was out keeping an eye on the streets of Stanford. He'd met Drew Tanner at the mayor's house this morning. Tanner looked a little young and seemed a little green, but he had some experience and he was eager.

As sheriff's offices went, this one was as good as any. Jared surveyed his desk, his racks of rifles, Wanted posters nailed to the walls, the little stove in the corner with the rocking chair next to it. Down the hallway were two cells, both empty at the moment.

Jared's living quarters were there, too. The room was small, but it held everything he needed: a bunk, a washstand, a bureau. A place he could hang his hat every single night.

No more meals around a campfire. No more cold nights on the trail. No more hunting down lawbreakers who would knife him in the back or blow his head off given a second's opportunity. He'd never have a daily dose of those kind of men again.

Jared smiled in the quiet office. The town of Stanford was peaceful as a Sunday morning, tame as a speckled pony. He could do his sheriff duties in his sleep.

Jared drew in a deep, satisfied breath. Yep, he was going to like it here in Stanford.

Pausing at the little mirror beside the stove, Jared straightened his badge and pulled his hat a little lower over one eye. He gave himself a brisk nod, then walked out into the streets of his town.

Spring had come to Stanford and should have been gone by now, but the pleasant weather hung on. The morning was warm. A hint of a breeze stirred.

Citizens crowded the boardwalks and the streets, going about their business. Jared strolled along, looking things over, watching for trouble, getting the lay of the place.

And looking for Mattie Ingram.

He stopped abruptly outside the Stanford Mercantile, realizing that his first walk-through of the town had taken him directly to the Cottonwood Café.

Well, why shouldn't he head here first? It was the heart of the business district, he told himself. Nearby was the bank, the assay office and most of the shops. Places likely to draw criminal activity. Mattie and her Cottonwood Café didn't have anything to do with it.

Jared pulled on his chin. No sense in lying to himself.

Mattie had been on his mind—and in his dreams— almost continually since he'd laid eyes on her. Since their night together.

Mattie was a widow, Jared reminded himself, her husband dead not quite three months yet. Of course, after what she'd told him about Ingram, Jared doubted she'd done too much grieving over him.

But after her proper period of mourning, dare he hope to court her himself? A little smile pulled at Jared's lips. Yep, that's exactly what he could do.

In the meantime, he'd have to settle for looking at her. Of course, he could talk to her, too. Have supper at her restaurant.

Think about rolling around in bed with her.

Heat rushed through Jared, pumping his blood faster. Damn, after all this time, thoughts of making love to Mattie still had the same affect on him.

He walked a little faster, trying to push those images out of his mind before he gave the townsfolk an impression of their new sheriff he didn't want them to have.

But, as if he didn't have a will of his own, Jared's feet carried him across the street to the Cottonwood Café. He peered through the window. Only one table was occupied.

Good, he thought. If the restaurant wasn't busy, that meant Mattie would have time to talk to him. But he didn't want their reunion to take place in front of an audience. Jared circled the building.

As he walked he allowed himself to indulge in a little fantasy. On those long, lonely nights on the trail he'd often found himself thinking about how Mattie might react when she saw him again.

His favorite conjured-up scene was the one where she took one look at him, shucked off her clothes and jumped into bed with him.

Jared pulled on his chin. A hell of a nice vision— one he'd about worn out—but not likely to happen.

Next was the one where she confessed that she'd pined endlessly for him, prayed for his return, then shucked off her clothes and jumped into bed with him.

He'd even imagined that she said she loved him— then shucked off her clothes and jumped into bed with him.

"Damn..."

Jared shook his head, getting himself under control. Fact was, the best he could hope for when Mattie saw him was a smile on her face. That would be plenty. A smile would mean she was happy to see him. A smile meant...everything.

Rounding the corner of the restaurant, Jared stopped. His heart thundered in his chest.

Mattie stood on the back steps, holding on to the railing, gazing up at the sky. His insides seemed to melt.

Lord, what a pretty woman she was. At times over the past months he'd wondered if his imagination had turned her into something she wasn't. But seeing her now, he knew that wasn't true. Mattie was as pretty as he remembered.

She had on a gray dress with a black lace collar and cuffs. Proper mourning attire for a widow, but it did nothing to hide her swells and curves.

Jared headed toward the back steps, anxious to see her up close, talk to her. What the hell? Maybe she *would* shuck off her clothes and jump into bed with him.

"Mattie?" he called.

She spun around. Only a second passed before recognition bloomed on her face. Her eyes widened.

A little whimper slipped from Mattie's lips. She splayed her fingers across her stomach.

"Surprise," he said.

Mattie slapped her hand over her mouth and raced to the outhouse.

Jared frowned as he pushed his hat back on his head and watched the outhouse door bang shut behind her.

"Well, damn..." he muttered. Never *ever* had he imagined the sight of him would send her running to the privy.

The restaurant door opened and a gray-haired woman stepped outside, wiping her hands on a linen towel.

Jared looked at her hopefully. "Something she ate?"

Mattie slumped against the door of the outhouse, the coarse wood digging into her forehead. She had to get out of this airless little shed. The smell, the heat…

Her stomach rolled. Mattie swallowed quickly, fearful she'd be sick again.

But she didn't want to go outside. *He* was there.

Her heart banged in her chest. What was he doing here? Why had he come back? And why did it have to be *now?*

Did he *know?* Had he somehow found out?

Mattie touched her palm to her stomach. Flat, still. No outward sign of the baby—*his baby.*

No, he couldn't know, she decided. He couldn't possibly know.

What should she do? Mattie thought frantically. Tell him?

Weeks ago when she'd found out she was carrying his child, she'd decided not to contact him. His presence would only complicate things.

Mattie twisted her fingers together. But now he was *here.* Did that change things?

Drawing in a deep breath, Mattie fought off the nausea that had plagued her for weeks, her spirits lifting a little as she realized that, like before, Jared McQuaid would be in town for only a day or so to pick up prisoners, probably. Then he'd be gone. All she had to do was keep her condition a secret from him—which would be a snap, since she didn't intend to speak to the man—and by tomorrow he'd be gone, none the wiser.

And her baby's future would be safe again.

Mattie gulped a few times, fighting off another wave of nausea and an unsettling nudge from her conscience.

"Mattie?" Mrs. Nance called from outside.

Bless her, the dear woman had been such a comfort—her only comfort, really.

Slowly, Mattie opened the door to Mrs. Nance's smile. The woman was stout, with a lifetime of lines on her face.

"Feeling better?" she asked.

"Well, no…not really."

Mrs. Nance patted her hand. "All perfectly normal. Come along, dear."

Mattie didn't move. "Is—is that man still out there?"

"The new sheriff, you mean?" Mrs. Nance asked.

"The—*what?*"

"Jared McQuaid. The new sheriff," she explained.

Mattie's stomach heaved. She fought it down, along with a rising wave of panic. "We have a new sheriff?"

"You hadn't heard?" Mrs. Nance nodded. "I guess not. You've had your mind on other things lately."

Yes, that was certainly true. Her queasy stomach—on top of all her other problems.

"He's the new sheriff? Stanford's sheriff?" Mattie asked. "Here permanently?"

"Just arrived this morning, and here to stay, he says."

Mattie clamped her lips together to hold in her groan.

"You need to get off your feet for a while," Mrs. Nance said, and led her from the outhouse.

Mattie's gaze fell on Jared McQuaid, standing across the yard. He was big, tall, sturdy. His sheriff's badge glinted in the morning sun.

Her heart thumped in her chest and her stomach squeezed into a knot again, making her footsteps drag. She watched as Jared's gaze touched her face, then dropped to her belly and hung there.

Mattie froze. He *knew*.

The world suddenly tilted and Mattie swayed. In the next heartbeat, she felt Jared beside her, holding her upright, bracing her against his chest—that chest…*that night*.

How familiar he felt. How comfortable. Part of Mattie wanted to melt against him, soak up his strength—goodness knows, the man had plenty to go around. But something inside her warned her to get away as fast as she could.

"I'll take you to the doctor," Jared said.

"No." Mattie pushed away from him. "No. There's nothing he can do, and besides I—"

She didn't finish the sentence. It was none of Jared's business that she couldn't afford another visit to the doctor.

"I'll take her home," Mrs. Nance said, as if reading Mattie's thoughts.

"I'll handle it," Jared told her in a tone that brooked no disagreement. He dipped his chin toward his badge. "It's my duty. Besides, don't you have to look after the café?"

"The restaurant is my responsibility," Mattie insisted. She tried to pull away, but Jared's long fingers remained folded around her arm and splayed across her back. "I need to stay here. The noon rush will start soon."

Mrs. Nance shook her head sympathetically, but didn't say anything. There was no need. Both of them knew how foolish Mattie's claim was.

"Let the sheriff take you home for a while, dear," Mrs. Nance said. "He…understands."

With that, Mattie realized Mrs. Nance had told Jared about her condition while she'd been in the outhouse.

How much more humiliation could she bear in front of this man?

"I can get myself home just fine," Mattie announced, though really, she hardly felt up to it.

Jared never gave her a chance to prove her words. With a little pressure at her back, he escorted her away from the restaurant.

When they got to the street, Mattie glanced at the

people passing by on the boardwalk and pulled away from Jared.

"I will not be paraded through town like a circus train," she told him.

Mattie looked up to see a frown on his face. He didn't say anything, but he didn't put his hand on her again.

When they reached her house, Mattie expected Jared would leave. He didn't. He walked inside as if he belonged there. Mattie was too tired, too nauseated to protest. She went straight to her bedroom with him on her heels.

Heat flushed Mattie's cheeks. This room. That night. Him.

"Do you need help with your dress?" Jared asked, his gaze traveling over her, lingering on her belly.

He'd already seen her naked. Suddenly, Mattie felt that way again. Vulnerable, exposed, but not in a sexual way. More like a bug in a jar.

"Stop looking at my stomach!" She slammed the door in his face, then dropped onto the bed and fell asleep.

When she awoke some time later, Mattie felt only marginally better. She splashed her face at the washstand, then took down her hair and pinned it up again. Leaning closer to the mirror, she took stock of her features. Pale, dark circles under her eyes... She looked terrible.

Almost as terrible as she felt.

With a deep sigh, Mattie went to the kitchen. Her stomach jolted again when she found Jared standing at her cookstove.

"What are you doing here?" she demanded.

He spun around. A moment passed while his gaze traveled the length of her, dipped to her belly for only a second, then landed on her face.

"I heard you stirring around in the bedroom," he said. "I made you something to eat."

"You've been here all this time?" she asked. He'd stayed? Gone through her cupboards? Sat in her chairs? Made himself comfortable in her house? Had he peeked into her bedroom while she slept?

Jared took a biscuit from the warmer and poured tea into one of her china cups. "You don't have much here to eat."

"I own a restaurant, remember? I usually eat there."

Jared pulled back a chair for her. When she glared at him instead of sitting down, he circled the table and eased into a chair across from her, then picked up the newspaper and began reading.

How casual and comfortable he'd made himself, sitting at her table. Honestly, the gall of this man.

Another minute passed before Jared spoke as he turned the page of the newspaper. "The tea and biscuit will settle your stomach, make you feel better."

He was right, of course, but it didn't particularly suit Mattie that he'd said it. Or that he'd prepared it for her. Or that he was sitting at her table, in her house.

But the tea did smell good, while so few things did these days. Mattie sat down and took little sips as she ate the biscuit. Jared kept reading the newspaper, his silence unnerving.

When she finished, he dropped the paper and laid his hand lightly on her wrist, keeping her in the chair.

"We need to talk," he said.

Mattie pulled away and got to her feet. "There is nothing we need to discuss."

His gaze dipped to her belly. "Are you sure you're pregnant?"

It was pointless to deny it. Mrs. Nance had told him. Her illness had confirmed it.

Mattie clenched her fists at her sides. "Three times in one night! How could I *not* be pregnant?"

Jared rose and stood beside her, his expression grim. "It's mine, isn't it?"

She raised her chin. "It's my husband's."

"It's mine." Jared's eyes narrowed. "Unless you had some other man in town *making you forget* after I left."

She slapped him. Hard, on the cheek with her open palm. Jared didn't flinch, didn't pull away, didn't move. Finally, he nodded, satisfied.

"It's mine," he declared.

"It's my husband's," Mattie told him again. "That's what the whole town thinks and that's what I'm letting them believe."

"Just your little secret. Is that it?"

Mattie gazed up at Jared and jerked her chin. "Yes, my little secret."

This baby *could* have been Del's, if they'd had a normal husband-wife relationship. The town didn't know any differently, and Mattie had decided to let them believe it.

After all, telling the truth would label her baby a bastard. What kind of choice was that?

"Did you ever intend to tell me?" Jared asked.

She turned away. "No. I was never going to tell you."

Jared drew in a big breath, then let it out slowly, as if he'd come to terms with everything she'd said, made some sort of decision about it.

"Let's go," he said.

Mattie frowned. "Go? Go where?"

"To the church."

"Whatever for?" she asked.

"We're getting married."

Chapter Four

"*Married?*"

"Yes. Married," Jared said. He took her hand. "Right now."

She pulled away from him. "I'm not going to marry you."

"Yes, you are." He eased closer, crowding her. "You're carrying a baby. My baby. I'm taking responsibility for what I did and we're getting married."

"Nobody knows it's your baby. I told you, the whole town thinks it's Del's."

"*I* know it's mine." Jared tapped his finger against his chest. "I'm not turning my back on you, or this baby."

Mattie lifted her chin. "I don't want your help."

"Maybe you don't want it but you sure as hell need it," Jared told her. He looked her up and down. "You're sick as a dog. You're pale. You've lost weight. You can't keep anything down."

For a lawman, he certainly knew a lot about having babies. Or he was just observant.

"Yes," Mattie admitted. "I've been sick. But that will pass."

"And you're dead tired, aren't you? You can't make it through the day without lying down."

"If I have time I lie down, but I'm usually too busy at the restaurant."

"And what effect do you think that's having on the baby?" he challenged.

Mattie turned away from those fierce blue eyes of his, uncomfortable under his gaze. She tried to think of a reasonable response, but couldn't.

Finally she said, "Just because I'm sick and I need to take a nap is no reason for us to get married, of all things."

"Yes, it is," Jared told her. "It's the best reason. The only reason. I'm marrying you so I can take care of you, and make sure our baby comes into this world healthy."

"But—"

"It's the right thing to do." Jared gave her a brisk nod. "And you know it."

She'd worried about all those things. Dr. Whittaker, Mrs. Nance at the restaurant—along with most every other woman in town—had cautioned her over and over again to take it easy.

She did feel terrible. She was worn out by midafternoon. Was she being thoughtless? Was she being a bad mother? Was she jeopardizing her unborn child?

More than anything, she wanted her baby to be healthy. Nothing was more important.

Jared seemed to read those feelings in her expression. He pulled on his hat and opened the back door. "Let's go."

Mattie hesitated a moment. "But—"

"This isn't about you and me," Jared told her. "It's about the baby."

What could she say to that? Mattie walked out ahead of him.

Just beyond the gate in the white picket fence that surrounded her house, Mattie slowed, gazing toward Main Street. Jared was a few paces ahead of her. He stopped and turned back.

"What about the Cottonwood?" Mattie asked. "What about my restaurant?"

"Close it."

"Close it?" Mattie shook her head, stunned by the thought. "How am I supposed to support myself? What am I supposed to do for money?"

"I'll take care of you."

Her gaze roamed once more to the Cottonwood Café. Close it? Walk away? It had belonged to her parents. She'd worked there with them, side by side, with so many wonderful memories. She'd turned the place around and built it into the most popular eatery in Stanford.

But that was before.

Images of Del Ingram floated in Mattie's mind. He'd drained every cent from her bank account without her knowing it. Had left her penniless. He'd also run up some sizable debts around town, debts she was saddled with.

With no money, she'd been unable to buy meat and poultry to serve to her diners. It hadn't taken long before her soups and vegetable platters lost favor with her customers. With no sausage or bacon on the menu, the businessmen who'd made the Cottonwood their spot for breakfast stopped coming.

She'd had to let her serving girls and dishwasher go, and take on those chores herself. She held on to Mrs. Nance by a thread, paying her salary with what little money she took in; if the Silver Bell Restaurant on the other end of town hired her away, Mattie would be lost for sure.

Her business had spiraled downward for months, since Del's death. For a moment, Mattie considered doing as Jared said, closing it. Free herself from the work, the worry. Could she do that?

Mattie shook her head. "I can't close the Cottonwood. I just can't."

Jared's brows drew together; obviously he was unhappy with her decision. "Then let Mrs. Nance run it. Or open it only part of the day. Hire more help. You can keep it open, but you're not going to be over there all the time."

Mattie's back stiffened. "I made the restaurant what it is. I can't just turn it over to hired help."

A little frown creased Jared's forehead. "Anybody

can run that restaurant, Mattie, but only *you* can have this baby.''

She wished he'd stop making so much sense.

Jared clasped her elbow and they walked to the church.

As they crossed the yard beneath the trees, Mattie's steps slowed again until he was nearly pulling her along. At the bottom of the stairs, she stopped completely, with Jared on the step above her, glaring down. The door stood open and Reverend Harris's voice drifted out. He was rehearsing his sermon, it seemed.

''We don't even know each other,'' Mattie said.

Jared raised an eyebrow at her. ''We know each other well enough.''

Mattie's cheeks flushed, remembering the extent of their intimacy. She'd spent many a night thinking about U.S. Marshal Jared McQuaid in the weeks after he'd left Stanford, left her bed. Their one night together had been like no other.

Then she'd found out she was pregnant.

Mattie lifted her chin. ''Don't think that just because we're married that you and I are going to...well, you know.''

''What?'' He looked a little confused, but Mattie saw the grin pulling at his lips.

''You know what I mean,'' she informed him, crossing her arms in front of her.

''Oh.'' Jared nodded broadly. ''You mean make love.''

Mattie flushed bright red. "Shh. Keep your voice down. We're at the church, for heaven's sake."

"It won't hurt the baby, you know," Jared said. His grin turned into a full smile. "And after that one night we were together, I figured you'd be anxious to—"

"Just hush!" Mattie pushed past him and stomped into the church.

Her bravado disappeared when she stepped inside. Where she was and what was about to happen smacked her in the face. Mattie backed up and bumped into the solid wall of Jared McQuaid standing behind her.

"Jared, I—I don't know—"

"Reverend Harris!" Jared's voice boomed over her head, carrying through the church and startling Reverend Harris, who was standing at the altar.

The reverend adjusted his spectacles and squinted at them, then smiled.

"Ah, yes, good afternoon," he called, closing his Bible and stepping into the aisle.

Jared's big, strong body pressed against Mattie's back, easing her between the rows of pews toward the front of the church.

"Jared, I'm not sure—"

"We want you to marry us," Jared called out.

Reverend Harris looked as stunned as Mattie felt, hearing the words spoken aloud. Jared splayed his hand over her back, urging her down the aisle. Mattie dug in.

Jared moved to her side and looked down at her.

"This is for the baby, Mattie. Not you. Not me. The baby."

He'd said it softly so only she could hear.

"It's the only sensible thing to do," Jared said.

Sensible. Yes, it was that. And Mattie had been sensible her whole life. Well, most of it, anyway.

"Let's get this over with," he said.

Jared pulled her down the aisle behind him, clutching her arm with one hand, offering his other to Reverend Harris. His palm felt rough, his fingers strong. Jared held tight to her as if he feared she'd bolt for the door.

Maybe she should.

"This is quite a surprise," Reverend Harris said, looking back and forth between the two of them.

"Like I said, Reverend," Jared said, "I want you to marry us. Right now."

Reverend Harris's eyebrows bobbed toward his hairline. "Well, now, this is sudden. You've just arrived in town, Sheriff, only this morning."

Jared leaned forward slightly and lowered his voice. "I guess you heard about Mrs. Ingram's...condition."

The reverend glanced at Mattie. His cheeks flushed. So did hers.

"Well, yes, I'd heard," he said. "But still, I don't understand. You want to marry her?"

"A woman alone? Having a baby?" Jared shook his head. "A woman can't raise a child by herself. It's not right. Not natural."

"Yes, that's true enough," the reverend agreed. "A woman needs a man to take care of her."

"Damn right—excuse me, Reverend—of course she does."

"But still…" the reverend said.

"It's my duty to do the right thing by her."

Reverend Harris frowned. "Your duty?"

Jared drew in a breath. "Del Ingram was my friend. We grew up together. Del saved my life. I owe it to his memory to take care of his wife and baby."

"Oh, I see." Reverend Harris nodded thoughtfully. "Saved your life, did he?"

"He did," Jared said.

The reverend mulled it over for a moment, stroking his chin, then nodded. "Well, all I can say is what a good man you are, Sheriff McQuaid, taking on this responsibility."

Reverend Harris smiled at Mattie. "You're a mighty lucky young gal to have this man stepping in the way he is. I hope you appreciate what he's doing."

"I want you to marry us right away," Jared said. "Today. Now."

"Well, all right. Can't see any point in waiting…considering." Reverend Harris glanced at Mattie's belly. "I'll go get the missus for a witness."

Anxious to get the ceremony over and done with, Jared grumbled under his breath as he watched the reverend leave the church. Beside him, Mattie stood rigid. A little pink blush highlighted her pale cheeks, emphasizing the dark circles under her eyes. He knew she didn't feel well.

He knew she might turn and run at any minute.

Mattie seemed docile enough right now, but he didn't know how long his luck would hold. He wanted this service over and done with before she changed her mind.

"Is it true?" Mattie asked softly.

She looked up at him, her eyes wide and hopeful.

"Is what true?" he asked.

"About Del. He really saved your life?"

"Hell, no." Jared snorted. "The bastard nearly got me killed twice."

"Oh."

Mattie turned away, disappointment turning down the corners of her mouth. Maybe he should have lied to her, confirmed the story he'd told the reverend. Surely she'd like to think there was something honorable in the man she'd chosen to marry, that there was some kernel of goodness in him.

Especially after the way things had turned out.

"Where's that reverend?" Jared mumbled, craning his neck to see out the window.

"Were you and Del—"

"There he is—about damn time." Jared strode to the doors of the church and escorted the reverend and Mrs. Harris to the altar.

Mrs. Harris, still wearing her apron, giggled behind her hand. "Oh, a wedding. How lovely. Why, I just love a wedding. Don't you want some flowers, dear?

I can get you some from the garden. Oh, and let me play something on the piano for the occasion. How about—''

"We don't have time for flowers or music," Jared said.

Mrs. Harris's tittering stopped and she looked properly admonished. "Oh, well, all right."

Jared waved toward the reverend. "Let's get this show on the road."

Reverend Harris opened his Bible. "Very well, let's see now..."

Jared glanced down at Mattie. She inched away from him. He latched on to her elbow and stepped closer.

"Reverend, you want to speed it up here?"

"Oh, yes, certainly." Reverend Harris adjusted his spectacles and held his Bible out in front of him. "Dearly beloved, we are gathered here today—"

"We don't need that part," Jared said.

"Hmm? What?"

"We don't need that part," Jared repeated. "Move it along."

"Well, then, let's see." Reverend Harris cleared his throat. "Do you, Jared McQuaid, take this woman—"

"Yeah, yeah, sure I do." Jared felt Mattie glaring up at him, but he refused to look at her. He made a spinning motion with his fingers. "Keep going, will you?"

The reverend adjusted his Bible. "And do you, Mattie Ingram, take this man to be your lawful—"

"We know all that stuff," Jared said. "Jump ahead."

The reverend exchanged a troubled look with his wife. "Very well. Mattie, will you marry this man?"

"Sure she will," Jared insisted. "Go on, pronounce us married. Now."

Miffed, Reverend Harris closed his Bible. "She must answer the question herself, Sheriff."

"Look, Reverend, she's here, isn't we? She agrees. Just say we're married and—"

"Mattie?" the reverend asked. "Do you agree to this marriage?"

Jared gave her arm a little shake. "Say yes."

Reverend Harris and his wife exchanged another look, then leaned a little closer to Mattie.

"Well..." Mattie gulped.

Mrs. Harris smiled gently at her. "Are you not sure, Mattie?"

"Of course, she's sure," Jared insisted. "Answer him, Mattie. Let's get this thing over with."

Reverend Harris smiled kindly. "Perhaps I can say a few words here that will help."

"Just say we're married!"

The reverend went on as if Jared's words weren't echoing off the church ceiling.

"Mattie," Reverend Harris said, "I admit I wasn't in favor of your marriage to Del Ingram. But look how well that turned out. I'm sure this marriage will be just as wonderful as your last."

Mattie gasped and went white.

Jared winced. He slapped his palm over his eyes, then dared to look at Mattie.

Her cold, sharp gaze impaled him. Her breath came heavier, causing her shoulders to rise and fall.

"Mattie," Jared said. "We talked about this. We agreed—"

He turned back to the reverend, his jaw set. "Hurry up. Say we're married. Say it."

"But she hasn't answered. I can't pronounce you two married unless—"

"Damn right you can," Jared told him. "Just get on with it before—"

"But—"

"Do it!"

"No!" Mattie shouted.

Mrs. Harris gasped. The reverend's eyes widened.

"No. That's my answer." She looked up at Jared. "No, I won't marry you."

"Now look here, Mattie, you know—"

"No!" Mattie wrestled away from him. "I won't marry you! Not now, not ever! No!"

She spun away from him and ran out of the church, slamming the door behind her.

Halfway across the churchyard, Mattie heard Jared calling her name. She didn't stop until she heard his footsteps behind her. She turned to find him towering over her.

"Listen to me, Mattie, we're going back into that church and we're—"

"No!"

"You can't raise this baby by yourself!"

"Yes, I can!" She looked up into his face and saw that Jared was as angry as she.

"Listen to me—"

"No, you listen to me," she told him. "I have a home and a business. I have friends to help me. I'm perfectly capable of raising this baby myself. And that's exactly what I'm going to do."

"You don't know what you're saying. You don't know what you're up against."

Mattie reined in her temper. "This doesn't concern you. Everyone thinks this baby is Del's and that suits me fine."

"It doesn't suit *me* at all!"

"I don't care if it does or not," Mattie told him. "You have no say in the matter. This baby is mine to take care of. Mine. Not yours."

A flash of pain came over Jared's face. Mattie looked away and softened her voice. "From now on, you are to stay away from me. That's my final word."

A minute dragged by, and Jared didn't speak. She knew it would be hard on him to accept her decision, but it was for the best.

Finally, she lifted her gaze to his face. His features burned with an intensity she'd never seen before.

"Like hell I will." He ground out the words in a low voice.

Mattie nearly buckled under the weight of his pronouncement. She forced her chin up a notch. "I insist you respect my wishes," she said.

"I don't give a damn about your wishes," he told her. "That baby is mine and I don't care who knows it."

A deep, sickening fear rushed through her. "You can't mean that. You can't poison this baby's future by telling everyone the truth."

"I'm going to have a say in everything that goes on with you and this baby. Get used to it."

Jared gave her a curt nod and walked away.

Chapter Five

The lantern light flickered as the night breeze blew through the open window, sending shadows dancing across the kitchen. Elbow deep in the washtub, doing the dishes, Mattie hardly noticed.

The restaurant was quiet now, closed for the evening. Mrs. Nance had gone home some time ago. She'd offered to stay, of course, and help Mattie finish up the day's dishes, but Mattie had told her no. She was lucky to still have Mrs. Nance working for her; she wouldn't impose any more than necessary.

Mattie didn't mind the solitude of the kitchen, but she sorely missed Billy Weaver. Billy had been her dishwasher...before.

With a jerk of her chin, Mattie sent unkind thoughts in the direction of Jared McQuaid. If not for him, she'd have been at the restaurant all day and could have done these dishes a little at a time, rather than standing here all night, doing them now, to ready the kitchen for tomorrow's business.

Instead, he'd taken her home to rest. Then hauled her to the church to *marry* him. Mattie shuddered at the thought. Good gracious, what had she been thinking, agreeing to the marriage? Luckily, she'd come to her senses in time.

She scrubbed the next plate in the tepid water, dipped it in the rinse tub and stacked it with the others. Maybe she should march to the jail and insist Jared come over and wash these dishes himself. Yes, that would serve him right.

For an instant the vision of Jared standing at her washtub bloomed in her mind. Sleeves rolled up, dark hair spread over flexing forearms, legs braced wide apart. So big, so strong. Unlike Mattie, he no doubt could work for hours and not even breathe hard.

Of course, Jared McQuaid didn't have another person riding around inside of him.

Mattie smiled to herself. The baby. Growing within her right now, this very moment. What did it look like? she wondered. Would it be a boy? A girl?

More sobering thoughts came to Mattie then, taking the smile from her face. She had so much to do before the child was born. Pay off Del's old debts. Build up her bank account. Get her business back on track. Prepare for the baby's arrival. Then insure the child's future.

"Well, gracious..." Mattie muttered, the sloshing of water muting her words.

So much to do. So much to do...alone.

She sighed, dipping the last plate into the rinse tub.

Better to do things alone than to depend on someone who wouldn't come through for her. She didn't need to learn that lesson twice.

True, her future was a tall order, but Mattie was confident she could handle it. The only question concerned Jared. And she intended to settle that tonight.

Mattie dried the dishes and stacked them in the cupboard, then dumped the wash water and took off her apron. This afternoon in the churchyard, Jared had threatened to make it known that he was the father of her baby. She couldn't—wouldn't—allow that to happen.

Slipping her shawl around her shoulders, Mattie gathered her handbag, blew out the lanterns and locked up. But instead of heading home, she went the other way.

The good thing about the day wearing on was that the nausea that marked her mornings faded. The bad thing was that fatigue took its place.

Bone weary, Mattie walked along the darkened street. Most of the businesses had closed long ago. Just a few windows glowed with lamplight. The only noise came from the Lady Luck Saloon at the other end of town.

Mattie stopped as she neared the jail, and glanced around. No one was about, but that didn't mean she might not be seen. Surely, word would spread that the new sheriff had offered to marry her and she'd turned him down. Mattie didn't want to add any more fuel to the gossip by being seen entering the jailhouse this late at night.

She cut through the alley to the rear of the jail. Glancing around, she opened the door and stepped inside.

From a doorway to her left, light spilled into the hallway, illuminating two empty cells. Straight ahead, through another opened door, lantern light burned in the sheriff's office.

Mattie paused, listening. She heard nothing. Maybe Jared wasn't here. He could be out walking rounds.

She ventured farther down the hallway, wanting to make certain. Mattie wanted to talk to him tonight, get this issue settled once and for all.

A shadow crossed her path and Jared leaped in front of her. Startled, she froze.

Good gracious, his chest was bare.

Which was an odd thing to notice, she realized a second later, given that he had a Colt .45 pointed at her head.

"What the hell are you doing, sneaking in here?" Jared demanded. "I nearly shot you."

Mattie pointed lamely down the hall. "You shouldn't have left your door unlocked. How thoughtless."

Jared grumbled and lowered his pistol. "Nobody breaks *into* a jail, Mattie."

"Oh."

"What are you doing here?" he asked, frowning.

Mattie twisted her fingers together, unsure where to

start. Of course, it would be much easier to think if he weren't standing only a foot away with no shirt on.

Dark, crinkly hair covered his chest and arrowed down his muscled stomach, disappearing into his trousers. His arms bulged as he shifted his wide shoulders. The sleeves of his long johns and his suspenders hung at his sides; the top button of his trousers was unfastened.

"Change your mind about getting married?" he asked.

The question shocked her back to reality. "No, of course not. I need to talk to you."

Jared stepped into the room and turned a cane bottom chair toward her. "Sit down," he said.

A tingle swept up her spine. This was his bedroom. She couldn't waltz inside and sit down. It wasn't decent.

"You've been on your feet all evening. Sit down." When she still hesitated, Jared gestured toward the bunk in the corner. "Unless you'd rather hop into bed?"

Mattie jerked her chin at him and plopped into the chair. He shoved the pistol into the holster that dangled from a row of pegs on the wall. His shirt hung beside it. He'd probably been getting ready for bed when she walked in. Her gaze bounced to the tidy bunk, then to Jared. He was already watching her. Mattie's cheeks burned. She busied herself straightening her skirt, refusing to look at him again.

"How are you feeling?" Jared asked.

"Fine."

He stopped in the center of the floor and sighed heavily. "How are you *really* feeling?"

She wasn't sure if the frown on his face meant he was angry or genuinely concerned. "Tired. A little tired."

"Did you eat a proper supper?"

She huffed. "That's really none of your concern."

His chest swelled and his frown deepened. "Did you eat a proper supper?"

"Yes," she told him. No sense in annoying him further, given the reason she was here tonight.

Jared nodded, apparently satisfied, then shoved his arms into his long johns and pulled them over his shoulders.

"What do you need to talk about?" he asked.

How odd, sitting in a chair in Jared's bedroom, watching him dress. Mattie couldn't recall any such moment with her husband.

Obviously, Jared thought nothing of her being there. He buttoned his long johns and slipped on his shirt, completely comfortable with her presence.

His long fingers fastened the shirt, then dipped into his trousers, tucking the tail inside. Mattie sat mesmerized by the simple action, the intimate details he shared so casually.

"Mattie?"

"Oh." She shifted on the chair. "I have to know if you'll keep my secret."

"You mean about the baby really being mine?"

"You can't be serious about telling everyone the truth. Can you imagine the scandal?"

"You'd rather live a lie than be gossiped about?"

Mattie rose from the chair. "I don't care so much for myself. I'm worried about the baby. This will throw a shadow over his whole life."

"*His* whole life? You think it's a boy?" His gaze dipped to her belly.

She touched her hand to her stomach. "I don't know."

"I want a girl," Jared said, pulling up his suspenders. "It'll be a girl."

"All the more reason not to jeopardize her future," Mattie said. "Surely you can see that."

Jared shrugged into his vest and fastened his gun belt on his hips. "I'm more concerned that she'll turn out as stubborn as her mama."

Mattie sighed heavily. "Jared, please—"

"You need to get home," he said, and put on his hat.

She pulled away when he reached for her arm. "Not until you give me your answer. I have to know this is settled. Surely you can understand that."

He leaned down, just a little, just enough to make her draw back. "And surely you can understand that, for a man, agreeing to give up his child isn't a decision to be made lightly."

The depth of his gaze held her captive for a moment, and in that moment she saw something unreadable in Jared. Something deep. Something old and timeworn. It touched her, frightened her a little.

"I can walk home myself," she said to him.

He sighed irritably. "I'm walking you home, Mattie, and that's that."

Jared strode out of the room, leaving her no choice but to follow.

A ray of morning sunlight streaming through the window bored into Jared's eyes, waking him. He sat up, groggy, looked around and finally remembered where he was after his first night in his new room.

He scrubbed his hands over his face and pushed his fingers through his hair. Then he tossed back the covers.

It had been a hell of a night....

His wedding night, or should have been. If Mattie hadn't been so hardheaded at the church yesterday, he'd have spent the night in bed with her. Jared didn't need to look down to be reminded of the missed opportunity. It had kept him tossing and turning for hours.

What the hell was wrong with that woman? Naked, Jared rose from the bed and poured water from the pitcher into the basin at the washstand. Every other woman in the whole country was champing at the bit to get married. Hell, most of them were tracking men down, dragging them to the altar.

Jared braced his arms on the corner of the washstand and squinted into the mirror. Sure, he looked a little ragged this morning, hair sticking up, eyes red, heavy whiskers, but he was a good catch, as husbands went.

He had a respectable job that paid well. He worked hard, had money put away. He was handsome enough. He knew how to treat a woman, take care of her needs…her womanly needs.

Jared groaned aloud as his body tightened, remembering how he'd taken care of Mattie's needs their night together—all three times. The ache worsened, just thinking about it.

She'd come here last night to talk to him, but all he'd been able to think about was getting her into bed again. He'd walked her home, but she hadn't let him come inside with her.

He'd told her he'd let her know his decision about telling everyone the truth about the baby. But that was just an excuse to get to see her again; he'd never poison his child's future by branding him a bastard.

Jared groaned softly, remembering the night the baby was conceived. Before, when he'd been a marshal riding the trail, thinking of her, and this happened, he'd just waited it out, concentrated on his job. But now that he was in the same town with her, seeing her, touching her, almost marrying her, his condition had grown worse, much worse.

It just wasn't right, wanting one woman this much, but he did. If he didn't do something about it soon…

"Damn stubborn woman," Jared muttered.

When he'd come to Stanford he'd wanted to make

himself a home here, court Mattie, get to know her. Many a night on the trail he'd wondered if he'd fallen in love with her.

Jared gazed into the mirror, but it wasn't his reflection he saw, it was the past. Ten years. Ten long years of loneliness, hurt and painful memories. Somehow, all of that had gone away after one night with Mattie.

Hell, maybe he did love her.

No matter what, Jared didn't intend to let her out of his life. He liked being around her, liked the way she looked, the way she smelled. He even liked that spirit of hers, though he'd have to find a way to control it.

And she was having his baby. A little grin pulled at his lips every time he thought of it. Him, a papa. Mattie, sweet Mattie, the mama.

He dipped his hands into the basin and splashed icy water on his face. He shuddered.

Mattie might think she could order him out of her life, or wish him away, or scare him away, but that wouldn't happen. Jared wasn't about to turn his back on her. And he certainly wasn't going to abandon his child. Not when he was this close to having so many of the things he wanted.

Jared sighed in the silent room. Hell, he *did* love her. He loved her and he wanted her. He'd figure a way to have her.

But that would be so much easier to do if he could just get himself under control enough to make it through the day without embarrassing himself in front of the whole town.

Jared ground his teeth together, picked up the pitcher and poured it down his front.

He sucked in a quick breath as the icy water splashed over him. His chest heaved from the shock. His body shuddered.

But at least it took care of one problem.

Until the next time he laid eyes on Mattie.

Chapter Six

Jared needed breakfast, but didn't dare go to the Cottonwood Café for it. He wasn't exactly Mattie's favorite person right now. He was liable to get the bowl of oatmeal he ordered dumped over his head.

And even that, he feared, would make him want her again.

He headed to the Silver Bell Restaurant at the other end of town to have his meal. After that, he'd get down to work. This was a quiet town, but he needed to learn his way around, make himself known, check for trouble spots. He didn't intend to let things get out of hand in his town.

Stanford came to life as he strode down the boardwalk. Shop owners swept up and set out merchandise, readying for the day's business. Horses and wagons rumbled down Main Street. Folks passed him on the boardwalk, giving him curious looks.

He hadn't seen his deputy, Drew Tanner, since yesterday evening, when he'd come by the jail. Jared would have to find him this morning; there were things they needed to go over.

But right now he needed to eat. He was hungry and starting to feel a little grouchy.

"Sheriff! Sheriff McQuaid!"

Jared spotted his young deputy waving his arms from the other side of the street. Drew darted between the wagons and stepped up on the boardwalk in front of Jared.

"Sheriff, I've been looking for you. I got to talk to you."

A strong, sturdy young fellow, Drew stood almost as tall as Jared. He'd lived in Stanford for most of his life and had been Sheriff Hickert's deputy for nearly a year.

"What's wrong?" Jared asked.

"Well, sir, I don't know how to say this, exactly." Drew shuffled his feet, stared at the boardwalk for a minute, then finally pulled a rumpled piece of paper from his pocket.

"I got a telegram this morning from my mama back in Texas. She's been living there with her sister since my pa passed on. She's sick, Sheriff. She wants me to come out there and be with her." Drew ducked his head. "So I reckon I've got to quit my deputy duties."

"Your mama's real sick?"

Drew looked up. "I hate to leave. I take my responsibilities seriously."

Jared had counted on Drew being here. He needed someone who knew the town, the people.

"I got to go right away," Drew said. "There's a train heading east at noon."

"Go see about your ma. And good luck to you." Jared offered his hand. They shook, and Drew hurried away.

Jared's stomach growled, reminding him that he was hungry. Now, thanks to Drew's mama, he was feeling more than a little grumpy, too.

Nearly all the tables in the Silver Bell Restaurant were taken when Jared walked inside. The mayor and the four members of the town council sat together, talking. He'd met the councilmen at the mayor's house the morning he was sworn into office. They all ran businesses or owned land in Stanford.

"Have a seat," Mayor Rayburn offered when he spotted Jared. He dragged up a chair from another table. "We got us a business proposition we're discussing and it looks like we'll be needing you in on it, too."

Jared thought it a little early in the day to discuss business, especially since he hadn't had a cup of coffee yet. The other men had eaten already. Dirty plates crowded the table.

"You getting settled all right over at the jail-house?" Gil Spencer asked. Gil owned the blacksmith shop.

"No problems so far," Jared said. He'd have to tell them about Drew Tanner quitting, but right now having his breakfast seemed more important.

Jared spotted a man and women working together

back in the kitchen, and figured they were the Everettes, the couple who owned the place. Their half-dozen children swarmed the restaurant, some serving diners, other working in the kitchen. One of the girls poured Jared a cup of coffee and took his order.

"Big doings coming our way here in Stanford," Mayor Rayburn said, rearing back in his chair. "Big doings."

The men at the table nodded in agreement, looking pleased with themselves.

Rayburn leaned a little closer. "Got us a group of investors coming from back East. They're making a sweep through some of the towns out here, looking for business opportunities."

"They're coming to Stanford?" Jared asked.

"Yessiree," the mayor said, smiling broadly. He nodded around the table. "Me and the boys here, we're planning to roll out the red carpet for these men. Show them that Stanford is the kind of town where they can put their shops and factories—and their money."

Everybody around the table nodded, mumbling their agreement.

"So here's what we need you to do, Sheriff," Gil said. "We want to make certain that everything in Stanford is running smooth as silk when those investors get here."

"We can't let them think this ain't the right kind of town for them," Hayden Langston said. "We don't want no problems while they're here."

"We're counting on you to keep everything under control," the mayor said.

"Yeah," Hayden said, "just like Sheriff Hickert used to do."

"When are these investors arriving?" Jared asked, glancing toward the kitchen, watching for his breakfast.

"In a few weeks," Marvin Ford said. "That don't give us much time. We've got all kind of plans to make, things to do."

"The whole town is getting involved," Mayor Rayburn said. "Why, just think—"

"Sheriff?"

Jared turned in his chair to see a man standing at the window, gazing outside.

"Sheriff, I think you ought to get over to the Lady Luck," he said, pointing. "Looks like that Ballard boy is shooting up the place again."

"Tarnation!" Olin Burrows, who ran Stanford's bank, thumped his fist on the table. "See there? This is just what we don't need with those investors coming out."

Jared didn't answer. He headed out the door.

The street had cleared when Jared stepped onto the boardwalk. A shot rang out. He drew back, then peered down the block. At the entrance to the Lady Luck Saloon, a man dangled by one arm from the batwing door, swinging back and forth, waving his pistol around and singing at the top of his voice.

Jared drew his gun and eased down the block. When

he got closer he saw that it wasn't a man, but a boy. Probably no more than sixteen years old and drunk as a skunk.

Drunk, but still dangerous.

It seemed the boy was more interested in swinging on the door and singing than firing, but Jared didn't take any chances. He crept down the boardwalk, keeping close to the building, taking cover in doorways until he reached the saloon. He ducked into the alley and waited until the boy swung the opposite direction.

"Drop the gun!" Jared came up from behind, aiming his Colt.

"Huh?" The boy swung around.

Jared backhanded him across the face. He went down like a wet sack of flour.

Jared scooped up the boy's pistol and nudged him with the toe of his boot. Blood trickled from his nose. He was out cold.

A half-dozen men came out of the saloon, staring down at the boy. They all looked up at Jared.

"What did you have to go and do that fer?" one of them asked.

"Yeah, Johnny was just having a little fun, that's all," another said.

"That there is Johnny Ballard. His pa is Jim Ballard. He owns the biggest spread around these parts."

"Yeah, Sheriff Hickert never done nothing like that," someone else said.

Rafe Duncan, the bartender, pushed his way through the crowd, wiping his hands on a towel. He shook his head gravely. "Big Jim ain't going to be happy when he sees what you've done to his boy."

Jared hoisted the kid to his feet, then heaved him over his shoulder.

"You tell this Big Jim when he gets here that he can find his boy at the jail."

Whispers, finger-pointing and some frightened looks from women followed Jared as he carried the boy to the jail. He dumped him on the bunk inside one of the cells and locked the door.

From what the men at the saloon had said, Jim Ballard wouldn't be pleased when he found out his son had been arrested. Jared didn't care. He wasn't pleased about having his town shot up.

Stomach rumbling, Jared pulled the ledger from the bottom drawer of his desk and sat down. He didn't especially like doing the paperwork that came with his job, so he made it his policy to do it as it came up, do it and get it over with.

He flipped through the pages of arrests, fines and incarcerations until he came to the one with Johnny Ballard's name on it. This wasn't the first time the boy had been in trouble with the law.

Jared wrote down the information, hoping the Silver Bell was keeping his breakfast warm. He was ready to leave when his office door opened and four women marched in—all well dressed, all pinch-lipped, all scowling.

Trouble. Just what he needed. Especially on an empty stomach.

The tallest woman stopped in front of his desk, the others crowding around her. "Sheriff McQuaid, I am Mrs. Pomeroy, and we are from the Ladies for the Betterment of Stanford Committee."

Jared frowned. "The Ladies for what?"

Mrs. Pomeroy drew herself up. "We are appalled— *appalled*—by the incident that took place only moments ago at that disgusting haven of sin and evil."

Jared frowned. "Haven for sin and what?"

"The saloon!"

Jared rocked back in his chair. "You mean the Ballard boy?"

"Exactly." Mrs. Pomeroy's lips curled down distastefully. "Imagine, drinking and shooting up the town. And at this hour of the morning, too."

The ladies behind her made little tsking sounds.

Jared's stomach growled. "Look, ladies, I arrested the kid and threw him in jail—"

"Woefully inadequate!" Mrs. Pomeroy declared. "We, of the Ladies for the Betterment of Stanford Committee, insist that you take steps to close down that saloon."

"*What?*" Jared came out of his chair. "What the hell do you expect me—"

"Really, Sheriff, your language," Mrs. Pomeroy admonished. All the ladies cringed.

"Look," Jared said, "I've got nothing to do with the saloon—"

"You most certainly do, Sheriff McQuaid, and I— we—insist that you—"

"I'm not going to do anything about that saloon," Jared told them. "Now, you ladies get on back to whatever it is you were doing, and—"

The door burst open and Tom Keaton from the feed and grain store stuck his head inside. "Better get over to the mercantile, Sheriff. Looks like trouble brewing."

"Oh, hell, what now?" Jared muttered.

"Sheriff!" Mrs. Pomeroy declared. "Don't you dare leave until this discussion is finished."

"It's finished," he told them, and headed out the door.

The ladies swarmed after Jared, crowding around him on the boardwalk, all of them talking at once.

"What's the problem?" Jared shouted to Tom.

He pointed to the Stanford Mercantile just down the street. "Old Ben and Abel. Looks like they're at it again."

Jared craned his neck toward the mercantile, trying to see over all the hats bobbing in front of him.

"Sheriff," Mrs. Pomeroy said, planting herself in his path, "I insist you give this issue your immediate attention."

He waved his arms. "Ladies, will you just— yeow!"

Pain shot through Jared's left knee and vibrated up his thigh.

"Goddamn, son of a—"

"Sheriff!" Mrs. Pomeroy gasped. "Such language! In front of *ladies!*"

Holding his knee, Jared whirled to see a little boy probably no more than five years old, dressed in a blue coat, disappear into the alley.

"You kicked me!" Jared yelled. "Get back here, you little—"

"Oh, my word, Millie's going to faint!" one of the women cried.

Two women screamed. Jared turned in time to grab Millie as she swayed.

"You insensitive brute! Look what you've done!" Mrs. Pomeroy swatted him over the head with her handbag. "Get away from her!"

The women pulled Millie from Jared's grasp and hustled her down the boardwalk. Mrs. Pomeroy turned back. "Rest assured, Sheriff McQuaid, the mayor and the town council will hear about this."

All the women threw him murderous looks as they walked away.

"Come on, Sheriff, better get over to the mercantile," Tom Keaton insisted.

Jared rubbed his aching knee and hobbled along behind Tom to the store across the street, getting stares from most everyone he passed. Once there, he saw two old men in buckskins and battered hats, nose-to-nose over a checkerboard balanced atop a barrel, shouting at the top of their voices.

"What the hell's going on here?" Jared demanded.

One of the men pointed at the other. "He cheated! Abel Conroy here is a low-down, cheating skunk. He took his hand off his checker, then claimed he didn't!"

"I never did such a thing, Ben Paxton, you lying dog, you!" Abel yelled.

"I seen you! With my own two eyes!" Ben shouted. "You took your finger off, plain as day!"

"And you're a-lying, plain as day!"

Ben put up his fists. "Nobody calls me a liar. Come on, let's go!"

Abel's fists went up, too. "I'll knock you flatter than your mama's pancakes!"

"Them's fighting words, for sure!" Ben's face turned red.

"Back off! Both of you!" Jared pushed between them, separating them and knocking over the barrel with the checkerboard resting on it. Red and black checkers flew everywhere.

Ben and Abel both froze, watching their checkers roll into the street and drop between the cracks in the boardwalk.

"Now look what you've gone and done," Ben said to Jared, the fight gone out of him.

"Yeah," Abel echoed. "What kind of man goes and ruins another man's checker game?"

Ben and Abel squared off at Jared.

"That's about the lowest thing I've ever seen done in my whole entire life," Ben declared. Abel nodded along with him.

Even Tom Keaton nodded. "Yeah, Sheriff, that's pretty bad."

Jared seethed. He was in no mood to argue. His

knee hurt, his stomach rumbled and now his head was starting to ache.

He pointed his finger at the two old men. "If I catch the two of you disturbing the peace again, I'm throwing you both in jail."

Jared whipped around. A little crowd had gathered behind him. They eyed him sharply as he pushed through and headed toward the Silver Bell.

But when he arrived, all he got was a sorrowful headshake from Ennis Everette.

"Sorry, Sheriff, we didn't think you were coming back. My wife, she served your meal to somebody else."

Jared grumbled under his breath. "This is a restaurant, isn't it? You've got something to eat in there, don't you?"

"We might have a little something," Ennis said, wringing his apron in his hands and glancing into the kitchen. "But we're just starting on lunch and it's not ready yet. Come on back in a couple of hours and—"

"Never mind."

Jared stomped out of the restaurant and stood on the boardwalk. He was hungry, and grumpy, and irritated beyond belief. What in the hell was *wrong* with all the people in this town?

A flash of blue streaked by. Pain shot through his knee.

"Damn it!" Jared limped after the boy, who'd kicked him again, until the child ducked into the alley.

Cursing, Jared sank onto the crates stacked outside the restaurant, rubbing his knee.

He sat there, cursing everything and everybody, ignoring the looks he got from passersby, until the pain died down enough that he could walk. He headed toward the Cottonwood Café.

Mattie. He wanted to see Mattie. Just the sight of her would soothe him. And if he didn't get soothed soon—and fed—all hell was liable to break loose in Stanford.

When he rounded the corner at the rear of the Cottonwood, he saw her coming out of the kitchen. Jared's heart lurched. A wave of calm passed through him.

Mattie had on a green dress today, one he'd never seen before. Little tendrils of brown hair bobbed against her neck as she walked. She looked pretty, so pretty. He could have stood there and looked at her all day.

But then his chest tightened when he saw her stop at the woodpile and load logs into her arms.

"What the hell do you think you're doing?" he demanded, charging toward her.

She gasped and spun around, juggling the logs in her arms. "Good gracious, you scared me."

He jerked the wood away from her. "Don't you know better than to carry heavy things in your condition?"

Her lips thinned as she glared up at him. "It's not

that heavy—I wouldn't carry it if it were. Besides, it's none of your business. I told you that last night.''

"It is my business!" Jared cursed again. "As long as you're walking around with my baby inside you, everything you do is my business!"

Red flashed across her cheeks and her eyes narrowed. She took a step forward. Jared backed up.

"You stay away from me, Jared McQuaid. You're not a nice person and I don't like you. I had a husband who bullied me and I'm not going through that again." Mattie jerked the logs from his arms. "And don't you *ever* raise your voice at me again!"

Jared watched her stomp up the steps and into the kitchen. He nearly went after her. He itched to. Instead, he turned and strode away.

By the time he got halfway through town, his temper was boiling. No breakfast, some kid shooting up the town, those ladies screeching at him about the saloon, two old men coming to blows over a checker game and, of all things, that kid kicking him. Then Mattie. Talking to him like that. Telling him to stay away. Saying she didn't like him.

Up ahead on the boardwalk he saw a woman gather her small children and pull them aside as a man staggered toward her. His gray hair was unkempt, his whiskers ragged, his clothes soured; he had a half-empty bottle of liquor in his hand.

Jared swore. He had little patience left, and none for a drunk.

"Hey!" Jared called.

The man lurched toward him, waving the liquor bottle. He grabbed the man's collar and slammed him against the side of the building; the bottle broke on the boardwalk. The man grunted, made a gurgling sound in his throat. Jared held him there for a minute, then yanked him away.

When he turned, he saw the woman and her children. They looked frightened. But of *him*, not the drunk.

Jared carted the man to the jail, half carrying him most of the way, and tossed him in the cell beside the Ballard boy.

When he walked into his office, he found Mayor Rayburn standing in the middle of the room. The older man slid his hands in his trouser pockets and rocked back on his heels. "Appears you and me need to have us a little talk," the mayor said.

"I got no time," Jared answered. He pulled the ledger from the bottom drawer and slammed it down.

"Oh, I think you do," Mayor Rayburn said. "We need to talk about whether or not you're going to be able to keep your job."

Chapter Seven

Jared glared at Mayor Rayburn. "Keep my job? What the hell are you talking about?"

"Seems you've had a busy morning," the mayor said, seating himself in one of the chairs in front of Jared's desk.

"What the hell is that supposed to mean?"

"Have a seat," the mayor said, gesturing to the desk.

Jared glared at him a few seconds longer, then dropped into the chair.

Mayor Rayburn stroked his side whiskers thoughtfully. He was a good twenty years older than Jared, graying and wrinkled, with a wizened gleam in his dark eyes. "Heard you locked up the Ballard boy," he said.

"Damn right I did."

"And I see you brought old Mr. Hopkins in just now."

"That drunk? Yeah, I brought him in. Liquored up like a blind owl, staggering through town."

Mayor Rayburn nodded slowly. "Mrs. Pomeroy and the Ladies for the Betterment of Stanford Committee paid me a visit a while ago."

Jared cursed. "Those women barged into my office making demands—"

"Seems you got Ben and Abel pretty riled up outside the mercantile."

"Yeah. So what?" Jared came to his feet. "Look here, mayor, you hired me to enforce the laws in this town."

The mayor drew in a deep breath, then let it out slowly. "Now, see, son, that's where you're wrong."

Jared blinked at him. "Wrong?"

"I hired you to keep the peace."

"That's what I'm doing."

"Nope, that's not what you're doing. Enforcing the laws and keeping the peace are two different things."

Jared just looked at him. "What the hell are you talking about?"

"Sit down. I'll explain it to you," Mayor Rayburn said.

Jared hesitated a moment, then sank into his chair.

"You see, Stanford is a good town, with a lot of good folks," the mayor said. "We have a little trouble from time to time, but nothing big."

"I wouldn't call a kid shooting up the town 'nothing big'."

Mayor Rayburn waved his hand for quiet, then went

on. "The kind of trouble we have here in Stanford means that sometimes you might have to be a friendly ear, instead of a lawman. A preacher, or a pa. A brother, sometimes. Usually, a lawman is the last thing you'll have to be. Understand?"

Jared shook his head. "That's not what you hired me to do."

"Well, maybe I didn't explain it good enough," Mayor Rayburn said. "But the long and short of it is that we don't need a lawman who causes more problems than he solves." The mayor got to his feet. "You think it over. And if you don't believe you can be the kind of sheriff we need, well, then we'll just have to find us somebody else."

He nodded pleasantly and left the office.

"Damn it..." Jared heaved the ledger across the office.

What was that mayor thinking, accusing him of not knowing how to do his job? He'd been a United States Marshal for ten years. Ten long years of distinguished service. He knew how to be a lawman. He'd proved it with the capture of hundreds of criminals.

From the sound of it, Mayor Rayburn didn't need a sheriff—he needed a nursemaid. And that wasn't the kind of lawman Jared was, and that's all there was to it.

He sat back in his chair and sighed heavily. To hell with them. He didn't need this job. With his record he could go anywhere and get hired. He could go back to the marshal service, if he wanted.

Maybe that's what he ought to do. Jared slumped

further into his chair, considering the possibility. Listening to a bunch of women bellyaching about the saloon, breaking up a fight over a checker game…well, it was beneath him, a man of his reputation. It was almost embarrassing. Maybe he should just march over to the mayor's office and resign.

Jared sat there stewing, and the longer he thought about what the mayor had said, the more quitting seemed like the thing to do.

His office door opened, and Jared was almost afraid to look up, fearing it was Mrs. Pomeroy and her committee again, or Ben and Abel expecting him to hunt down their checkers.

Instead, he saw a tall, lanky young man with a shock of brown hair hanging over his forehead, dressed in clothes a couple of sizes too big. He walked right over to Jared's desk and offered his hand.

"Sheriff, my name is Billy Weaver. Glad to know you."

Good Lord, what now? Jared took his hand cautiously.

Billy folded his long legs into the chair in front of Jared's desk. "I heard about your arresting Big Jim Ballard's boy, so I come right on over, soon as I could. My aunt Frannie had me cleaning out the fireplaces, and I couldn't just get up and leave."

Jared frowned. "Is that so?"

"Yes, sir," Billy told him. His gaze roamed the office for a moment, then settled on Jared again. "Is it all right if'n I talk to you before I get started?"

"Get started?"

"Yes, sir. Get started. On the cleaning." Billy waved his hands around. "I clean the jail. Sheriff Hickert hired me. I do the cooking, too, for the prisoners."

Jared's stomach rumbled. "You can cook?"

"Oh, sure. My aunt Frannie taught me. Aunt Frannie says that anybody who can't cook for themself is just about as worthless as a button on a hat. That's what my aunt Frannie says."

Jared nodded toward the stove in the corner. "How about you get something started and we'll talk."

"Yes, sir," he said. "Them prisoners will be hungry by now."

Billy got a fire going in the stove, then went through the cupboard, putting beans on to heat and cutting off a hunk of bread from a loaf in the biscuit jar.

"Give me a plate of that, will you?" Jared told him. "The prisoners can wait awhile."

Billy served him, then sat down in the chair again. He glanced around, then leaned forward.

"Now, if'n I tell you this you got to promise you won't tell nobody," Billy said. He glanced around again. "'Cause if my aunt Frannie finds out, she'll take a switch to me for sure."

The boy looked a little big for anybody to be taking a switch to him. Jared tasted the beans.

"How old are you, Billy?"

"Nineteen," he announced, and sat up a little straighter. "Twenty, come fall."

"You live with your aunt?"

"Yes, sir. My folks passed on when I was a kid. I

don't rightly remember them. Aunt Frannie, she raised me.''

Jared paused over his plate. "Does your aunt happen to be a member of the Ladies for the Betterment of Stanford Committee?"

"Shoot, no." Billy waved his hands expansively. "Aunt Frannie says those women got no business poking their noses where it don't belong."

Jared grunted. He liked Aunt Frannie already. "So, what is it you want to talk about?" he asked, biting into the bread.

"Well, sir, here it is. I'll just say it straight out. My aunt Frannie, she says that's the best way." Billy drew in a big breath. "I want you to hire me as your deputy."

Jared's chewing slowed as he gazed across the desk at Billy. The boy looked well suited for sweeping up and cooking, but as a deputy?

"'Cause now, see, Aunt Frannie says I need to be getting me a job. A real job. Not the little ones I've been doing around town," Billy explained. "She's done gone and taken a notion to send me back East to her brother to work in his can factory, and well, I just don't want to go. So you see, that's why I want you to hire me as a deputy. That way I'll have a real job."

Jared scraped the last of the beans from his plate. They weren't particularly good, but at least they were filling. "Being a deputy is a serious job," he said.

"Yeah, I know. But you need a deputy now that Drew's gone to see about his mama."

"How did you know about that?"

Billy just shrugged. "So, how about it, Sheriff? I'll make a good deputy. I swear I will."

The town needed a deputy now that Drew Tanner had left. And the way things were going, they'd need a new sheriff, too.

"Don't decide right now," Billy said. "You think it over. You just watch how I do my work. Aunt Frannie says that's the real measure of a man, how he does his work."

"Your aunt Frannie sounds like a wise woman."

"Yes, sir, she is." Billy smile faded. "And I don't care what everybody says about you arresting old Mr. Hopkins or that Johnny Ballard, I think you done the right thing."

Nice to hear that someone in this town agreed with him.

Pushing his plate away, Jared got to his feet. "I got to go out for a while."

"Don't you worry about nothing, Sheriff. I'll take care of everything while you're gone. You'll see."

Jared walked outside and surveyed the town. Just yesterday he'd stood on this very spot, thinking how happy he was to be here. Yesterday. Was it just yesterday? Seemed like a long time ago.

And now he had to leave. No way in hell could he let the mayor and town council dictate how he'd do his job. Jared was a professional lawman. He knew what he was doing. And he wouldn't kowtow to anybody.

Be a friendly ear, a preacher, a brother? What the

hell was the mayor thinking? That was no way to run a town. Even a quiet little town like Stanford.

Jared straightened his shoulders. Better to get it over with quick. No sense waiting.

But instead of going to the mayor's house, Jared found himself heading toward the Cottonwood Café and Mattie. She'd probably dance a jig when she found out he was leaving.

Jared's stomach started to hurt.

She'd said this morning that she didn't like him, that he wasn't very nice. She'd compared him to Del Ingram, too. That didn't make Jared feel very good, either.

He'd come to Stanford with high hopes of finding a home, finding a place he belonged. Putting his past behind him. Starting fresh.

Now he was leaving it all.

Leaving Mattie. Mattie and his baby.

Jared stopped at the front of the Cottonwood Café and gazed through the window. No one was seated in the dining room.

He caught a glimpse of Mattie straightening the cloths on the tables, and his heart lurched. What would it be like to never see her again? To never see the baby? To never know…?

Standing there feeling like a lovesick puppy, Jared couldn't bear the thought of leaving Stanford. He wanted to stay.

He didn't want to be the town nursemaid, but he wanted to stay. He wanted a home. He wanted Mattie.

But how would he go about it?

For the past ten years he'd dealt with hardened criminals. On the trail, he'd had no one to answer to. As long as he got the job done, that was all that mattered.

The truth was, he didn't know how to deal with people when their biggest problem was whether or not they'd taken their finger off their checker. What was he supposed to do with drunks but throw them in jail? How was he supposed to deal with a gaggle of women making ridiculous demands on him?

Jared didn't know. He just plain didn't know.

He had no training for this aspect of his job. No experience. No inkling of what to do. He needed help.

The knot in his stomach wound tighter. Mattie could help him, if she would. She'd know what to do. She'd lived in this town for a long time. She knew everyone.

The only problem was that she had no reason to help him. She'd just as soon see him ride out of Stanford for good. Though, honestly, he didn't see why. He'd done nothing but try to help her, do the right thing by her. Maybe he needed to remind her of that.

Jared pulled his hat lower on his forehead. Mattie was going to help him whether she liked it or not. And the sooner she got started, the better.

Chapter Eight

"I'm almost afraid to say it aloud, but we're doing better today," Mattie said.

Seated on a stool at the worktable in the kitchen of the Cottonwood Café, she smiled at Mrs. Nance, who was standing at the stove.

"Seems the noon crowd was the best turnout we've had in a while," Mrs. Nance said, "thanks to the train passengers."

Mattie dropped the coins she'd just counted into her lock box and closed the lid. Before, the Cottonwood routinely sent a wagon to the train station to transport passengers to the restaurant during layovers. But that was before Del died. Shortly thereafter, when the new owner had showed up at her house and claimed them, she'd learned Del had lost the team and wagon in a poker game.

Nearly twenty train passengers had arrived at noon to eat. The hale and hearty travelers from Minnesota thought nothing of making the walk, it seemed. Mattie was thankful. While it wasn't the repeat business she needed to keep her Café going, she'd take it.

Tapping her pencil against her ledger, Mattie pressed her lips together. "I've got to come up with more money. I've got to improve the menu if I'm going to get my old customers back."

Mrs. Nance nodded. "Most any merchant in town would gladly extend you credit."

Mattie cringed at the thought. That was her biggest problem. All the merchants had already extended credit—to Del. And now Mattie was left to pay them back. They were willing to let her repay them a little at a time, thanks to Del's sterling reputation in Stanford, but even that was nearly impossible. It took almost every cent the restaurant earned.

"I wouldn't feel right asking for credit." Mattie hadn't told anyone, not even Mrs. Nance, about the debts Del had left her with.

"Then how about talking to Mr. Burrows at the bank?" Mrs. Nance suggested. "He gives loans to the businessmen in town when they need it."

Mattie had considered the possibility. Mr. Burrows was pompous and uppity, used to looking down his long nose on people. She didn't want to go to him for a loan unless she absolutely had to.

Which might be any day now.

Mattie looked over the columns of figures in her ledger. Her heart sank. How would she ever pull out of this hole?

If only she could offer the hearty, robust meals she

used to, her customers would come back. But to restore her menu she needed beef, poultry, pork—and lots of it.

The problem was that meat cost money, and after paying Mrs. Nance's salary, Del's debts, and buying what meager supplies she could, there simply wasn't enough money left.

The restaurant was spiraling downward, and unless she got cash from somewhere, she'd be out of business.

Her parents weren't wealthy people. They'd left Mattie nothing of value except the home she lived in, and it made no sense to sell that. If the house were gone, where would she live? Perhaps with only herself to consider, she could make do with living in the restaurant. But Mattie had a baby on the way now, and a baby needed a home.

Of course, there was the modest jewelry that had belonged to her mother. Only Mattie couldn't bring herself to sell it—yet.

"I'll make my offer again," Mrs. Nance said. "I'll be glad to help you out. You know that."

Mattie smiled. Mrs. Nance had offered to lend her money from her own savings, but Mattie had turned her down. Mrs. Nance wasn't a young woman. She couldn't afford to risk her small savings on the restaurant. Mattie couldn't bear the thought that Mrs. Nance might lose everything, and it would be her fault.

"You're a dear, Mrs. Nance, and I appreciate your

offer. But you know I can't let you do that,'' Mattie said.

"There's someone you haven't asked yet."

Mattie's spirits lifted. "Who?"

"The new sheriff."

She groaned and slid off the stool. "Don't start about Jared McQuaid again."

"The man wanted to marry you, Mattie. How many other men in this town have stepped in to offer help?"

Mrs. Nance was the only person Mattie had told about her near nuptials. Yet, somehow, most everyone who'd come into the restaurant had mentioned it. The news was all over town.

Mattie waved away the thought. "I'm not marrying Jared McQuaid."

Mrs. Nance grinned. "I don't know. Being wed to a big man like him—"

"Mrs. Nance!" Mattie's cheeks flushed. Heat wafted through her body. She turned away quickly, praying Mrs. Nance wouldn't see how her words and the images they brought affected her.

"Gets pretty cold around here at night," Mrs. Nance added. "Having him in your bed would sure warm things up. And often, too."

Mattie fanned her flaming cheeks. If only Mrs. Nance knew.

"Well, anyway," Mrs. Nance said, "I think you ought to at least talk to the sheriff about it. I'll bet he'd help you out."

"No." Mattie shook her head. "This restaurant belongs to me. If I ask Jared—or anybody—for money it will be like taking on a partner. Then I'd have to share whatever money I make, and I don't want to do that.'' Her hand went to her belly. ''This restaurant is my baby's future. I have to keep it going for him.''

Mrs. Nance smiled sweetly. ''Still thinking it's a boy, are you?''

Jared had said he wanted a girl. All the more reason to hope for a boy.

''A boy would suit me just fine,'' Mattie declared.

Mrs. Nance looked past Mattie to the back door, then smiled broadly. ''Well, seems you've got yourself a visitor.''

Turning, Mattie saw Jared walk through the door. Her heart beat a little faster at seeing him, which annoyed her no end. She didn't even like the man, for goodness sake.

Mattie crossed her arms and blocked his path. ''We're closed.''

Jared frowned. ''I've got to talk to you.''

''I don't have time. Go away.''

He shifted his weight. ''Now, look, Mattie, I—''

Mrs. Nance breezed by. ''I've got to run to the store. I'll be back in a bit,'' she called, disappearing out the door.

The kitchen seemed suddenly smaller, crackling with some unknown energy as Mattie stood face-to-face with Jared. She pressed her lips together. ''See how easily Mrs. Nance left? Why don't you do the same?''

"Because I need to talk to you," Jared insisted. "I need your help."

Taken aback, Mattie just stared at him. The forceful sheriff needed help? Her help? She'd never imagined him saying such a thing to her, but for some reason, it pleased her.

Still, she wouldn't give in so easily. "Seems to me you never answered my question about the baby. Are you going to keep my secret, or not?"

Jared frowned, then shook his head. "I don't like it, but I'll go along with it."

"Oh." Surprised, Mattie smiled. "Well, thank you. Now, what sort of help do you need?"

Jared rocked from foot to foot, pulled on the back of his neck as if he were working up to whatever it was he had to tell her. Finally, he blew out a deep breath.

"Seems the mayor isn't too happy with the way I've been doing my job," he said.

"Ah, yes. You've been the talk of most everyone who's come into the restaurant today. The way I hear it you've arrested half the town and offended the other half."

"Yeah, that's about the size of it," Jared muttered. "It doesn't make any sense to me. All I did was lock up a couple of prisoners and break up a fight."

"The Ballard boy. Yes, I heard. Jim Ballard's Three B Ranch employs dozens of men who patronize Stanford. He buys a lot of supplies from here. Nobody wants to make Big Jim mad."

"Even if his boy was shooting up the town?"

"Well, yes, I see you have a point there," Mattie admitted. She clucked disapprovingly. "But really, Jared, locking up poor old Mr. Hopkins?"

"He was drunk. Staggering through town."

"He's always drunk," Mattie told him. "Always staggering through town."

"How the hell was I supposed to know that?" Jared demanded.

Mattie wagged her finger at him. "It's just *that* attitude and *that* kind of language that offended Mrs. Pomeroy and her committee."

Jared rolled his eyes. "Those old biddies…"

"They do a lot of work in this town. A lot of good work. You shouldn't have treated them so disrespectfully."

"Oh, well, thank you. I know that *now*."

Mattie huffed. "So, what do you want me to help you with?"

"I want you to tell me what I'm supposed to do with the likes of old man Hopkins. How I'm going to handle those two old coots fighting over a checker game. How I'm going to get on Mrs. Pomeroy's and her cohorts' good side."

"And just why on earth would I do that? Why would I want to help you?"

Jared came closer, pinning her with his intense gaze. "Because I'm asking you to," he said softly.

Mattie's stomach twisted, but not from the nausea

she usually felt. It was something else. Something she didn't understand.

Something she didn't intend to think too hard about.

She waved her hands around the room. "Even if I wanted to help you, I can't. I don't have time. I have work to do."

Jared grunted. "Okay, look. I'll help you with your chores if you'll tell me what I need to know. How's that for a fair trade?"

"Well..." Behind him on the other side of the kitchen, the sideboard was running over with dirty dishes. Thanks to their unexpectedly large noon crowd, she hadn't had time to do the morning dishes, either.

A little grin pulled at Mattie's lips, and she struggled to keep it from blooming into a full smile. "Well, all right, if you're sure?"

"I'm sure." Jared gave her a quick nod. "I'll fetch more firewood."

"I have plenty of firewood."

"Oh. Well, okay, then I'll bring in those crates stacked outside."

"They stay outside."

"How about if I tighten up that porch railing? One of the boards seems loose."

"Well, actually, I was thinking you could..." Mattie gestured grandly to the sideboard.

Jared turned. A frown cut deep lines in his face. "Now just a damn minute. You don't mean..."

She smiled sweetly and nodded.

His back stiffened. "You want me to wash dishes? *All* of those dishes?"

"Every last one of them."

"But—"

"Do you want me to help you or not?" she asked. "If you want my help, you're going to have to give me a hand with chores. It's up to you."

Jared glared at her, then stomped over to the sideboard, grumbling and cursing.

"I'll get you an apron." Mattie pulled one from the drawer. It was pink, with flowers embroidered on the pockets and bib.

Jared raised an eyebrow at it. "Don't you have one with a few *more* ruffles on it?"

She swept off his hat, then rose on her toes to loop the apron over his head.

Mattie stopped in midstretch. Would this be what her son would grow into? A man like his father, tall and sturdy? Would the tiny babe inside her one day tower over her? Whose eyes would he have? Jared's deep blue or her own brown ones?

Jared's gaze met hers, held her captive. Warmth radiated from him. His body pulsed with it. Though he stood perfectly still, he seemed to beckon her. Mattie wanted to lean forward, press herself against him. Feel his taut muscles, his strength…again.

She hung there, suspended in some web he'd cast over her. And for a moment, a long troubling moment, Mattie wanted to be no other place but here.

Finally, she ducked behind him and tied the apron strings. Without really meaning to, she found her hands lingering while her gaze swept him from head to toe. Black, wavy hair. He'd need a haircut soon. Wide shoulders. A long, hard back. How did he ever finds shirts that fit? Her gaze dipped lower, hovered as she remembered their night together when she'd—

"You done back there?" he asked.

Heat plumed up Mattie's neck. She spun away and hurried toward the dining room. "I have to straighten the tables."

"Didn't you already do that?" he called.

Damn the lawman in him. He noticed everything. Mattie didn't answer, just kept going until she couldn't feel his gaze on her any longer.

She had, in fact, straightened the dining room after the noon crowd left, but now she performed the task all over again. She took her time, waiting for her hands to stop trembling and her face to cool.

Finally, she ventured back into the kitchen and found Jared at the washtub standing in a puddle of water, sleeves rolled past his elbow, apron and shirt soaked from the water he'd splashed on himself.

Mattie couldn't hide her smile. "You're really getting into your work, I see."

He threw her a sour look, then shook his head. "The least you can do is talk to me while I'm washing all these damn dishes."

His request seemed reasonable enough, and really, what excuse could she give him not to? That his nearness made her uncomfortable—in a delightful way?

Mattie pulled a stool over to the sideboard and sat down close enough to be sociable, but not near enough that she'd get splashed. Jared was the most aggressive dishwasher she'd ever seen.

And that really didn't surprise her.

"So, what made you move here to Stanford?" Mattie asked.

Jared glanced up. For a moment it seemed he wanted to say something, but didn't. He shrugged. "Stanford appeared to be a good town."

"That's certainly true."

"I guess it will be getting a lot bigger, with what the mayor and council have planned."

"What's that?"

"You mean there's one bit of gossip that hasn't made it through Stanford yet?" Jared chuckled. "There's a big group of investors from back East coming through this part of the country. The town council's planning a big shindig for them, trying to get some of their investment money for Stanford."

Mattie's stomach bounced. "Investors? When?"

"They'll be here in a few weeks, according to Mayor Rayburn." Jared dipped a bowl in the rinse tub, sloshing more water on the floor. "What's got you so interested in Eastern investors?"

Mattie clamped her lips together, tempted to tell him the truth. At the moment, it seemed easy to include him in her troubles, her problems...her life.

But she decided to say nothing. She was on her own now. That's the way she wanted to keep it.

Mattie changed the subject and Jared didn't seem to notice. Surprisingly, they talked continuously until he'd finished the dishes, dried and stacked them in the cupboard, then mopped up the water from the floor.

Jared peeled off his wet apron and hung it on a hook beside the back door; underneath, his shirt and long johns were soaked through.

He planted himself in front of Mattie, still perched on the stool.

"I've washed every dish in the whole restaurant, maybe even the whole town," Jared said. "So let's have it. How am I going to deal with all these people in Stanford?"

"Simple," Mattie said. "Be nice."

"Huh?"

"Be nice," Mattie said again.

Jared stared expectantly at her. She stared back.

"Yeah?" he asked. "And…?"

Mattie shrugged. "That's it."

"That's it? *That's it?*" The corner of his lip curled up in a snarl. "I stand here and wash three hundred dishes for you and all you can say is *be nice?*"

She lifted her shoulders. "What did you expect? That I would wave a magic wand and make everything all right?"

"Hell, no. But I did expect some real help from you," Jared told her. "After all I've done for you—"

"All you've done for me?" Mattie hopped off the stool, anger shooting through her. "All you've *done for me?*"

"Damn right. I never asked for a word of thanks, but the least you could do is—"

"Oh, dear, did I forget to thank you? For getting

me pregnant? For that heartwarming marriage proposal? For that romantic wedding ceremony? For making me the object of the town's gossip—again? Please,
excuse my poor manners! What in the world was I
thinking?"

"Now, look here—"

"Just leave." She turned her back and headed toward the dining room.

"Mattie!"

She didn't stop. A moment later, she heard the back
door slam. Mattie turned. Jared was gone.

The afternoon dragged by, with few diners coming
to the Cottonwood. The boom earlier in the day wasn't
repeated. Mattie stayed busy, cleaning things that
didn't need cleaning, straightening the pantry, cupboards and shelves. She sent Mrs. Nance home early,
then closed up and left.

She was tired. But somehow it wasn't all the physical activity she'd done around the restaurant that had
worn her out. Thoughts of Jared McQuaid had done
it.

Certainly she was happy that he'd agreed to keep
her secret about the baby. That in itself was a huge
decision, and a favorable one, leaving one less thing
for her to worry about. But that wasn't the only reason
he'd been on her mind.

Though she didn't want to, Mattie admitted to herself that she'd liked having him in her restaurant today. Something about his presence was comforting.
His strength, perhaps. She wasn't sure.

So it was hard to understand why, at the same time,

he could cause her to get so riled up. The man evoked all sorts of emotions in her, no matter how she tried to steel her feelings against him.

A little sliver of moon hung in the sky, offering only a bit of light to guide Mattie home. Few people were out at this time of the night. Somewhere, a dog barked.

As she walked, Mattie considered telling Jared about her declining business and financial problems. Might he help? Maybe he could send some of those Eastern investors her way. If she asked, maybe he'd invest in her restaurant himself, give her the cash she so desperately needed.

Mattie sighed heavily in the still, cool air. As easy as that sounded, she didn't really want it. She'd depended on Del, when she'd first married him, and he'd taken over everything himself. Taken everything away from her. And ruined it.

No, Mattie didn't want to count on anyone but herself—couldn't afford to. Not with her baby to take care of.

And really, that suited her all right. She was on her own now. No one to depend on but herself. No one to interfere with her life.

Everything would run smoothly, now that she was in charge.

Mattie stopped outside the gate in front of her house and squinted in the darkness. Her heart tumbled.

Jared McQuaid waited on her porch.

Chapter Nine

A fresh wave of fatigue washed through Mattie as she stopped in front of Jared, who was sitting in the swing on her front porch. She was tired. She didn't want to fight with him anymore. Tonight, at the end of this long day, she just didn't have it in her.

Mattie pinched the bridge of her nose. "Jared, would you please leave? I—"

"I'm sorry."

She blinked at him in the darkness, sure she hadn't heard him right.

"I'm sorry," he said again. "Seems I keep saying and doing all the wrong things around here."

Did he mean in Stanford? Or with her?

He rose from the swing and held out a small bouquet of flowers tied with a ribbon. "Is this 'being nice'? You said I should be nice. Does this count?"

He must have sat there for a while waiting for her because the flowers were slightly crushed and wilted from his big hand. Even so, they were the prettiest things Mattie had seen in a long time.

She accepted the bouquet from him. "Yes, this is being nice."

"Hallelujah." Jared wiped his hand across his forehead. "I finally got something right."

Mattie forced the smile from her lips. "You didn't come all the way over here to bring me flowers."

"No, I didn't," Jared admitted. "I came here because you owe me."

Her brows rose. "I owe you?"

"Damn right. I figure that I made a big enough fool of myself in your kitchen this afternoon, wearing an apron and washing dishes, that I deserve more help than what you gave me."

"Is that so?"

"That's so, and I came over here to tell you that." Jared grinned. "I didn't think the flowers would do my cause any harm."

She should send him on his way. Mattie knew that. There was something about Jared McQuaid that could worm its way under her skin—if it hadn't already.

Mattie tossed that thought aside, refusing to consider it. She'd made her decision on running her own life and wouldn't be swayed.

But the thing she couldn't push away was the fact that Jared was right. At least about this. She did owe him.

"All right, you can come inside," Mattie said. She looked at him sternly. "But only for a few minutes."

Jared took the key from her, walked inside to the kitchen and lit the lanterns. He hung her shawl and handbag on pegs by the door. When Mattie opened the top cupboard, he reached over her head and picked up the vase she was going after, then pumped water into it.

"Did you arrest anybody else after you left the restaurant this afternoon?" Mattie asked, arranging the flowers in the vase. "Yell at old ladies? Frighten any small children?"

Jared leaned against the sideboard beside her. "I know this is hard for you to understand, Mattie, but I'm pretty much lost when it comes to this 'being nice' business. Up until I came to Stanford, being nice would have gotten me killed."

"When you were a marshal, you mean?"

"Riding the trail, hauling in desperados…I couldn't let my guard down, not for a minute."

"I see your point. All right, let's see what we can do for you." Mattie stepped in front of him, tapping her finger against her jaw, assessing him. He just stood there, letting her look him over from head to toe, not the least bit uncomfortable under her scrutiny.

And just why this made Mattie's stomach tingle, she didn't know.

"Let's work on your appearance first," Mattie decided.

"What the hell's wrong with the way I look?"

She rolled her eyes. "Maybe we should work on your language first."

He sighed irritably. "Nothing's wrong with the way I talk."

"Didn't you come here for my help?"

"Yeah, but—"

"Then hush up and listen," she told him.

"Yes, ma'am."

Mattie looked him up and down one final time. "You should try not to make that face so often."

He squinted at her. "What face?"

"The one that looks so mean."

He frowned. "I don't know what you're—"

"There. That's it. Don't tell me you didn't practice that in the mirror." Mattie touched the deep ridges between his eyebrows, making little swirls with her fingertips. "Relax your forehead. Relax. There, that's better. Now smile."

"I am smiling."

"No, you're not." She tugged at the corners of his mouth, then leaned back a little. "Well, that's somewhat better. You look nicer already."

The crease came back between his brows. "Is that so?"

She shrugged. "It's a place to start."

Jared straightened away from the sideboard, towering over her. He used his size to bully and intimidate. She'd seen him do it.

"And another thing, you shouldn't crowd people," Mattie said.

She placed her palm against his chest to demonstrate. Heat suddenly radiated up her arm. Her fingers began to tingle.

Jared froze. The little lines between his brows disappeared in earnest now. But instead of backing up, he eased forward.

"You don't like me being close?" he asked softly.

Mattie looked up at him. "N-no, I don't."

"Do I frighten you?"

"No," she whispered, "of course not."

"Then what is it?" Jared asked. He rested his hands on her shoulders and inched closer.

Mattie knew she should insist he take his hands away; she should pull her own hand off his chest. But she could do neither. Her gaze locked with his and she couldn't turn away.

Jared leaned down. "Does it make you...remember?"

She gulped. "Remember...what?"

"You know what." His breath brushed her cheek. "Is it because you're afraid if I get too close *this* will happen?"

He kissed her on the lips. Tenderly, so tenderly, as if she were a fine wine and he wanted to savor the taste. He slid his mouth over hers, tightening his arms around her. Mattie trembled with the delight of it.

Jared ended their kiss but didn't release her. He pressed his forehead against hers, keeping her in his embrace.

"This afternoon at your restaurant you asked why I came to Stanford," he said softly. "I didn't tell you the truth, not all of it, but I want you to know now, Mattie. I came to Stanford because I was lonely. I wanted a home. I wanted to live in a place where I belong.''

Mattie gazed up at him. ''Is that the only reason?''

''No. I came because you were here.''

''Because you thought that I—that we—would...you know?''

''Make love again?'' Jared smiled sweetly. ''I thought about it, Mattie. I won't lie to you about it. Sometimes, on the trail, thinking about you was the only thing that kept me going.''

''I'm not like that, usually,'' Mattie told him. ''That night, the night of Del's funeral, I don't know why I...''

''I know why. You were lonely. You needed somebody,'' Jared said. ''I guess I'd been lonely, too, and didn't realize it until that night. That's why I came back to Stanford. Not because I wanted to bed down with you again, although it would be nice, but because I couldn't quit wondering about you. What were you doing? How were things going for you? I wanted to get to know you better, Mattie.''

She eased away, needing distance from Jared. He didn't let her go far.

''Jared, I don't have the time or energy for anyone else in my life right now. I have a home to take care of, a business to manage, a baby to get ready for.''

''I don't want to add to your burden, Mattie. I want to ease it.''

''That's just it,'' she said. ''It's *my* burden to carry. I don't want any help. I don't want any more complications. It has nothing to do with you, Jared.''

"The hell it doesn't," he said.

Mattie stepped back, escaping his grasp. "I'm living my life and raising my baby. Alone."

"And you won't even give me a chance?"

"I gave Del a chance and look what happened." She shook her head. "I'm not going through that again."

Jared glared down at her, sure that crease she'd cautioned him about was cutting into his forehead, giving him the "mean look" to end all mean looks.

Where the hell had this woman gotten that stubborn streak of hers? Rolling around in bed with him that night, she'd been warm and giving beyond his wildest dreams. He'd never imagined she'd be this hardheaded, this determined.

But still, Jared found it captivating, like most everything else about Mattie. Knowing this about her just made him wonder what else there was to learn. Made him want to fight that much harder to make a place for himself in her life...in their baby's life.

For a moment he considered telling Mattie he was in love with her. That his heart ached just thinking of her. That his body yearned for her—only her.

But he didn't dare say the words. He'd scare her off for sure. Mattie was already retreating. His confession of love would undoubtedly send her hightailing it away from him at a dead run.

He didn't want that. He wouldn't stand for it. Jared wasn't about to let the woman he loved—or his baby—get away from him.

Getting Mattie to open her heart to him would require some finesse. Too bad finesse wasn't one of his strong suits. Jared preferred a straight-on confrontation. Just as he'd have to work at getting the townsfolk of Stanford to accept him, he'd have to earn his way into Mattie's life.

None of which particularly suited Jared. But what choice did he have?

"Does that mean if I asked you to marry me right now you'd say no?" Jared asked, a little grin tugging at his lips.

For an instant, Mattie looked angry. Then she saw that he was teasing, and smiled. "That's exactly what it means."

"Just thought I'd ask."

Jared ambled down the hallway to the front door and stepped outside. "Be sure to lock up."

Mattie nodded from the doorway. "I hope you understand why I feel the way I do."

"I understand."

"It's better this way," she said.

"If you say so."

"Just put me out of your mind," Mattie said.

"Can't do that." Jared shook his head. "In fact, I'm going to think about you naked all night."

"Jared!"

"'Night."

"Jared! Don't you dare do that!"

Mattie fumed as he sauntered across her yard, then she slammed the door shut. Oh, that man!

Think about her naked? How dare he!

Mattie stopped dead in her tracks. Him thinking of her naked made her think about him the same way.

Another wave of heat washed through her, warming her as his kiss had done earlier in the kitchen. Memories. So many memories of that night, their night.

"Oh, gracious…"

Determinedly, Mattie went to the kitchen and blew out all but one of the lanterns. She'd put that man out of her head—if it was the last thing she ever did.

She stopped then, lantern in hand as the flame danced across the bouquet of flowers Jared had brought her. It was silly, really, to be so pleased by such a small thing. She should toss them out—along with all thoughts of Jared McQuaid.

Instead, Mattie took the flowers to the bedroom with her, placed them on her bureau and readied herself for bed.

Seldom did she come to this room without thinking of the night Jared had been here with her. Tonight, with his kiss still fresh on her lips, he raged like a storm in her mind…in her heart.

Sliding beneath the covers, Mattie took one last look at the flowers and blew out the lantern. She fell asleep almost at once.

But when she woke in the middle of the night, it wasn't thoughts of Jared that had jarred her awake.

Mattie sat straight up in bed.

She knew how she'd save her restaurant.

Chapter Ten

As plans went, it wasn't much of one. But it was all Jared had. He'd have to make it work.

Be nice, Mattie had advised him. Damn...

Standing outside the sheriff's office, Jared nodded pleasantly to the men who passed by, and tipped his hat to the ladies. This morning he'd practiced his smile in the mirror while shaving—and nicked himself in the process—and was now trying it out on the towns-folk.

So far, it wasn't going well.

But truthfully, his heart wasn't in this "being nice" campaign Mattie had suggested. As a lawman, it went against his grain. So lying awake most of the night, Jared had come up with another plan he could defi-nitely sink his teeth into.

"Morning, ma'am." Jared touched the brim of his hat as a woman passed in front of him. She spared him a brief glance as she went by; at least she hadn't crossed the street to avoid him as others had done this morning.

Jared held his smile in place until the woman was gone, then hung his thumbs in his gun belt, thinking.

The plan that kept him tossing and turning all night, the one he was most concerned with, was the one that would win Mattie's heart.

Somewhere around midnight it had occurred to Jared that Mattie didn't know him. Not really. Sure, she knew him in the intimate way a man and woman knew each other, thanks to their night together. But in view of the fact that Mattie had ended up pregnant, Jared didn't think the experience had done much to endear him to her.

On top of that, Del Ingram had been her first husband. Her only husband. And a poor one, to boot. Surely, marriage to that man was enough to sour any woman's view of the holy state of matrimony.

"Morning, ma'am." Jared stretched his mouth into the smile he'd practiced this morning, and tipped his hat to a woman and her three little children who walked by. She grabbed the youngsters and scurried as far away from him as she could without venturing into the street, keeping a wary eye on him as she hurried down the boardwalk.

Jared swallowed a mumbled curse and kept smiling.

Despite the havoc he'd caused as sheriff, and what the townsfolk thought of him, Jared knew he could make Mattie come around. It would take some doing, but he'd show her the good man he was, the good husband he could be.

He knew how, knew what to do, even if he hadn't done it in years.

So if it took kissing up to every old biddy in town to keep his job and stay in Stanford, close to Mattie, he'd do it. He wasn't about to leave. Whatever the cost, he would win Mattie's heart.

And she would marry him before their baby came into the world.

Jared straightened as he spotted Mrs. Pomeroy heading his way. He didn't know if he was up to "being nice" to that old battle-ax; he'd had only an hour or so of practice this morning. But here she came, her wide hips taking up most of the boardwalk, her lips pursed and her gaze deliberately, he was sure, avoiding him.

"Good morning, Mrs. Pomeroy," Jared crooned, touching his finger to the brim of his hat.

Her expression grew more sour, though Jared hadn't thought that possible, as she spared him a brief glance.

"Ma'am, I'd like to—"

"Humph." Mrs. Pomeroy put her nose in the air and steamed right past him down the boardwalk.

A curse rumbled in Jared's chest. It tickled his lips, begging to be spit out, and might have, too, if Mattie hadn't appeared at his elbow.

She nodded toward Mrs. Pomeroy. "Thinking of *her* naked, too?"

"Oh, damn..." Jared grimaced and splayed his

hand across his belly. "Don't say that. I just ate my breakfast."

Mattie tossed him a smug smile, and even that pleased Jared. He smiled back—and not his practiced smile, either. This one was genuine.

"How are you feeling this morning?" he asked, forcing himself not to look down at her belly.

"Better than usual."

Mattie always looked beautiful to him. But today her cheeks seemed a little pinker, not so pale and drawn from the morning sickness she experienced. In fact, today she looked as if she felt better than he'd seen her look since his return to Stanford.

"Actually," Mattie said, "I've had so much on my mind this morning, I haven't had time to think about being sick."

"What's on your mind?" he asked, and couldn't help hoping she'd say it was him.

Instead, Mattie glanced away. "Business. Just business. I have to run."

She scooted around him before Jared could stop her. He watched her, though, as she headed down the boardwalk, admiring the sway of her skirt. She stopped as Billy Weaver approached. They talked for a few minutes, and she was on her way again.

"Morning, Sheriff," Billy said, as he walked up.

Jared nodded down the boardwalk. "You know Mattie Ingram?"

"Oh, sure," Billy said. "I washed dishes for Miss Mattie…before."

Jared straightened. "Before what?"

"Before her husband passed on."

"What was she talking to you about just now?"

Billy shook his head sorrowfully. "Well, the thing is, Sheriff, I can't tell you."

"Why not?"

"'Cause Miss Mattie asked me not to."

"She told you not to tell anyone?" Jared asked. "Or just me?"

Billy winced. "Well, truth is, Sheriff, she said not to tell you."

"It's a secret?"

"Well, yeah." Billy shifted from one foot to the other. "I'm sorry as I can be, Sheriff, but I can't tell you. I gave my word I wouldn't. My aunt Frannie, she says that a man is only as good as his word, so I can't tell you what Miss Mattie's up to."

Jared nodded thoughtfully. "Why don't you go on in and take care of the prisoners?"

Relieved, Billy smiled. "Sure thing, Sheriff," he called as he disappeared into the jailhouse.

So Mattie had a secret, huh? Jared rubbed his chin as he watched her fade into the crowd down the street. A secret. One she didn't want him to know about.

Jared felt his "mean look" creep over his features, and he did his best to plaster a smile in its place as he nodded at passersby.

Why would Mattie not want him—only him—to know what she was up to this morning? From her comment, he figured it was something to do with her business. What was wrong with letting him in on it?

The whole thing just didn't sit right with Jared. He didn't like being on the outside of anything concerning Mattie.

He waited around on the boardwalk, smiling and nodding until his cheeks hurt, and finally Billy came outside again.

"I don't know about you," Billy said, dragging his hand across his forehead, "but I'll be glad when Big Jim gets here to post bail for that boy of his."

Jared agreed. Johnny Ballard had done nothing but whine and complain since yesterday. At the same time, old Mr. Hopkins had yet to utter a sound.

"How about you and me take a walk?" Jared asked. "I've got a few things we need to discuss."

"Deputy things?" Billy asked.

"Exactly. Let's—damn!" Jared howled and swiveled on his throbbing leg in time to see the little boy who'd kicked him yesterday race down the street. "That little brat did it again! Who is that kid?"

"That's Chuckie," Billy explained. "Chuckie Waldron. His pa owns the barbershop."

Jared rubbed his knee, cursing. "Why the hell does he keep kicking me?"

"'Course, I ain't no lawman, not yet, anyway," Billy said. "But seems to me he don't like you."

Jared huffed. "Let's go."

They walked down to the Lady Luck Saloon. But when Jared got inside, he realized Billy wasn't with him. He looked over the bat-wing doors and saw him standing outside, rooted in place, his eyes wide.

"What's wrong?" Jared asked, stepping outside.

"I can't go in there," Billy fretted. "Aunt Frannie will take a switch to me for sure."

"You're a grown man, Billy. Plenty old enough to go into a saloon. Now, come on. I've got business to discuss with you." Jared caught his arm and pulled him inside.

Just inside the door, Billy froze, refusing to take another step. He squeezed his eyes shut and plastered his palm over them.

"I'll go blind!" he wailed. "Aunt Frannie told me I'd go blind if I ever came into this place!"

"You won't go blind, Billy." Jared pried his fingers away from his face. "Open your eyes."

Slowly, Billy lifted one eyelid, then the other. "Well, dang, you're right, Sheriff."

"Go sit down."

The saloon was quiet at this time of day, with only a couple of men playing cards. Jared bought two beers at the bar and joined Billy at a table in the back of the room.

"I want to talk about you becoming my deputy," Jared said.

Billy sat on the edge of his chair, his gaze bouncing from ceiling to floor, wall to wall.

Jared leaned into his line of sight. "Billy, are you listening?"

"Huh? Oh, yes sir, Sheriff. I'm listening."

"Good, because I—"

"This is beer!" Billy's eyes bugged out. "Oh, goodness, you got me beer!"

"You've never had beer before?"

"Shoot no. My—"

"Aunt Frannie. Yeah, I understand. Don't drink it if you don't want to."

Billy leaned closer and sniffed the glass. "Well, I don't reckon it would hurt nothing if'n I just tried it one little ol' time."

"Okay, fine, Billy. Now listen, I want to talk to you about being my—hold on, there." Jared pulled Billy's arm down as he gulped about half the beer from his glass.

"Whew!" Billy's eyes glistened as he smacked his lips. "That stuff's pretty darn good."

Jared pulled at the back of his neck. "Listen up, Billy, this is important."

"Oh, sure thing, Sheriff." He gazed steadily across the table at Jared.

"First off, I want you to know that I'm taking you seriously about being my deputy. But the thing is, a sheriff has to trust his deputy. He has to know he can count on him for anything, no matter what."

"You're trying to get me to tell you what Miss Mattie's secret is, aren't you?"

Jared shifted in the chair. Maybe this kid was a little smarter than he'd thought.

"Yes, Billy, that's exactly what I'm trying to do,"

Jared admitted. "But not because I want to do anything that will hurt Mattie. I only want to help her."

Billy nodded thoughtfully. "I heard about you being friends with that husband of hers, and how you offered to marry her, just to make things right." Billy glanced around the saloon, then leaned closer. "If you ask me, that Del Ingram wasn't nothing but trouble."

This was the first time Jared had heard anyone in Stanford say anything against Ingram. "Why do you say that, Billy?"

"You know how my aunt Frannie says I got to go back East and work for my uncle because I don't have a real job here? Well, that's because I work at a whole bunch of different places in town. The mercantile, the blacksmith, the feed and grain store, the bank, just about everywhere in Stanford. So that's how I know what all's going on."

Jared's frowned. "And what is it, exactly, that you know?"

Billy glanced around again, then lowered his voice. "Miss Mattie's about to lose her restaurant. That's why I don't wash dishes over there no more. That's why she let the Spencer sisters go, too. She can't afford to pay nobody to wash dishes and wait tables, so she does it herself."

"What does that have to do with Ingram?"

"He left accounts all over town. Miss Mattie's been trying to pay on them. That's why she can't buy meat for her restaurant. That's why she don't have hardly no customers anymore."

"Damn..." Jared grumbled, hating Del Ingram all over again.

Why hadn't Mattie told him this? He could help her. He had a good chunk of money put aside. He'd give her every cent, if she'd just ask for it.

"Anyhow," Billy said, "that's what she was talking to me about this morning. Miss Mattie's figured out how to save her business."

"Yeah? How?"

"Well..."

"Look, Billy, if you're going to be my deputy, you have to tell me what's going on in this town. Mattie's not planning something illegal, is she?"

"Oh, shoot, no. She's going to talk to the mayor about those investors that are coming to town."

Anger spiked through Jared. Mattie would ask the investors—total strangers—for help, but she wouldn't ask him?

"Miss Mattie wants the town to throw a big shindig at her restaurant for those investors," Billy explained. "She told me that if the town has it at her place and pays her good, she can get the restaurant back on its feet again."

Jared shook his head. "There're dozens of men coming out here, plus everybody from town. That's a hell of a lot of work for her."

"Yeah, I know. Especially in her...condition," Billy said, his cheeks flushing. "That's what she was asking me about this morning—if I could help out that night. That is, if the mayor and the town council let her do it.''

Jared fumed silently. Mattie was biting off a big chunk with this idea of hers. Too much, in his opinion. She wasn't well. She was having a baby, for Pete's sake. She had to take care of herself. And this plan of hers would be nothing but hard work.

Jared didn't like it. He didn't like it one bit.

He folded his hands cross his chest, thinking. If what Billy said was true, Mattie would likely lose her restaurant without this financial boost. And without her restaurant, she couldn't support herself.

A little smile tugged at Jared's lips. Mattie would have to marry him then. She'd have no other choice.

Billy drained his beer. ''Miss Mattie's on her way over to the mayor's house to talk to him about it.''

''Right now?''

''Yes, sir.'' Billy hiccuped. ''Shoot, she's probably already settled it with him.''

Jared pushed himself out of the chair. ''We'll see about that.''

Chapter Eleven

Darn that mayor! Darn him!

"Oh!" Mattie clenched her fists as she stood in the shade of the general store near Mayor Rayburn's house. She was so upset she thought she'd explode.

He'd liked her plan, the one she'd come up with in the middle of the night, the one that would save her business. He'd thought it a fine idea and intended to propose to the council Mattie's suggestion that the town host a supper for the Eastern investors. A grand celebration to welcome them and to showcase Stanford's many fine qualities and business opportunities.

The problem was that Mayor Rayburn had refused to let Mattie's restaurant host the supper.

Just thinking about it made Mattie's blood boil, made her ache inside, pushing her emotions to near the breaking point. And lately, for some reason, all those things seemed more intense.

Her *condition,* Mayor Rayburn had explained, lowering his voice and ducking his head as if it were something shameful. She had a baby on the way. She wasn't up to hosting the supper.

It had taken all of Mattie's willpower not to shout at him, not to burst into tears. Calmly, she'd explained that she was perfectly healthy, well enough to host the supper, something she did for a living, anyway.

But Mayor Rayburn had been adamant. The Cottonwood Café would not be considered for the supper. She wasn't up to it. It wasn't decent, in her condition. People would talk. The mayor simply wouldn't hear of it.

And that was that.

Mattie gulped down the lump that rose in her throat. She *needed* that job. Without it and the money it would generate, her restaurant would continue its decline. It would wither away. She'd have to close it. Close the Cottonwood Café.

Unbearable. Mattie pressed her fingertips to her lips, trying desperately to hold her raging emotions in check.

The Cottonwood and all its memories, gone? Taking her future with it?

What would become of her? Her and her baby?

"Mattie?"

Jared. The sound of his voice washed through her. She turned and there he stood, tall, strong and sturdy. Jared, who always seemed to be in front of her at her worst moments, who somehow seemed to make them better.

Tears sprang to Mattie's eyes. She blinked, trying to hold them back, and gulped hard.

He came forward, frowning. "What's wrong, Mattie? What happened? Are you hurt?"

Her throat tightened, and despite her efforts, tears spilled onto her cheeks. "I—I'm all right."

"Then why are you crying?"

"Because I'm mad!"

He just looked at her for a few seconds, then wrapped his arms around her and pulled her against his chest.

Mattie didn't resist him. She sobbed into his shirt, twisting her fingers in the fabric.

How easy it was to lean against him, to let her problems flow into him, knowing he would soak them up. Just as he had the night of Del's funeral.

But it wasn't like her to fall apart like this. She almost never cried.

"I—I don't know why I'm carrying on so," she managed to say between sobs. "It's just—"

"The baby. I know," Jared said, and gently rubbed her shoulders.

Finally, when her tears subsided, Jared gave her his handkerchief. Even as she wiped her eyes and blew her nose, he kept his arm around her.

"What's got you so mad?" Jared asked.

Mattie hesitated. She stepped away from him and tucked the handkerchief in her pocket.

"You can tell me," he said. "Maybe I can help. I'd do anything to make you happy."

She glanced up at him. "Anything?"

"Anything."

"*Anything?*"

Jared paused. "I'd prefer not to have to sing or dance, but yes, I'd do anything."

A little laugh bubbled up, and like quicksilver, it turned to tears. Mattie fell against him again, crying. Jared held her tight without saying a word, until she quieted.

"I heard about your plan for those Eastern investors," Jared said. "Is that what this is all about?"

She looked up at him, wiping her nose again. "How did you find out what I was doing?"

"I'm the law in this town. It's my job to know everything that goes on." Jared nodded toward the mayor's house. "I take it Rayburn didn't like your idea."

"Oh, he liked it, all right. Only he won't consider me for the job. Just because I'm having a baby. Women all over Stanford are having babies, and they're going about their business just fine. But for some reason I can't, according to the mayor."

Jared nodded. This morning, standing in front of the jailhouse, he'd noticed a half-dozen expectant mothers, something he'd never paid much attention to until Mattie became pregnant.

"Putting on that supper will be a lot of work, Mattie. To tell you the truth, I'd be worried about you myself."

"Yes, it is a lot of work. But that's not a good

enough reason for the mayor to forbid me to do it,'' Mattie said. "No one has better food than the Cottonwood. Not the Silver Bell or any of those other, smaller restaurants in town.''

"I know how bad you need this work,'' Jared said.

Mattie gasped, then huffed. "Oh, wonderful. Now I suppose the whole town knows, too?''

"No, I was told in confidence. It's not common knowledge,'' Jared said. "But if you need money, Mattie, I could help you out.''

She looked up at him and shook her head. "I intend to handle my business myself. I don't want your—or anyone's—money.''

Hearing her say those words annoyed Jared, but he couldn't fault her for them. She had her pride, and there was nothing wrong with that. She'd told no one her problems, hadn't gone around whining or conniving or complaining when things got tough. She'd not even mentioned what a bad husband Del Ingram had been, or how he'd left her with his debts.

Just one more reason to love her...as if Jared needed another.

Suddenly, Mattie looked tired, the emotional distress of the situation taking its toll. Jared saw it as the opportunity he'd been looking for.

"You know, Mattie,'' he said softly, "if you do have to close the Cottonwood, there's no need to worry about your future. I told you I'd take care of you, and I meant it. I'll marry you—you just say the word.''

She seemed to steel herself, drawing on some internal well of strength. Mattie straightened her shoulders.

"Marriage isn't something to be tossed around casually," she said. "You have no idea what it means."

"Yes, I do."

"No. You can't possibly know unless you've been married." Mattie shook her head. "If what you said earlier is true, Jared, if you really want to help, if you'd really do *anything* to make me happy, figure some way for me to host that supper."

"Look, Mattie—"

"*That* is what would make me happy. *That* is the kind of help I need."

He stood fuming silently as Mattie walked away. The pride she'd displayed a few minutes ago that he'd thought so highly of seemed downright irritating all of a sudden.

Still, he couldn't blame her. Mattie wanted to run her own life. It would take her a while to warm up to the idea of letting him be a part of it, too.

So that left him with a dilemma.

Jared glanced at Mattie, then back at Mayor Rayburn's house. If he didn't go talk to the mayor, convince him to give Mattie that job, she'd lose her restaurant for sure. If he didn't say anything, Mattie would be forced to marry him. He'd have her for his wife.

But was that how he wanted her? Penniless? Her spirit broken?

Sure, she'd marry him. But would she love him?

"Damn it…" Jared took another look at Mattie, then at the mayor's house.

He wasn't exactly the mayor's favorite person right now. In fact, Rayburn had threatened to fire him.

Still, Jared had to do something. He rubbed his chin thoughtfully. Yeah, he'd help her. But he'd do it *his* way.

"Maybe if I talk to the mayor on your behalf it will help," Mrs. Nance offered.

"I doubt it will do any good. He didn't seem of a mind to listen to reason," Mattie said, seated at the worktable in the Cottonwood's kitchen. She looked up from her writing tablet. "Maybe if I approach Mrs. Pomeroy. If I can get her and her committee on my side, perhaps then the mayor will be convinced."

Mrs. Nance didn't appear encouraged. "Well, maybe."

Mattie sighed and turned back to her tablet. Even Mrs. Pomeroy wasn't likely to change the mayor's mind. But something had to be done. Tonight, Mattie had once more closed the Cottonwood early. There just weren't enough diners to keep it open. Here it was, not quite dark outside, and the restaurant was closed.

"What if I talk to the town council myself?" she mused.

"Go to the council after the mayor's told you no?"

Mrs. Nance made a little tsking sound. "You're not likely to win any favors from the mayor like that."

Mattie hopped off the stool. "I have to do something. I can't stand idle and let this golden opportunity pass by. Those Eastern investors are just what I need. Something like this isn't likely to happen again."

"Too bad Del's gone. He could have convinced the mayor to let you have the supper." Mrs. Nance took off her apron and plucked her shawl and handbag from beside the back door. "Well, good night, dear. See you in the morning."

Mattie slumped onto the stool again and leaned forward, covering her face with her palms. Del...would that man ever stop haunting her?

She sat there, bone weary, trying to muster the energy to come up with a plan to secure the supper for her restaurant, trying to make herself get up and wash the dishes piled high on the sideboard. Both, it seemed, were impossible tasks.

With a deep breath, Mattie dragged herself off the stool. The sooner she got these dishes done, the sooner she could go home and lie down. And at the moment, that prospect seemed the only bright spot in her life.

A commotion out back drew her attention. A second later Jared opened the door and strode into the kitchen.

"Evening, Mattie," he called. He looked behind him. "Come on in here."

She craned her neck and saw Mr. Hopkins follow Jared inside. "What's going on?"

"The sheriff's office has a new policy. I'm calling

it my community assistance program," Jared announced, looking altogether pleased with himself. He turned to Mr. Hopkins and pointed to the sideboard. "Get to it. And if you break anything, it'll cost you another day in jail."

Mr. Hopkins ambled to the sideboard, shucked off his rumpled coat, turned back his sleeves and began washing dishes.

Mattie had seen Mr. Hopkins in town often. Everyone knew him, though no one knew much about him. Nearly fifty years old, from all appearances, he led a solitary life, finding odd jobs, sleeping here and there, spending what little money he earned drinking silently at the Lady Luck, talking to no one.

"Didn't you arrest Mr. Hopkins yesterday?" Mattie asked.

"Yes, ma'am, I did."

She looked at the old man, elbow deep at the washtub, then at Jared. "I don't understand."

"Seemed to me to be a useless waste of time to have able-bodied prisoners lying around the jail when there was work in the community that needed doing," Jared told her. "That's how I got the idea for my community assistance program. Mr. Hopkins is working off one day of his sentence by washing dishes."

The load on Mattie's shoulders lifted considerably.

"Really?"

"Really."

"He's washing dishes? Here? For me?"

"Yes, ma'am."

"You can do that?"

Jared dipped his chin toward his badge. "I'm the law. I can do as I see fit."

"Oh, my..." Mattie shook herself. "Well, the least I can do is dry."

Jared stepped in front of her as she headed for the sideboard. "If you did that, I couldn't knock a whole day off his sentence. You don't want Mr. Hopkins to have to serve more time on account of you, do you?"

"Oh, well, no. Of course not."

"Besides," Jared said, "I've got some business to talk over with you. Come over here and sit down."

Mattie allowed him to lead her to a stool at the worktable. He nodded toward the stove as she sat down. "Is that coffee still hot?"

"Yes, I'll get you some," she said, and started to rise.

Jared waved her onto the stool again, then poured coffee into two china cups.

"You got any pie or cake?"

"There's apple pie. I'll get it—"

"Just sit still and point." Jared followed her finger to the pie safe, cut a wedge for each of them, then sat down beside her, positioning himself to keep an eye on Mr. Hopkins.

Mattie raised an eyebrow at the pie and coffee sitting in front of her. "I don't believe I've ever been served in my own restaurant."

"All part of the service, ma'am," Jared announced, biting into his pie. "How are you feeling?"

She nodded. "All right."

He glanced at her belly and lowered his voice. "My little girl moving around yet?"

"It's a boy," Mattie told him, touching her hand to her stomach. "And no, not yet."

"You'll tell me when it happens, won't you?"

An odd sensation passed through Mattie. Without realizing she was going to, she reached across the worktable and touched Jared's arm. "Sure. If you want me to."

"I want you to."

"Then I will," she promised.

"Thank you."

How odd it seemed that he'd have to ask for the tiniest detail of his child's life. How humbling that he would. How endearing that he'd thank her for it.

Mattie sipped her coffee, pushing the thought from her mind. "You have business to discuss?"

Jared scraped the last bite of pie off his plate. "As it stands, Billy Weaver comes to the jail to fix meals for my prisoners. But the way I see it, even criminals deserve better than beans and bread three times a day. So the sheriff's office is offering the business to the Cottonwood Café."

"You want me to provide meals for your prisoners?"

"Nothing fancy, just something decent," Jared said. "You'd be paid for your food, of course."

Mattie's back stiffened. "Oh, I understand. Charity. A pity job."

"Business," Jared told her sternly. He shrugged. "Of course, if you don't want the job I'll offer it to the Silver Bell. With all those young-uns they've got, they'll jump at the chance."

Mattie laid her hand on his forearm for a second time, unable to keep from doing it, for some reason. "You're serious? You really want me to do this?"

"The sheriff's office has a budget for prisoners and the like, but don't go thinking you're going to get rich off of this. It's steady income as long as I have a prisoner that needs to be fed."

Mattie mulled it over, but there was really only one decision she could make. "Sheriff, I do like your offer." She nodded toward Mr. Hopkins. "And I'm very pleased about your community assistance program."

Jared smiled. "So you're agreeable?"

"I'm agreeable."

Footsteps clattered up the back steps and Billy hurried into the kitchen, wild-eyed and breathing hard.

Jared lurched from the stool. "What's wrong?"

"You'd better come to the jail, Sheriff," Billy said, holding his heaving chest. "Big Jim Ballard's come to get his boy back. And he ain't happy."

Chapter Twelve

Jared jerked his thumb toward Mr. Hopkins. "You stay here, Billy, keep an eye on the prisoner."

The young man gulped hard, catching his breath. "You mean it? You want me to watch him? Like a real deputy?"

"Yep." Jared headed out the door.

"But, Sheriff? Don't I have to be deputized or something?"

Jared stopped. "Raise your right hand. Do you swear to uphold the laws of this state to the best of your ability, so help you God?"

Billy nodded solemnly. "Yes, sir, I do."

"Okay, you're a deputy—temporarily."

"Lordy me!" Billy smiled broadly and puffed out his chest. "Do I get a gun, Sheriff?"

"No." He nodded toward Mr. Hopkins. "Any deputy worth his salt can watch this prisoner without a gun."

"How about a badge? Do I get a badge?"

Jared pressed his lips together. "No badge, Billy. Not this time."

"Well, all right. I'll do my best, even without a badge."

"Jared?"

He turned back from the door as Mattie crossed the room.

"Big Jim is a very powerful man in Stanford," she said cautiously. "You should know that he's very protective of his sons, especially Johnny."

"'Scuse me, Miss Mattie, but that ain't exactly so," Billy said. "It's 'cause of his wife, that's all."

"What do you know about the Ballards?" Jared asked.

"Well, for one thing," Billy said, "Big Jim ain't happy about his boy being locked up. But that's mostly because Big Jim's got that cattle ranch to run and he don't like having to come into town during the week."

"What else?"

"You see, Big Jim's got seven other sons. His wife is partial to Johnny because he's the youngest. Fact is, she's real partial to that boy. My aunt Frannie says that's the reason Johnny is always causing trouble, and why he ain't worth hardly nothing."

Jared nodded thoughtfully. "Okay, Billy. Keep an eye on the prisoner. I'll be back."

"Yes, sir. I'll watch him good. I swear."

"Good luck," Mattie said, touching Jared's arm.

He knew what she really meant was *be nice.*

Jared kept to the alleys behind the storefronts as he headed for the jail. He just didn't have another smile or pleasant word for passersby in him tonight. When he entered the jailhouse, Jim Ballard was pacing the floor.

Big Jim had gotten his nickname from his large cattle ranch, Jared figured, as well as his size: he was tall and broad shouldered. His face was tanned and lined from years in the sun, and Jared decided the scrawny, fresh-faced Johnny must have taken after his mama. Ballard wore a leather vest, an open collar and a Stetson pulled low on his frowning forehead.

"Sheriff McQuaid, I don't like having my boy arrested and locked up," he growled, squaring off in the middle of the floor.

Jared resisted the urge to tell Ballard that Johnny was an embarrassment to young men everywhere, whining like a girl and complaining the whole time he'd been locked up.

Instead, he nodded in understanding. "Truth is, Mr. Ballard, I didn't like having to arrest him or lock him up."

That seemed to take some of the starch out of Big Jim. He relaxed marginally.

"The boy was just blowing off steam," Ballard said.

"Can't say I haven't done that a time or two myself." Jared nodded toward the chairs in front of his desk. Big Jim hesitated, then finally the two men sat down.

"The problem is, Mr. Ballard, that your boy started shooting up the town." Jared shook his head solemnly. "I can't have that kind of thing going on, with women and children on the streets."

Ballard grumbled and pulled on the back of his neck.

"I know it puts you in a tough spot," Jared said. "You've got a ranch to run. You don't have time to come into town for something like this."

"I'd just as soon leave that boy locked up, teach him a lesson, but—"

"His mama?" Jared murmured. Ballard looked up sharply, and Jared nodded sympathetically. "Yeah, I understand. You've got to keep his mama happy."

Ballard ruminated silently for a few moments, then puffed out a big breath. "And you can't have him shooting up the town. I'll pay his fine and get him out of here."

Jared pulled the ledger from the bottom drawer of his desk and flipped it to the page with Johnny Ballard's name at the top.

"This isn't the first time the boy's been arrested," he said. "I've got to tell you, Mr. Ballard, if he causes any more trouble in town, it's going to take more than a five-dollar fine to get him out of jail."

Wearily, Ballard dropped the money onto the desk. "I understand, Sheriff."

Jared got the keys and went back to the cells. Johnny, in rumpled clothes, with a feeble beard darkening his chin, looked smug when he unlocked the door. The boy started whining before he made it into the office.

"Pa, that sheriff gave me nothing but beans to eat, and it stunk in there, smelled like—"

"Shut your mouth, boy." Ballard yanked his collar and sent him out the door. He looked back at Jared. "He won't give you any more trouble, Sheriff."

"Glad to hear it," Jared said.

After they left, he dropped the money in his cash box and made a notation in the ledger. Really, he should have released Mr. Hopkins this evening, too. But the man could surely use a decent bed to sleep in tonight, even if it was in a jail cell. He'd likely appreciate a hot meal in the morning, too. One that Mattie and her Cottonwood Café would provide.

After that, the cells would be empty. No more meals to buy from the Cottonwood, no one else to wash dishes for Mattie.

Jared pushed himself out of his chair. Hell, maybe he'd hang on to Mr. Hopkins for another day.

Mattie watched glumly as the last of her noon diners left the Cottonwood. Three of them. Only three. And they were strangers, probably passing through Stanford, not likely to come back again.

Mattie stacked their dishes, the remains of the food causing her already queasy stomach to roll anew, and mentally tallied the price of the food and her cost in preparing it. Not much profit.

The breakfast she'd taken to the jail this morning for Mr. Hopkins was a welcome addition.

The bell over the door jangled and Mayor Rayburn stepped inside. Mattie's spirits lifted. He'd come for lunch. Oh, thank goodness, the mayor had come for lunch.

Would he bring the whole town council with him, as he used to? Would others follow? The reverend? The businessmen who used to make the Cottonwood their regular meeting place?

"Good afternoon, Mayor. Have a seat by the window. Mrs. Nance has outdone herself today. We have—"

"Oh, no." The mayor rested his palm on his stomach. "No, no. Couldn't eat another bite."

"Oh." He'd eaten at the Silver Bell. As usual.

"I need to have a word with you." He stopped in front of her. "About that supper you proposed for our visiting investors."

"Yes?" Mattie asked cautiously, daring to let her spirits rise again.

Mayor Rayburn tugged at his side whiskers. "I talked it over with the council this morning, and everybody liked your idea."

"I was sure they would," Mattie said.

"Yes, yes, you were right." He cleared his throat. "And, well, we've decided to give you a chance to host the supper."

Mattie's knees nearly gave out. Her future—her secure future—sprang into her mind. "You have? Oh, Mayor Rayburn, thank you. I—"

"Hold on a minute." He held up his palms and shifted his feet. "We've decided to let the Cottonwood and the Silver Bell, and all the other restaurants in town, present a proposal to the town council."

"A proposal?"

He nodded. "Give us your ideas on how you think the supper should go. The kind of food you'd cook, anything special you'd do. Things like that. Then we'll make a decision on which restaurant will host the investors."

It wasn't exactly what she needed—what she'd hoped for—but she'd certainly take it. At least now she'd have a chance at hosting the supper.

"That seems fair," Mattie said.

"That's what the council figured."

"And it's all right with the council if I participate?" Mattie asked. "I mean, with the baby coming and all?"

Mayor Rayburn shifted uncomfortably. "Well, you've been in this town a long time. You've always run a sound business. Well, almost always—but that's understandable, what with your husband dying and a baby on the way."

It took all of Mattie's strength not to throw her arms around the mayor and plant a big kiss on his cheek.

"Thank you, Mayor. Thank you so much. I'm glad you and the council agree that I'm worthy of hosting that supper."

Mayor Rayburn seemed put off by her gushing words of thanks. He studied the tips of his shoes for a moment, then the ceiling, and finally shoved his hands in his trouser pockets.

"To tell you the truth, Mattie, the council's not crazy about the idea. And neither am I."

Her soaring emotions plummeted. "But you said—"

"It was the sheriff who convinced us."

"The sheriff?" A prickly tingle swept up Mattie's spine. "Jared?"

"He said that showing favoritism by giving the supper to the Silver Bell might cause hard feelings in town. And we don't want any problems when those investors are here."

"Problems? What sort of problems?"

"Well, you know, a disagreement. Different factions of the town up in arms against one another. Like, say, maybe Mrs. Pomeroy and her committee taking offense to you being left out, or something like that."

Anger bubbled deep inside Mattie. "Jared suggested that might happen? I might cause trouble?"

Mayor Rayburn waved his hand. "Now, don't go getting all upset. It's the sheriff's job to look out for things like that. And the important thing to remember here is that you're having a chance to host the supper. That's what you wanted, isn't it?"

"Yes, but—"

"You can make your case for the Cottonwood at the next council meeting. We'll be deciding then." Mayor Rayburn hurried out of the restaurant.

Mattie curled her fingers around the back of a nearby chair, clenching her other fist at her side. So, it wasn't her years of hard work that meant anything to the men of the town council. It wasn't the strong business she ran. Nor was it her loyalty to the town, her desire to bring in new business or her idea to impress the Eastern investors.

It was merely the fact that they were afraid she'd cause trouble.

Thanks to what Jared had told them.

"Oh!" Mattie stormed out of the restaurant.

"Afternoon, ma'am…good day to you, ma'am. Howdy, ma'am…"

Jared smiled and nodded pleasantly as he strolled down the boardwalk, tipping his hat to the women who passed. Still, despite his ever-present smile, he hadn't done much to improve his standing with the folks of Stanford, or dispel their initial impression of him. Most people continued to skirt around him, eyeing him warily.

Jared sighed resolutely and kept walking. Up ahead, outside the Stanford Mercantile, he spotted Ben and Abel playing checkers. Maybe he'd have better luck making up to these two old men.

"Afternoon, boys," he called as he approached.

Both men looked up at him, then moved protectively closer to their checkerboard.

"How's the game going?" Jared asked.

Ben pulled a sack from his pocket and scraped the checkers into it. Abel folded the board. Both men turned their chairs away from Jared, pointedly ignoring him.

Well, so much for being nice.

"Sheriff McQuaid?" Hayden Langston waved from the entrance to the Stanford Mercantile. "Can you come in here?"

Jared followed Hayden inside, glad for something to do, some official function to perform.

Tall and thin, Hayden wore a crisp white shirt, arm garters and a string tie. He owned the mercantile and served on the town council.

Across the aisle, Billy Weaver swept around a display of blue speckled dishes. He waved and went back to his chore.

"Got a problem, Hayden?" Jared asked, peering about the store.

The shopkeeper led him to the back counter, where he pulled out a ledger and opened it. He flipped through the pages. "I need you to ride out to the Bishop place," Hayden said, "and collect his account."

Jared stilled. "You want me to what?"

"Cecil Bishop hasn't paid one thin dime on his account in nearly two months. I need you to go out to his place and get my money."

Jared stifled a groan. "I guess Sheriff Hickert did this sort of thing for you?"

"Oh, sure. All the time."

Jared's first inclination was to tell Hayden Langston that if he was stupid enough to extend credit, he could go collect his own damn accounts. But since Langston was on the town council, and Jared wanted to keep his job, he kept his comment to himself.

"I'll see what I can do," he said.

"Don't let him give you some lame excuse why he can't pay," Langston insisted. "If he doesn't pay, I'm swearing out a warrant against him. You tell him that. Then I want you to arrest him and lock him up."

"A warrant?" Jared eyed the page in the ledger. "For a three dollar account?"

"Money's money," the merchant declared, and closed the ledger.

Jared ambled out onto the boardwalk again. Damn. Old Sheriff Hickert probably shot *himself* in the leg just to get out of this job.

A familiar scent tickled Jared's nose. He turned, and a warm rush went through him at the sight of Mattie coming down the boardwalk. This morning when she'd brought breakfast to the jailhouse, she hadn't felt very well. But now, hours later, the color was high in her cheek. She glided through the crowd easily.

No, wait. Jared's brows drew together. Mattie wasn't gliding, she was striding. And that pretty pink hue in her face wasn't from good health, it was anger.

Her gaze locked with his. Jared gulped and fell back a step.

"How dare you?" she demanded, stopping in front of him. *"How dare you?"*

Jared worked his jaw, but no words came out. He spread his palms and finally uttered, "I don't know what you're—"

"Yes, you do!"

"Well, all right, if you say so." Jared pushed his

hat back on his head. "But maybe I could explain things to you if I knew what you were upset about."

"There is no explanation for what you did!" Mattie clenched her fists at her sides.

"Mattie, please don't get so worked up. It's not good for the baby."

She swatted at his hand. "I wanted to host that supper because I deserve the opportunity. Because I run a good business. Because my food is the best in town. *Not* because you convinced the town council that I'll raise some kind of ruckus if they don't give me a chance!"

Jared flung out both hands. "Look, you wanted them to consider you, and that's what they're doing. What difference does it make what I told them?"

"You convinced them I'm some kind of troublemaker."

"That's not what I told them…exactly."

"I wanted to be accepted on my own merits."

"You said you wanted help, Mattie. I just—"

"Not that kind of help."

"Oh, well, pardon me all to hell if I don't know exactly what *kind* of help you want."

Mattie drew herself up straighter, and for a few dreadful seconds Jared thought she might burst out crying. He softened his voice. "Look, Mattie, I didn't mean to upset you. I was just trying to help."

She swallowed hard. "Del took over my business. He took it away from me and nearly ruined it. I won't let that happen again."

"I'm not trying to do that, Mattie. I just want to help you."

"Don't help me," she told him. "Just leave me alone!"

Mattie spun around and disappeared down the boardwalk.

"Damn it..." Jared sank onto a crate stacked against the side of the mercantile and braced his palms on his knees, watching Mattie walk away.

"And you want to marry her?"

He glanced over and saw Ben and Abel sitting in their chairs; they'd had front row seats for the whole confrontation.

Jared sighed wearily. "Yeah, I want to marry her."

"Still?" Ben asked.

He nodded. "Still."

"Looks like you've got your work cut out for you, Sheriff," Abel offered.

Jared pulled off his hat, dragged his sleeve across his forehead and settled it in place again. He rose. "That's for damn sure."

Jared leaned inside the Stanford Mercantile. "Hey, Billy!"

He sprang onto the boardwalk. "Yes, sir?"

"Go get the horses. We're getting out of town."

Chapter Thirteen

"You sure it's all right for us both to be gone like this, Sheriff? To leave the town unprotected?"

Jared took in a big breath, drawing in the sweet smells of the open trail as he and Billy rode away from Stanford at a leisurely pace.

"They'll manage just fine without us for a few hours," he declared.

"Well, okay. You're the sheriff, Sheriff. And I'm just the deputy." Billy's brows rose hopefully. "I'm still your deputy—temporarily—right? You never un-deputized me."

"Sure thing, Billy."

"The town council's trying to find you a new deputy, aren't they?"

"They're pretty busy with these Eastern investors. I don't think they're working too hard on it."

Billy nodded. "So, where are we going?"

Really, Jared didn't much care where he was going at this particular moment, as long as it was away from

Stanford. He'd had enough of the town, the people and their problems. As he gazed toward the Sierra Nevadas, the days when he'd ridden free through those mountains seemed dear to him.

"I guess we're going out to the Bishop place, huh?" Billy said. "Mr. Langston at the mercantile was raising a fit about Mr. Bishop and his bill, wasn't he? Well, my Aunt Frannie says that you ought not to buy on credit, and I think she's right."

Normally, Jared would have agreed with him. But today he couldn't bring himself to criticize Cecil Bishop, since he'd provided Jared with the perfect opportunity to get out of Stanford.

"That's Mr. Pitney's place. He lives by himself," Billy said, nodding to a little farm off the road. "He don't come into town much, and when he does, he don't talk to nobody. Sort of like Mr. Hopkins."

"Why's that?" Jared asked, content with Billy's chatter.

He shrugged. "Aunt Frannie says it's because he served in the war. Fought for the Union at Gettysburg. Made him sort of crazy in the head, she says. I don't know myself, 'cause I never been in no war. You think that's true, Sheriff? Can it make you crazy?"

Jared had been too young to serve in the War Between the States, but he'd heard the talk, the stories. "Yes, Billy, I surely believe it can."

"You reckon that's what's wrong with Mr. Hopkins? He sure acts crazy in the head," Billy said. "'Course, Aunt Frannie says she thinks Mr. Hopkins had his heart broke a long time ago. That's why he turned out the way he did.''

Jared sighed. Would that be his own future? Spurned by Mattie, would he turn into the town drunk, wandering the streets aimlessly, speaking to no one?

''Mayor Rayburn hasn't invited you to supper yet, has he?'' Billy asked.

Jared shook his head, grateful for this change in the conversation. ''No. He said he would, though.''

''Well, if you don't mind me saying so, you'd best better eat before you go.'' Billy held his nose as if he'd smelled something bad. ''That wife of his can't cook for nothing. Aunt Frannie says it's a disgrace. Watch yourself at church, too. If there's a social afterward, you gotta scout out what Mrs. Rayburn brought. You'll know because everybody puts a little bite of whatever it is on their plate, but don't nobody eat it. Just watch. You'll see.''

Jared nodded. ''I'll remember that.''

''And if you don't mind a word of caution, you'd better keep an eye out for Mrs. Spencer.''

''Gil Spencer, the blacksmith? His wife?''

''Yes, sir. Now, most everybody in town knows that you've offered to marry Miss Mattie, so it's not likely Mrs. Spencer would draw a bead on you, but the fact is that you're not married.''

''Yeah? So?''

Billy rolled his eyes. ''The Spencers' got themselves nine daughters, three of marrying age, and Mr.

Spencer is pushing his wife to get them girls out of the house, if you get my meaning.''

"How come you don't marry one of them?''

Billy's face and neck turned a deep red. "Shoot, Sheriff, them Spencer girls are pretty. Real pretty. Mrs. Spencer's got it in her head to marry them off to just a certain kind of man. Like the Ballard boys, maybe. Somebody important. See?''

Billy went on talking and Jared listened easily. The boy always had something to say, some information to pass on. He sure knew all there was to know about everyone in Stanford.

"Is it much farther to the Bishop place?'' Jared asked.

"A few more miles,'' he said, looking around, judging the terrain.

Jared nodded toward a farmhouse coming up on their left. "We'd better stop and water the horses.''

"That's the McCafferty place. I don't think it's such a good idea to bother them.''

"Why not?''

"Well, I don't know exactly,'' Billy said, rubbing his chin. "My aunt Frannie, she says there's something not right about that Mr. McCafferty. 'Cause, see, he likes to keep to himself, and that's all right, I reckon. He and his wife just moved here a little while ago, but she hardly ever comes to town. They don't even come to services on Sunday. And, see? They live just a stone's throw from the Pitney place, and they don't even speak to each other like neighbors ought to, Aunt Frannie said.''

Jared gazed at the carefully tended farmhouse and gray, weathered outbuildings. ''Why do you suppose that is?''

''I don't rightly know. It's got Aunt Frannie stumped, too.''

''Let's stop by and introduce ourselves.'' Jared pulled his hat lower on his forehead and guided his horse to the front of the McCafferty house. The door and windows stood open, white curtains fanning in and out with the breeze. They dismounted and Jared called out a greeting. No one answered. No one came to the door. Leading their horses, they circled the house.

A woman pulled bed linens from the clothesline. She looked thin and drawn, struggling with the billowing sheets and the loose strands of her hair. From a distance she looked old and weathered. But up close, Jared saw that she was young, hardly much older than Mattie. She wore a shapeless dress that did nothing to disguise her belly bulging with a baby.

''Afternoon, ma'am.'' Jared stopped in front of her and touched his finger to the brim of his hat. ''I'm Sheriff McQuaid and this is Deputy Weaver.''

''Howdy, Mrs. McCafferty,'' Billy said.

Her gaze darted from Jared to the house, then quickly back to him again. ''Nothing's wrong. I swear.''

"We're just passing through," Jared said, "and wondered if we could water the horses."

"Well...well, I suppose it would be all right." Her gaze jumped to the house again.

"Where's your husband?" Jared asked.

"Inside. Sleeping. I—I'd appreciate it if you wouldn't wake him," she said, "if you'd just tend to your horses and be on your way."

"Yes, ma'am. We'll do that." Jared nodded toward the basket of bed linens. "Can I carry that inside for you, ma'am?"

"No." Mrs. McCafferty shook her head quickly. "No, I can manage."

Jared and Billy watered their horses at the trough near the barn, then mounted up and rode away.

"See, I told you they were strange," Billy said, turning in the saddle, looking back at the McCafferty house. "Ain't they strange?"

Jared shrugged. "I've seen stranger folks."

"Well, yeah, I reckon so. But still..."

While the McCafferty farm had been neat and well run, the Bishop place looked a little rundown by comparison. Weeds sprouted, the front porch sagged, boards were missing from the corrals. An air of neglect hung over the farm.

Six—or maybe it was seven—children swarmed in the yard when Jared and Billy rode up. Jared wasn't sure, there were so many of them. The oldest he spotted didn't seem to be more than ten years old; the youngest was riding on her mama's hip as the woman walked out the front door.

"Afternoon," Polly Bishop called, smiling and waving from the porch. "Hi, Billy."

"Hey, Mrs. Bishop," Billy said, dismounting. "This here's the new sheriff, Sheriff McQuaid."

"Ma'am," Jared said in greeting, climbing down from his horse and tethering the reins to the hitching post. The woman looked to be nearly thirty, with blond hair tied back in a neat bun. She was wearing a crisp apron.

"Is your husband at home?" Jared asked.

"He's inside," she said, smiling. "Come on in. Cecil's not getting around too well these days since he broke his leg."

Jared and Billy followed her inside to the kitchen. Though the house was small, it was neat and clean. Cecil, teetering on a crude crutch, stood at the table sorting through a box of tools. He greeted them warmly, shook hands and offered them something to drink.

"Pleasure to have you out to see us," Cecil said. "I can't get into town as often as I'd like, with this busted leg of mine. Shoot, I can hardly get my chores tended to around the farm."

"The kids are helping out as much as they can, and the neighbors, too," Polly said, serving them coffee. She slid her arm around her husband's waist. "But we're doing fine, and with the good Lord's help things will get back to normal just as soon as Cecil's leg heals.''

He gave her a quick, confident nod. ''They sure will, honey.''

Jared and Billy stayed awhile visiting, watching the Bishops' clean, mannerly brood pass through the house. Then they mounted up and left. The sun dipped toward the horizon as they rode back to Stanford.

Billy started chattering again, but Jared didn't listen. For some reason, his mood had soured considerably.

He didn't know why, exactly. Maybe it was Hayden Langston sending him out to collect a piddly-ass account from a man with a broken leg, a man struggling to keep a roof over his family's head.

Or maybe it was the way Cecil and Polly Bishop had clung to each other in the kitchen of their warm little home, surrounded by their children. The two of them looking at each other in that special way husband and wives did, knowing they'd work things out together.

Jared's mind strayed to Mattie. While that wasn't an unusual occurrence, and he often thought of her, this time the recollection made him a bit angry.

She'd been annoyed at him for getting the town council to agree to let her have a chance to host the supper. But wasn't that exactly what she wanted? The opportunity to try?

Only Mattie didn't like the *way* he'd gone about it. He'd sniffed around the subject with the mayor and seen that the man's mind was firmly made up. Mattie wasn't participating and that was that. So Jared had come up with the only idea he could, at the time. And it had worked. So what the hell was wrong with what he'd done? Couldn't Mattie have said thank you for trying?

Silently, Jared fumed. In fact, the more he thought about it, the more worked up he got.

By the time he and Billy rode down Main Street, the businesses were closing up for the night and music was drifting from the Lady Luck Saloon. Despite himself, Jared found himself relaxing.

Home. Coming back to Stanford felt like coming home. And nothing had felt like home to Jared in years.

For all their shortcomings, all their problems, all their petty annoyances, the folks of Stanford were good people. He wanted to be here.

He was home. Even if Mattie wasn't speaking to him at the moment.

And, Jared realized, being "nice" wasn't so hard, after all.

At the Stanford Mercantile, Jared and Billy dismounted and went inside. Hayden Langston stood at the counter, counting the money in the till.

The man didn't get out of his store often, so maybe he didn't know that Bishop was laid up. Jared decided to give him the benefit of the doubt.

"Did you know Cecil Bishop had a broken leg?" he asked.

"Oh, sure."

Jared frowned. "Did you know he's having trouble keeping his farm running, taking care of his family and feeding his children?"

"Of course."

"And you need that three dollars so bad you'd swear out a warrant for a man in his situation?"

"Look, Sheriff, I've got a business to run here. I've got to stock my shelves, take care of my own family." Hayden frowned. "You didn't let Bishop talk you out of my payment, did you?"

Jared glared at him for a moment, then drew money from his pocket and slapped it down on the counter. "No. Here's your damn three dollars."

"Sheriff?" Billy called, following him out of the store. "Mr. Bishop didn't give you any money. He—"

"Take the horses down to the livery, will you, Billy?"

"But—"

"I need you to work at the jail all day tomorrow. I'll pay you full wages. Can you do that?"

"The whole day? How come? We don't have no prisoners."

"Can I count on you, Billy?"

"Well, sure, Sheriff, but—"

"Good. Come to the jail first thing in the morning."

Jared headed for his office, but didn't make it that far. Instead, he went to the Cottonwood Café and stood across the street staring at the darkened windows. He circled the building. No sign of life in the kitchen.

Mattie had closed up for the night and gone home

already. He was tempted to go to her house and try to talk to her. Maybe if he explained things better she'd understand and wouldn't be mad at him. Maybe she'd come to her senses and have the good grace to say she was sorry for talking to him the way she did.

But he decided he shouldn't. He didn't want her upset. It wasn't good for the baby.

Jared rocked on his heels and toes, staring at the restaurant. His chest grew a little tighter, as he wished he could go to Mattie, wished she would welcome him. He loved her. He wanted her badly. In his bed and in his life.

With a heavy sigh, Jared headed toward the jail. So, Mattie didn't appreciate his brand of help, didn't like the things he'd done for her? Fine, he could fix that. Starting first thing in the morning.

Chapter Fourteen

As plans went, this one was by far the worst Jared had come up with.

He moved along with the rest of the congregation leaving the church, anxious to go, craning his neck for a glimpse of Mattie, who was already outside.

At the door, Reverend Harris shook hands with his flock.

"Nice sermon," Jared said.

"Thank you, Sheriff," the minister replied. "And I appreciate you not shouting out for me to hurry it up, or skip over parts."

"Yes, sir," Jared mumbled, moving on. He supposed he deserved that, after the way he'd tried to rush Reverend Harris through his near wedding ceremony with Mattie.

Standing at the foot of the church steps, Jared located Mattie on the other side of the yard amid the Sunday morning congregation. His heart ached at the sight of her.

Stay away from her. That's what his latest plan had called for. Make her want him. Show her what it's like not to have him around. That would teach her.

Jared sighed heavily. Oh, yeah. Great plan. So great, in fact, it seemed he was the only one suffering for it.

Days had passed since he'd been in Mattie's company. Sure, he'd seen her on the street and when he'd walked past her restaurant—in the line of duty, of course. But catching an occasional glimpse of her through a window was as close as he'd gotten.

For days he hadn't had the pleasure of hearing her voice or smelling her delicate scent. He hadn't heard her gentle laughter, or seen the way she pushed her hair behind one ear when she was too warm, or crinkled up her nose when she concentrated. His ''plan'' had kept him away from her.

And now, all these days later, Jared could say without hesitation that his ''plan'' had backfired completely.

The first day he'd enacted this brilliant idea of his, he'd sent Billy down to the Cottonwood to help Mattie carry the prisoner's breakfast tray to the jail, then made certain he wasn't in his office when she got there. Let her wonder where he was, he'd thought. He'd done the same at noon, then at supper. But when he'd taken his prisoner down to the Cottonwood that evening to wash her dishes, Mattie had been gone.

The next day and every day after that, Billy had come back from the restaurant with the prisoner's meals—but no Mattie. And not once—not one single time—had she been in the kitchen when her dishes were being washed.

Watching her across the churchyard, Jared thought she hardly looked worse for the experience. Seemingly, she hadn't missed him at all. He was the only one, apparently, whose heart was aching.

The murmur of conversations drifted around Jared as Reverend Harris bade his flock goodbye and the congregation clustered to chat. A group of small children played at the edge of the churchyard, squealing, laughing and running. One of the little boys yanked on a girl's pigtails. She hit him. He hit her back. Two other children joined in before their mothers broke it up with stern words, leading them away, two of the children crying.

A chill ran through Jared as he saw Mattie standing by herself, watching them. She stared in silence, unblinking, unmoving.

Jared approached her. "You must hate me," he said quietly.

She turned, and for a flash of a second he thought she was pleased to see him. Jared wasn't sure. Wishful thinking, maybe?

He nodded toward the three children who'd resumed their game. "You must hate me for saddling you with this baby to raise."

She gasped and her face blanched. Jared's belly twisted into a knot. Seemed his guess had been right.

Then Mattie gazed up at him with those big brown

eyes of hers, pinning him with a look that seemed to seep into his soul.

"Good gracious, no, Jared," she said, as if the very idea were so foreign she didn't really understand it. "I never felt that way about this baby. Never."

A little grin tugged at his lips. "I'm glad to hear you say that, Mattie."

"I love this baby." Mattie touched her hand lightly to her stomach. "Somehow, I love him already—and I've not even met him."

Jared's knees weakened. Never more than at this moment had he wanted to take Mattie in his arms. He wanted to hold her. Kiss her. Love her. Keep her near him forever and always.

He jammed his fingertips in his hip pockets to keep from doing just that.

"This baby keeps me thinking about the future," Mattie said. "Without him, goodness knows how I might have dwelled on the past, on Del and everything that happened."

"So you're really happy about the baby?"

"Oh, of course." Mattie's smile faded. "I figured you'd stayed away from the jail on purpose when I brought over the food trays, before I started sending them with Billy."

Jared shifted from one foot to the other, feeling like an idiot. "Well…"

"I appreciate it. It was wise of you to do that."

"It was?"

She nodded. "That's why I had Billy carry the other

meals over without me. I needed some time to think about things.''

''And seeing me clouds your thoughts?'' Jared's heart thumped a little faster as he waited for her answer.

''Well...yes.''

''Why? Because you were thinking about me naked?''

Mattie gasped, then burst out laughing, pressing her fingers to her lips. Jared grinned, unable not to.

''You were,'' he said. ''Don't try to deny it.''

Jared glanced around and saw that they'd attracted some attention. Everyone in town knew their situation. He wasn't inclined to make Mattie the object of any more gossip, speculation or unsolicited advice from well-meaning townsfolk.

He moved in front of her, sheltering her. ''Would you allow me the privilege of walking you home?''

She glanced past him, aware, too, that stares were turning their way. ''No, thank you.''

''Are you doing something for supper?'' he asked. Usually after church services, families went home to a quiet meal, often inviting friends to join them.

''I've got things to take care of at the house,'' Mattie said. ''The Cottonwood is closed on Sundays.''

''You're not doing any heavy work, are you?''

She shook her head. ''No, nothing like that.''

Jared didn't say anything for a moment, hoping— praying, actually—that she'd ask him to come home with her for Sunday supper.

Instead, she shook her head. "I'd better go."

Mattie was sure she could feel Jared's gaze on her back as she crossed the churchyard. It warmed her, made her stomach tingle. And while part of her—an ever growing part of her—wanted to ask him to come to supper with her, the rest of her—the ever shrinking logical part of her—knew that she shouldn't.

Mattie let herself into the house, thinking of the things she needed to do, on her only day away from the restaurant. Silence hung heavily in every room. It was odd not being at the Cottonwood. Mrs. Nance and the few diners who came by were good company. They kept her from thinking too much about things she didn't want to think about. Things that kept nagging at her.

In her bedroom, Mattie undressed, freeing herself of her bustle, corset and stockings, and slipped into a simple gingham dress. A breeze floated in through the open window, cooling her bare feet as she straightened the room.

A knock on the door drew her to the front of the house. She opened it and found Jared standing on her porch.

"I figured you wouldn't have much chance to do any cooking for yourself, so I brought supper for you," Jared said, lifting a covered basket for her to see.

"Where did you get that?"

"The Silver Bell," he said. "Besides, I thought you'd like to sample what your competition is doing."

Cautiously, Mattie lifted the checkered cloth covering the basket. "Oh, my, so much food. I can't possibly eat that much. Why, it's enough to feed—"

Mattie steeled herself. "Two people," she said.

Send him on his way, a little voice somewhere in Mattie shouted. *Take the basket, thank him and tell him to leave.*

But wait, another voice countered. *Don't make him go. Look at him…just look at him.*

She couldn't resist the temptation to do just that. Jared was a fine-looking man. Mattie knew. She'd seen him naked.

A plume of heat rose in Mattie. Fearful it would color her face, that Jared would see it and somehow guess her thoughts, she stepped back from the door. "You can come in and have supper," she said. "There's something I want to talk to you about."

Jared headed straight for the kitchen, hung his hat and gun belt on a peg beside the back door, then unloaded the basket.

"You just sit down and rest," he said. "I'll fix supper for you."

"You don't have to do that."

He looked up. "I know I don't have to. I want to."

Mattie let him have his way.

After another glance around the kitchen, Jared disappeared down the hallway, then came back carrying her rocker and footstool from the parlor. He placed it near the stove.

"You'll be more comfortable in this," he said. "How have you been feeling?"

"No more morning sickness," she said, sitting down in the rocker. "Just tired."

"Well, you'll get plenty of rest today." Jared knelt in front of her. "Just put your feet up on this stool and—"

He froze as Mattie placed her bare feet on the stool. Her toes actually warmed under his scrutiny, sending a rush through her. All Mattie's senses crackled to life.

Slowly, he lifted his gaze to her bare ankles, then to her legs. Though her dress covered her, she may as well not have had on a stitch of clothes. Mattie's knees trembled beneath her skirt. She was conscious of how little she wore, keenly aware that Jared knew it, too.

She moved to rise from the chair and murmured, "I'll go put on—"

"No." He shook his head, his voice a little desperate. "No, don't do that. Please. Just…just sit here."

They gazed at each other for a moment, then Mattie nodded. "All right."

He lurched to his feet and busied himself lighting the stove and putting on a pot of coffee, accomplishing it awkwardly, as he kept his back to her as much as possible.

Finally, he spoke, his voice a little hoarse. "You said there was something you want to talk to me about?"

"I never did thank you for talking to the mayor for me."

Jared paused as he took plates from the cupboard, his gaze scanning her in a hot sweep, as if the layers of fabric covering her meant nothing.

"So, thank you," she said.

"You're welcome," he answered, and went about setting the table.

Mattie started to rise from the rocker. "No, really, Jared, I—"

"Don't get up." It was a warning, not a courtesy. Jared waved his hand at her. "Just don't get up."

She settled into the chair again, her dress and petticoat feeling thinner and thinner with each moment that passed.

"Even if you didn't go about it the way I'd have liked, you still convinced the mayor to give me a chance," Mattie said. "I was thinking about that for the last few days. I shouldn't have been so angry at you. I shouldn't have—"

"Compared me to Del?"

Mattie's stomach rolled. A new warmth—this one different—crept through her. She dipped her gaze. "That's what I did, didn't I?"

Jared nodded as he set the table. "I'm not like him, Mattie. I'm nothing like him."

Mattie smiled. "Del certainly never made supper for me."

"He didn't do a hell of a lot of other things for you, either," Jared declared, and it was clear he wasn't referring to the household chores.

"Anyway," Mattie said, trying to ignore the heat

in her cheeks, "I appreciate your help with Mayor Rayburn, and I'm sorry I shouted at you."

Jared finished getting the meal on the table, something he obviously seldom did, and seated Mattie in the chair across from him. He dished out the Silver Bell's fried chicken, potatoes and carrots for both of them, and poured coffee.

"Billy and I took a ride out west of town the other day," Jared said, after they'd eaten awhile.

"Did you catch sight of Mr. Pitney?" Mattie asked.

"The old recluse from the Battle of Gettysburg?" Jared shook his head. "No, but Billy told me about him."

"Did you stop at the McCafferty place?"

"Just for a few minutes," Jared said. "Mrs. Mc-Cafferty was outside doing laundry."

"Has she had the baby yet?" Mattie asked.

"Looked like it could happen most any time."

"I feel sorry for her," Mattie said. "Out there all by herself, expecting a baby, and no other woman to talk to about…things."

"She's got a husband. He'll take care of her."

"Some husbands don't do that."

"Some *do*."

Mattie was certain Jared knew she was thinking about Del again.

"Anyway," she said, "there's something odd about that Mr. McCafferty. You're the sheriff. Can't you do something?"

"If I started locking up everybody in this town who

acted strange, there wouldn't be anybody left walking the streets.'' Jared nodded toward the food on the table. ''What do you think of your competition?''

''Not bad,'' Mattie was forced to admit. She smiled confidently. ''But the Silver Bell doesn't stand a chance of winning that supper away from the Cottonwood.''

''Have you decided what you're serving?'' Jared asked. He ate greedily, as if he were starving. Mattie wondered if it was really his belly he was trying to satisfy.

''Yes. Roast beef, chicken and ham, four kinds of vegetables, two kinds of bread and three desserts.''

''That's more than a full meal, all right. I don't see how the council can turn it down.''

''You haven't heard my whole plan yet,'' Mattie said. She'd spent days working on it, consulting with Mrs. Nance. ''I'm going to deck out the Cottonwood in red, white and blue. I'll get mama's old white tablecloths mended and freshly laundered, and put a red rose from Mrs. Donovan's garden on each table, then hang blue bunting around the room. Mr. Langston at the mercantile said he'd give me a good price on it.''

''Sounds fancy.''

''And that's not all. I'm going to cook the full meal and serve samples to the town council the night I make my proposal.''

Jared grinned. ''I guess that means they're having the meeting at the mayor's house.''

''You heard about Mrs. Rayburn's cooking?'' Mattie asked. "Well, after facing one of her meals, the town council won't be able to resist the Cottonwood's offering."

"Have you got plenty of help cooking and getting everything over to the mayor's house?"

"Billy is helping, of course."

"If you don't mind a suggestion, how about having the Spencer girls help you out that night, too? According to Billy, they're pretty girls, and ol' Gil is anxious to marry them off."

Mattie considered the idea. "I guess it wouldn't do any harm for him to know they'll spend a fair amount of time with those investors, if the Cottonwood wins the supper."

"Seems like a lot of expense involved with proposing this supper to the council, what with buying the food, paying Billy and the Spencer sisters, and giving Mrs. Nance something extra for all the cooking," Jared said, biting into another chicken leg. "Can you handle it?"

"Yes."

He glanced up from his plate. "You're sure?"

"I'm sure." Mattie toyed with her carrots for a moment. "I sold something."

He chewed slower. "What?"

Mattie laid her fork aside. She could hardly bear to think about what she'd done. How she'd sold one of the few family treasures she possessed. She'd wrestled with the idea, unsure of what to do, but in the end the survival of the Cottonwood Café and her baby's future had won out.

"My mother's brooch. I didn't want to sell it, of course. Her mother had given it to her, and I was supposed to pass it on to my daughter. But it was the only thing I had of value that I could sell quickly, and..."

Jared just looked at her for a moment. Mattie could imagine his thoughts. She'd had all the same ones herself leading up to the decision to sell the brooch.

"It must have been a tough thing for you to do," Jared said softly.

Mattie allowed herself a small smile, pleased he hadn't chastised her for selling her grandmother's jewelry, making her feel worse about it than she already did.

When they finished eating, Jared insisted Mattie rest in the rocker again, then cleared the table and washed the dishes.

"What about these chores you were doing today?" Jared asked, placing the last plate in the cupboard. "Anything I can help with?"

"Actually, I was planning to spend the afternoon working on my knitting," Mattie said. "For the baby."

He grinned. "Can I see?"

"Well, sure, if you'd like." Mattie left the kitchen and returned a moment later with her knitting basket. She laid the things she'd already completed on the table—a sweater and two pairs of booties. She was still working on a cap.

"Blue, huh?" Jared asked.

"It will be a boy," Mattie said. "I know I should be sewing for myself. I'll be needing proper clothes before the baby needs these things. But I just can't resist."

For a long moment Jared looked at the items on the table. Finally, he picked up a bootie and laid it in his palm. It looked tiny against his big hand, soft compared to his ruggedness.

He turned to her, his eyes burning with an intensity she'd seen only a few times. Deliberately, his gaze dipped to her belly.

A heat, an energy—something—arced from him to Mattie. She felt it pulling her toward him, binding her to him.

"Mattie..." Jared dropped the bootie and wrapped his arms around her.

She didn't step away, didn't try to escape. Instead, she looped her arms around his neck and met his lips with hers.

He sealed their mouths together, pulling her close. Mattie sank into his embrace, into his kiss, twining her fingers through his hair.

Jared's lips trailed down her cheek to the hollow of her neck. He raised his hand to cup her breast.

With a gasp, Mattie pushed herself against him. He groaned, then caught her behind her knees and lifted her onto the table. He fumbled with her skirt until his fingers found the flesh of her thigh.

Mattie's head spun as he kissed her and she kissed

him, both feverish in their need. She pulled open the buttons of his shirt and long johns and splayed her hand over his chest. He pushed his hand farther under her skirt.

"Mattie," he whispered, his breath hot against her face, "I want you."

"I—I guess it wouldn't be a sin, really, since I'm already pregnant."

"It wouldn't have to be a sin at all." He kissed her hard. "Marry me, Mattie. We'll go to the church. Now. The reverend can marry us. We'll be back here in twenty minutes. Then we'd have all afternoon to-gether…all evening…all night."

Mattie's head fell back as Jared's mouth trailed down her throat. "But…but I don't want to get mar-ried. Can't we…you know…just this one time?"

"I don't want to make love to you just one time." Jared eased back and caught her cheeks between his palms. "I want to make love to you forever."

They looked at each other, their passion cooling.

"I don't want to get married," Mattie whispered.

"Can't you see how much I care about you? How much you mean to me?"

"I…" She turned her head, unable to look at him.

"What is it, Mattie? Tell me."

"I—I…I don't know…."

He stepped away then, giving her one last hungry look. Mattie pulled her skirt down.

"I'd better go," Jared said, buttoning his shirt. He

got his hat and gun belt, and the basket he'd brought supper in, and left the kitchen.

Mattie followed him to the front door. He stepped outside but didn't leave the porch, just stood there for a long time looking at her, his expression unreadable.

Wishing she could think of something sensible to say, Mattie remained motionless in the doorway. Finally, Jared turned to leave, then looked back.

"Who did you sell your mama's brooch to?" he asked.

The question was so far removed from her own thoughts, Mattie couldn't answer for a moment.

"Mrs. Pomeroy," she finally said.

Jared walked away.

Chapter Fifteen

The door to his office burst open and Mattie stormed inside, cheeks flushed, eyes blazing.

Seated at his desk, Jared pushed aside the packet of Wanted posters he'd just picked up from the express office, wondering what he'd done since the last time he'd seen her to make her so angry.

Mattie planted one fist on her hip and pointed outside. "I want you to go arrest that awful Mr. McCafferty."

Relieved that, for a change, it wasn't him she was mad at, Jared took a minute to note how enticing Mattie looked when she was all riled up. Pink cheeks, jaw set, breasts straining against her dress...

He squirmed in his chair. God help him, everything this woman did made him want her.

Calmly, he laid his hands on the desk. "Did Mr. McCafferty happen to break a law?"

"No!" She pointed out the door again. "Just go arrest him!"

"Okay." Jared rose from his chair and nodded to the rifle rack on the wall. "Do you want me to shoot him, too?"

"Yes!"

"Kill him outright, or just wing him?"

Mattie huffed loudly, realizing, apparently, how unreasonable she sounded. She flapped her arms at her sides. "You have to do *something*," she insisted.

Jared sat down on the corner of his desk. "What's this all about?"

"That awful Mr. McCafferty is in town, right over there at the mercantile, and his wife isn't with him."

Jared frowned, trying to get the gist of her concern. "And…?"

That sparked her anger again. "She hasn't been into town in months! Didn't he consider that maybe she'd like to come along, too?"

"Maybe he figured the ride would be too rough for her."

"So he left her home alone? All by herself with a baby due at any minute?"

"They might have needed supplies, things they couldn't do without. Maybe he's buying something special and wanted to surprise her."

Mattie planted her fists on her hips again. "Would you just stop making so much sense?"

Jared left the corner of the desk and draped his arm around Mattie's shoulder. "You're worried Mrs. McCafferty might have the baby out there by herself?"

Mattie leaned against him, soaking up some of the comfort he offered. "What if her labor starts and she's alone?" She pressed her lips together, then nodded decisively. "I'll just go out to their farm myself and check on her."

Jared fought back his immediate reaction—to forbid her to go. Instead he said, "Do you think that's a good idea? You bouncing around in a wagon for that long?"

Mattie looked away. "No, I don't suppose it is. But somebody has to do something. Could you go, Jared?"

The last thing he wanted was to show up at their place and find Mrs. McCafferty giving birth. "I don't think she'd get much comfort from me calling on her, me being a man, and the sheriff."

"Yes, you're right. I'll ask Mrs. Pomeroy. She and her committee could go out there."

"Let's just suppose that Mrs. McCafferty is not having the baby at this very minute. Do you think she'd want all those women showing up on her doorstep? She probably hasn't felt up to keeping her house neat as a pin, and might be embarrassed for those ladies to see it."

Mattie looked up at him. "How do you know so much about expectant mothers?"

Jared didn't answer. "Tell you what, I'll go talk to Mr. McCafferty and see if his wife has had the baby yet. And if she hasn't, I'll ask the reverend and his missus if they can go out there. The two of them are always visiting people, so it won't seem unusual. And the reverend's wife can talk to Mrs. McCafferty about…whatever. Will that handle things to suit you?''

Mattie smiled. "Yes. Thank you."

"Good." Jared got his hat from beside the door. "I'll walk you back to the Cottonwood. Are you busy this morning getting everything ready for the town council meeting tonight?"

"A little," Mattie explained, as they stepped outside and moved down the boardwalk. "Most of the work will be done this afternoon. Billy's coming over and so are the Spencer sisters."

"So you've got a little free time?" When she nodded, Jared said, "Good. I'll come back by the Cottonwood in a bit. There's something we need to take care of."

She raised her eyebrows at him. "What?"

"I'll explain it to you later."

"You're sounding very mysterious."

"Stop frowning. It will be fun. I promise."

Jared left her at the Cottonwood, then headed over to the mercantile and found McCafferty. He was a big man, young, and not much for conversation, but Jared got enough out of him to learn that their baby hadn't been born yet. He circled back to the church, let Reverend Harris know the situation, then went back to the Cottonwood.

Mattie smiled when he walked through the back door into the restaurant's kitchen. Mrs. Nance was at the stove, while Billy packed dishes into a small crate.

"Big night," Jared said, surveying the scene.

"The Cottonwood has the best cook and staff in Stanford," Mattie bragged. "The council won't be able to refuse us that supper."

"Miss Mattie?" Billy called. "I know you told me how many plates to pack, but I think we'd better bring a few more, just in case."

"All right. I trust your judgment." Mattie turned to Jared. "You haven't heard anybody talking about what we're proposing to the council, have you? I've sworn everyone to secrecy."

"Not a peep. Of course, Billy's the one you ought to ask."

"Not a peep. Just like the sheriff said," he confirmed. "There ain't no other restaurant planning on actually serving the council samples of their menu, I can tell you that for a fact."

"Perfect," Mattie declared, smiling broadly.

"Okay, then let's go," Jared said to Mattie, nodding toward the door.

She looked anxiously around the restaurant. "I don't think I should leave, Jared. Something might come up."

"Billy? Mrs. Nance?" Jared called. "Anything happening you can't handle?"

"Shoot, no," Billy answered.

"Go on now, you two," Mrs. Nance said, waving a spoon at them and smiling sweetly. "If anything comes up, we'll find you."

Mattie hesitated another moment. "Are you sure this is important?"

"It can't wait much longer," Jared told her.

"Well, I suppose it will be all right, just for a while." Mattie took off her apron. Billy could handle most any problem that came up at the Cottonwood. He'd washed dishes for her before, but really, he'd been involved in every aspect of running the business. Mattie hadn't realized how much she'd depended on him until she'd had to let him go.

The streets of Stanford were busy as ever at midday, as Mattie and Jared left the restaurant. Shoppers crowded the boardwalk and wagons filled the roadway.

But unlike other times, Mattie realized things were different today. Different, because Jared walked beside her.

Men nodded to him as they passed and a few women spoke; apparently, the townsfolk had gotten over their initial negative impression of him.

But being beside Jared meant something else. He was tall and wide and sturdy. People got out of his way. Not simply because of the badge pinned to his chest, either. There was an air of command about him, a strength that couldn't go unnoticed or ignored.

Mattie glanced up at him. Though he'd kept up a steady conversation with her since leaving the Cottonwood, and he'd spoken politely to all who'd passed, Jared's gaze never stilled. He scanned the boardwalk ahead, the traffic that passed, the businesses across the street, taking in everything. Watching for trouble.

A little tremor jarred Mattie. She couldn't remember

ever feeling so safe on the streets of Stanford as right now at Jared's side.

When they reached the Stanford Ladies' Fashions and Millinery Shop, Jared opened the door. Mattie leaned back, eyeing the sign again.

"This is Mrs. Dixon's ladies' clothing store," she said. "Did you realize that?"

"Yes, ma'am, I did." Jared waved grandly and Mattie preceded him into the shop.

A display of hats took up about half the store, bolts of fabric the rest of the room. Colors and textures abounded. Boxes of buttons, ribbons and lace were everywhere.

While most of the women in Stanford, like Mattie, made their own clothing, there were enough ranchers', mine owners' and businessmen's wives to keep the dressmaker busy, to say nothing of the painted women who worked at the parlor house on the outskirts of town.

Colleen Dixon, the owner, dressed stylishly, her red hair beautifully coifed, came forward. "Why, Sheriff McQuaid, there you are. I was beginning to think something had come up. Good afternoon, Mattie."

Though Mattie had never bought clothing here, she'd purchased a number of hats from Mrs. Dixon.

"I don't understand," Mattie said. "Why am I here?"

"The sheriff has arranged for your upcoming fashion essentials and accessories." Mrs. Dixon waved her long, elegant hand toward Mattie, wiggling her fingers at her belly.

"My…?" She gasped sharply as she realized what Mrs. Dixon meant. Mattie turned to Jared, color flooding her cheeks. "You think you're going to buy my—"

"Mrs. Dixon, would you give us a minute?" Jared called. She nodded her understanding and disappeared into the back room of the shop. "Now, Mattie, before you get upset—"

"No."

"Please listen—"

"No!" Mattie folded her arms. "No, you can't buy my clothing. It's too personal."

"So getting you pregnant wasn't too personal, but buying clothes to accommodate your condition is?"

Mattie's cheeks flamed anew.

"Just hear me out before you get all worked up," Jared said. "You're getting far along now. It won't be long until you'll need proper clothes. And at the same time, you'll be in the middle of getting ready for those Eastern investors. These clothes aren't the kind of thing that can wait until you have time to make them yourself."

Mattie continued to fume. "No, I will not allow you to do this."

Jared didn't say anything for a while, just studied her. "This isn't about the clothes, is it? It's not about being too personal. It's something else." His expression hardened. "It's about Del, isn't it?"

A man trained in law enforcement, observing, watching, piecing things together, missed little. Mattie saw no reason not to tell him the truth. "I can't help wondering if you're being nice to me just to get me to marry you," she told him.

"Mattie, I really do care about you."

"That's what Del said."

"I want to be with you all the time."

"Del said that, too." Mattie looked up at him. "He said the sweetest, kindest things to me, bought me all sorts of gifts, and after we were married everything changed. Del changed. He wasn't the man who'd courted me."

Jared just looked at her for a long moment, as if thinking hard about what she'd said.

"If I were in your shoes, I might feel the same," Jared stated. "But even if you don't believe I'm sincere in my feelings for you, at least let me help out with the baby. I know it's God's way and you can't help it, but you get to have the baby with you all the time. Can't you let me take part in this baby, Mattie? Let me do a little something? Let me make the mother of my child comfortable and happy?"

Her heart melted. And she didn't want it to melt. She wanted to be strong and noble and declare her independence from him yet another time. This was her life. Her baby. She'd handle everything herself.

The anger went out of Mattie. Jared looked hurt and sweet and concerned all at the same time. The urge to press her palm to his cheek and soothe him nearly overcame her.

And the truth was that Jared had a right to participate in what happened with the baby, with her. As much as she didn't want to think about it, the baby was his, too.

What's more, he actually wanted to be involved. Some husbands—in fact, most husbands—kept their distance from the whole process. Mattie couldn't find fault with what Jared wanted, what he was asking for. Really, when she allowed herself to think about it, the whole idea of his involvement pleased her.

Pleased her, yes, but didn't make her lose sight of her situation.

"Good gracious, Jared, what will the whole town say when they find out you're buying me these clothes?"

He gave an exaggerated shrug. "They'll probably say, 'what a wonderful husband that Jared McQuaid would make,' and 'what's wrong with Mattie Ingram that she won't marry him?'"

She gave him a sour smile.

"Of course, if you don't want that kind of talk, you could always—"

"—buy my own clothes."

"—marry me." Jared smiled gently. "Being married isn't so bad, if it's to the right person."

"You don't know that," Mattie told him.

"Yes, I do."

"You don't," she insisted, then turned away. "I don't want to argue with you."

"Then you'll let me buy you the clothes?"

"All right," she decided. "But this is it. Nothing else. I don't want you spending another cent on me. Are we agreed?"

Jared rolled his eyes toward the ceiling. "Well..."

At that moment, Mattie knew this was what her own son would one day look like when he was guilty of something. When he'd done something he knew wouldn't please her. When he needed to confess and didn't exactly know how.

"What did you do?" she asked.

Jared pulled on the back of his neck. "Doc Whittaker...I already paid him for taking care of you and delivering the baby."

She sighed heavily. "Jared..."

He squared his shoulder. "I paid for it, and that's that. I don't want to hear one word from you about it."

"Is there anything else you've done and haven't told me?" Mattie asked.

"No. That's it."

"All right, fine. So we're agreed that you won't do anything else like this?"

Jared grunted. "Seems like the craziest thing a man could ever say to a woman, but yes, I won't buy anything else for you."

"Promise."

"I promise," he said.

Mrs. Dixon breezed in from the back of the shop. "Are we ready to look at patterns and fabrics?"

Jared raised a hopeful eyebrow at Mattie. She nodded. "Yes, I'm ready."

Mrs. Dixon pulled two gold upholstered chairs up to a small table, where Jared and Mattie sat, and brought out an array of fabrics for them to consider.

"Get whatever you want," Jared said, when he saw her hesitate. "Get as much as you want."

"No sense in buying too much," Mattie said. "After all, I'm only having this one child. I'll never need these clothes again."

Mattie picked out fabric for a few blouses and skirts, all in dark greens, blues and grays, with Jared sitting beside her, looking at what she pointed to, nodding thoughtfully at everything.

It felt strange and awkward at first, having him at her elbow, discussing clothing. But he seemed to enjoy it and gave his opinion on most everything. In the end, Mattie grew comfortable with both the clothing and Jared's presence.

"Excellent choices," Mrs. Dixon declared, writing up the order. "Now, Mattie, if you'll just come in the back room, I'll get your measurements."

As Mattie disappeared into the little curtained area at the rear of the shop, Jared approached Mrs. Dixon.

"Everything she ordered, triple it," he said in a low voice. "I know she asked for dark colors, but it will be hot this summer, so make some of her things lighter. And throw in anything else she'll need—underclothes or whatever.''

Mrs. Dixon smiled pleasantly. ''Of course, Sheriff.''

Jared paced in front of the window, listening to the soft feminine voices floating from the back of the shop.

He didn't like to think about the past. Too much sorrow. Too much pain. Only since he'd met Mattie had he been able to recall what had happened and not have his gut wrenched.

But right now, at this moment, Jared would give most anything to go back. Not for himself, though. For Mattie.

He wished he could have met her before Del did. Before Del had hurt her, tainted her view of men, marriage and life. Jared wished he didn't have all Del's damage to undo.

He gazed out on the streets of Stanford, taking solace in his new home, and drew in a fortifying breath. Forging this life with Mattie would only make their marriage stronger.

A little smile pulled at his lips as he thought about her modest selections of clothing, reasoning she'd have only this one baby.

One baby.

He'd be damned if that would be true. Not if he had any say in it.

Chapter Sixteen

What if he held the town council at gunpoint? What if he threatened to arrest every one of them?

Jared walked toward the mayor's house, ruminating over what he could do to convince the council to let Mattie host that supper. They were all assembled right now, getting ready to go over the town's business, and very shortly would be hearing proposals from all the restaurants in town.

Mattie would probably win the supper on her own, with what she had planned. But still, Jared didn't like leaving it to chance.

"Evening, Sheriff."

He stopped as Abel and Ben waved to him from their checkerboard in front of the mercantile. Since they'd witnessed Mattie berating him, they'd been a little friendlier. "Evening, boys."

"You headed over to the mayor's house?" Abel asked.

"Yep," Jared said.

"Figured you would, what with Miss Mattie being over there," Ben said.

Abel squinted at Jared. "You eat already?"

"I sure did."

Both old men nodded sagely. It seemed no one in town didn't know about Mayor Rayburn's wife's cooking.

"How's your game—yeow!" Jared grabbed his knee and whipped around as little Chuckie Waldron raced down the boardwalk. Damn, that kid had kicked him again!

"Get back here!" Jared stumbled along after him, gritting his teeth and cursing at the same time. He was going to get his hands on that boy, and when he did—

Chuckie darted into the alley. Jared followed, but came up short at the sight of Mrs. Waldron holding the struggling boy by the hand.

"Sheriff, I'm so sorry," she said. "I saw what Chuckie did and—oh, Chuckie, please be still."

"Settle down!" Jared's voice boomed, freezing both Chuckie and his mother.

"Sheriff, I'm sorry." Mrs. Waldron, young and obviously at wit's end over her son, pushed a stray lock of hair behind her ear. "Please don't be mad at Chuckie. He hears the older boys talking, pretending to be outlaws, making it sound so glamorous. He thinks he's some sort of lawbreaker."

Chuckie narrowed his eyes at Jared, frowning and glaring, pushing out his jaw.

"I've talked to him, really I have," Mrs. Waldron

said, still holding her son's hand. "But he won't listen."

"A good swat on the backside would make him listen."

"He won't kick you again. I promise."

"If he does, I'm taking matters into my own hands," Jared told her, resisting the urge to rub his knee.

"All right, Sheriff, that seems fair. Come on, Chuckie." As Mrs. Waldron led the boy away, he looked back at Jared and stuck out his tongue.

Mumbling another curse, Jared left the alley. Ben and Abel craned their necks in his direction, as if they expected him to drag little Chuckie out by his ear and haul him off to jail.

Jared shook his head. "Looks like I've got a real desperado on my hands."

Ben and Abel relaxed and chuckled.

"Better get on over to the mayor's house," Abel advised. "You don't want to be late. Miss Mattie can sure use a friendly face among that bunch."

"That's for dang sure," Ben agreed.

Jared hurried on his way, anxious to see Mattie and put the unpleasantness with Chuckie behind him. But an even greater unpleasantness loomed ahead of him on the boardwalk.

Mrs. Pomeroy.

Fighting the urge to dart across the street and avoid the woman, Jared drew in a deep breath. He needed to talk to her, and he may as well get it over with.

"Evening, Mrs. Pomeroy." Jared tipped his hat.

Nose in the air, she glared at him and walked by without speaking.

"Ma'am? I'd like to have a word with you, if you don't mind."

Mrs. Pomeroy stopped and turned ever so slowly, raising a haughty eyebrow at him. "Is that so? Well, Sheriff, you have already made it perfectly clear that you have nothing to say to me or my committee."

"Well, that's just the thing, Mrs. Pomeroy," Jared said, managing to sound contrite. "I know we got off to a bad start when you and the ladies of your committee came by my office. And I feel terrible about that. Truly, I do."

She pinched her lips together. "Is that so?"

"Yes, ma'am, it is," Jared said. "And I wanted to let you know that I intend to talk to the barkeep at the Lady Luck and see what can be done."

Mrs. Pomeroy's frosty expression hardened into something of a challenge. "You'll discuss curtailing their hours? Limiting the number of drinks served? Holding down the noise? Adopting a policy of not corrupting our youth by serving young men?"

Jared managed a nod. "Yes, ma'am. I'll talk about all those things."

"And you'll report back to me and my committee?"

"Yes, ma'am."

Still, nothing remotely resembling a smile spread

across her face. "Very well, then, Sheriff. Thank you."

"Mrs. Pomeroy?" He followed as she headed off down the boardwalk again. She turned once more, raising that same skeptical eyebrow. "I understand you recently bought a brooch from Mattie Ingram. I'd like to buy it from you."

A smug smile lifted the corners of her mouth. "Is that so?"

She knew why he wanted it. Plain as day, it was written all over her face. Seemed everyone in Stanford—including Mrs. Pomeroy—knew how he felt about Mattie.

Now, seeing the look on the woman's face, Jared figured she'd refuse to sell it to him, just to get back at him for being rude to her and her committee. But to his surprise, Mrs. Pomeroy nodded. "I'll be happy to sell you the brooch, Sheriff."

"Thank you, ma'am, I—"

"*After* you get the saloon to agree to *all* the changes my committee wants." Mrs. Pomeroy gave him a final nod and walked away.

Jared pulled at the tight muscles in his neck. He'd intended to talk to Rafe Duncan at the Lady Luck and see if anything could be done, but really hadn't expected the barkeep to agree to Mrs. Pomeroy's demands. Certainly not all of them. Jared had thought that simply *trying* would appease her and her committee. But now that wouldn't be nearly enough.

"Hellfire..." Jared headed for the mayor's house.

By the time he arrived, supper was over, evidenced by the hungry looks of the town councilmen who'd managed to avoid eating much of Mrs. Rayburn's meal. Jared accepted a cup of coffee, which he nearly gagged on, and took a seat in the parlor with the other men to discuss Stanford's business.

"You holding things together all right at the sheriff's office without an official deputy?" Mr. Burrows, the town banker asked.

"Doing fine," Jared assured them. "Billy's been helping out."

"We'll get you a new deputy as soon as we can," the mayor said. "In the meantime, we've got a few fellas in town who used to help out Sheriff Hickert every now and then. We'll hire them for duty when the investors get here."

Marvin Ford, owner of the Stanford Hotel, read the list of activities planned for the investors, everything from a parade to a performance by the schoolchildren to a tour of the town. The men talked for a while, making suggestions, asking questions, quizzing Jared on what he saw as potential problems.

Finally, Mayor Rayburn declared it was time to listen to proposals from the local restaurants wanting to host the official welcome supper. The Everettes, who owned the Silver Bell, came in with four of their children in tow.

When the curtains separating the parlor from the rear of the house opened, Jared shifted in his chair, hoping for a glimpse of Mattie. He'd been by the Cottonwood and helped load the wagon she'd rented for the evening. It had pleased him that Billy had taken charge, easing some of Mattie's responsibilities.

Jared had urged Mattie to make her presentation first, thereby knocking the competition out of the running right away. But Mattie had wanted to give her proposal after the Silver Bell, sure her ideas would look even better in comparison.

And she'd made the right decision, Jared thought, as the Everettes went through the list of foods they intended to serve. Admittedly, the meal sounded impressive, and the town council was familiar with the quality of their food, since they ate there so often. But the Everettes planned nothing compared to what the Cottonwood had in mind.

A few minutes later, when Mattie came into the parlor, Jared realized his palms were sweating. This afternoon when he'd gone by her restaurant, she and her whole staff had been in a flurry of activity, getting everything ready. But right now, Mattie seemed poised and confident.

"Good evening, gentlemen." She smiled and greeted each of them by name, and thanked them for allowing her the chance to make a proposal. "I think you're going to like what the Cottonwood Café has to offer."

It was all Jared could do not to smile proudly as Billy and Meg and Molly Spencer brought in plates of food from the kitchen and served the councilmen.

When Mattie brought Jared a plate, he couldn't help giving her a secretive wink.

The councilmen looked skeptical at first, but the food was too good not to eat, especially after Mrs. Rayburn's meal. Before long, the councilmen were asking for seconds, and Mattie was explaining the details of her plan, including how she planned to decorate the Cottonwood, and seat the distinguished visitors and town officials.

"Of course, Molly and Meg will serve," Mattie explained, speaking in Gil Spencer's direction. "Those investors should see the *finest* Stanford has to offer. All in all, I see the Cottonwood as the perfect restaurant to host the supper."

"Well, I don't know," Mr. Burrows said around a mouthful of potatoes, "we'll have to think this over."

"Did I mention I brought cake tonight?" Mattie asked. "And pie?"

When the men had finished off all the coffee and desserts, Mayor Rayburn thanked her for her presentation.

"We have to hear from the other restaurants in town, and then we can decide," he said. The other councilmen nodded in agreement. "Send them in here."

Billy stuck his head in from the adjoining dining room. "Uh, sorry, Mayor. Everybody else went home."

"Well, I guess that's it then," the mayor said. "All

in favor of the Cottonwood Café hosting the supper say 'aye.'"

A chorus of aye's rose from the men, along with an indiscreet belch.

"Nay?" the mayor asked. When no one spoke, Mayor Rayburn nodded. "The Cottonwood it shall be."

While the councilmen finished up some of the town's business, Jared slipped into the kitchen. Mattie's face lit up like a July sunrise when she saw him.

"We did it!" She flung her arms around his neck, bouncing up and down, and planted a big kiss on his cheek.

"Good job, Mattie," he said, resisting the urge to squeeze her too tightly. He waved his hand to Billy and the Spencer girls. "Good job, all of you."

Mattie turned around. "I couldn't have done this without you. Thank you!"

Billy smiled bashfully. "We'll get all this stuff loaded up and back to the restaurant. Don't you give it a thought, Miss Mattie."

She turned back to Jared and took both of his hands, a mist of tears in her eyes. "I guess it was worth it, selling Mama's brooch."

Jared nodded, wishing to hell she'd let him give her the money to pay her debts. Wishing that he'd gotten the brooch back from Mrs. Pomeroy. Wishing he could solve every problem Mattie had for the rest of their lives.

She sniffed and blinked away her tears. "But I get to keep the Cottonwood. That's what's important."

"You did fine, Mattie. Just fine." Jared wrapped his arms around her and she leaned against his chest. "I'm proud of you. The hard part is over. All you have to do now is put on the supper."

No, that wasn't quite right, Mattie thought, her jubilation fading. All she had to do now was find a way to *pay* for the supper.

It looked like business as usual at the Cottonwood Café when Jared walked through the kitchen door and found Mrs. Nance leaving for the night and Mattie busy at the worktable.

Except that Mattie's smile seemed wider, her eyes brighter as she looked up, making his heart tumble. She was one happy woman—not surprisingly, after being awarded the investors' supper at the council meeting last night. And that made Jared happy, too.

"Good evening, Sheriff," she called, then nodded pleasantly to the prisoner who followed him inside. This one was a wiry, weathered fellow, who, like most of the other prisoners Jared brought to do her dishes, looked as if he'd seen better days.

"See you tomorrow." Mrs. Nance nodded pleasantly to everyone, then left.

"Who's he?" Mattie asked quietly, after Jared got the prisoner situated at the washtubs and took the stool beside her.

The land around Stanford was rich with silver, a

fortune waiting for any man smart enough and lucky enough to find it. Few were. Those whose claim hadn't panned out, or whose strike had played out, found their way to Stanford. Some were looking for work, some for a handout. Some were looking for trouble.

"Says his name is Smith," Jared told her.

"What did he do to get arrested?"

"Disorderly conduct."

"Another disorderly conduct?" Mattie asked. "Good gracious, Jared, I've never seen most of the prisoners you bring in here. Are they from around here? People passing through? Who are they?"

Jared cleared his throat. "No need to look at this too closely."

She glanced up at him, concerned. "Mayor Rayburn isn't upset with you for making so many arrests, is he?"

"He hasn't said anything so far. Of course, with that fine food you're bringing to the jail, I'm liable to have men coming in from the next county to commit crimes here in Stanford."

"No complaints from the prisoners about having to wash dishes for your community assistance program?"

"Not a one." Jared laid a mail order catalog on the worktable in front of them. "Take a look at this, will you, Mattie? I could use your help."

That sweet little smile of hers turned to a frown. "You promised you wouldn't buy me anything else. You gave me your word."

"I wasn't going to buy anything for you."

"Oh."

"It's for the baby."

Her eyes narrowed. "Jared, we agreed—"

"You never said anything about not wanting me to buy for the baby, now did you?"

"Well, no, but—"

"Okay, then, give me a hand. Mrs. Dixon let me borrow this catalog of hers, and truth is, I've never seen one of these before." Jared held it up, pointing to the five-story building on the cover. "See? Bloomingdale Brothers Fashions, Dry Goods and Housewares. All the way from New York City."

Mattie leaned closer. "Oh, my…"

"Mrs. Dixon says they sell baby things," Jared said, flipping through the pages. "What I want—Holy smoke! There's women in their underwear in here!" Jared pulled the catalog closer, eyeing the pages. "Damn…where was this when I was a kid?"

"Give me that." Mattie pulled the catalog from his hands and primly turned the page. "Honestly, carrying on as if you never…"

"Never what?"

Mattie blushed. "Never…*you know*. I mean, there's a parlor house just outside town, and—"

"For your information, I haven't *you knowed* with any woman since *you know when*."

She looked up at him, surprised, and wagged her finger back and forth between them. "Since you and I—?"

"That's right."

Mattie frowned. "But I thought men always wanted to…you know."

"I never said I didn't *want* to. I'm just particular about who I'm with," he grumbled. "Thanks to you."

Mattie gazed up at him, looking both skeptical and pleased. "Really?"

"Really." Jared pulled the catalog away from her, anxious to put this topic of conversation behind them. His condition was difficult enough to endure without talking about it—to Mattie of all people.

"I want everything for the baby in pink," he told her, leafing through the catalog pages.

"Pink? All pink?" Mattie asked. She shook her head. "Your son is going to look mighty foolish swaddled in anything but blue."

"It'll be a girl," Jared told her. "I want pink."

"You're wasting your money. It's going to be a boy."

Jared grinned. "Maybe we'll get one of each?"

"Heavens, Jared, twins?" Mattie touched her hand to her throat. "I can't imagine."

"It's not so hard. I've got brothers who are twins. Two sets of twin cousins, too. They came to live with us after their folks died."

"My gracious, how did your parents manage?"

"That wasn't the half of it. There were twelve of us kids altogether, counting my cousins and those my folks took in. Gathering strays, my pa used to call it. Any kid who needed a home found one at our house."

Mattie sighed wistfully. "I didn't have any brothers or sisters, but I used to wonder what it would be like."

"Suited me fine." Jared smiled at the memory. "There was always somebody to go fishing with, somebody to get into mischief with, somebody to back you up in a fight."

"But your parents? How did they manage all those children?"

"They had a way of making all of us feel important." Jared shrugged. "Of course, there were times when one of them would be at their wit's end with us, but then the other one would jump in and take up the slack. My folks were good about looking out for each other. Seemed to me to be the point of them being together."

"Do you see your folks very often?" Mattie asked.

"I haven't been home in…a long time," Jared told her, pleased that thoughts of his home didn't upset him like they used to. He smiled down at her. "So how about helping me pick out some baby clothes?"

They pored over the pages of the catalog together, looking at the drawings, reading the descriptions. Jared pulled a sheet of paper from his pocket and started a list. Stewart's nursery pins for four cents per dozen. Infant bibs for fifty-nine cents each. A flannel infant wrapper trimmed with lace and satin ribbon, priced at $2.25.

"How about one of these?" Jared asked, turning the page. "'Infants' Outfit C,' it says here. 'Fifty-one pieces. Each set includes all the necessary articles, and nothing is forgotten…proven very popular.' What do you think?''

Mattie leaned closer. ''My goodness, Jared, it costs over fifty dollars.''

He pointed to the list of infant items included in the package. ''Will the baby need all these things?''

''Well, yes, but—''

''Then I'll get it.'' Jared added it to his list. He searched through more pages. ''Here. This is what I need.''

''A baby carriage?''

He studied the drawings on the pages and read the descriptions, then pointed to one. '''Fine rattan carriage, lined in silk plush, extra quality, satin parasol with lace edge. This is one of the finest rattan bodies that can be had.' Do you like it?''

''It's beautiful,'' she said. ''But only a few women in Stanford have baby carriages, and certainly not one as fine as this. I'm not sure the baby will need it.''

''Her mama will,'' Jared said, adding the carriage to his list. ''If you're dead set on keeping the Cottonwood, this will make it easier to get you back and forth every day. Now, let's see. What else?''

''Jared, you've really bought plenty for the baby already.''

''Just one more thing. Okay, here we go.'' He turned the catalog toward her. ''One of these dolls.''

She rolled her eyes. ''A doll? It will be years before she can play with a doll.''

"I know, but I want to give her a present the day she's born."

"Jared—" she touched his arm "—that's so sweet."

"I could buy you a present for that day, too," he said, adding to his list, "if you weren't so confounded hardheaded."

"Sheriff McQuaid?" the prisoner called. "I've finished the dishes, sir."

Jared scrutinized the sideboard, made sure the dishes were stacked in the cupboard and that there was no water on the floor.

"Okay, Smith, you're released from custody."

The man pulled off his battered hat and cast an apologetic look in Mattie's direction. "Well, sir, if'n I could have a word with you?"

When Jared walked over, Smith twisted his hat in his hands. "Well, Sheriff, I don't think I ought to be released just yet."

"Why's that?"

"Truth is, I feel another spell of disorderliness coming on."

More likely, night was coming on and the man had no place to sleep. Jared nodded. "Okay, get on back over to the jail."

"Yes, sir." Smith crammed his hat on his head and went out the back door just as Billy came up the steps.

"Sheriff?" he called. "I think you ought to get over to your office. There's a whole gang of men gathered out front and they're pretty riled up. They want to talk to you. Right now."

Chapter Seventeen

"It ain't right, Sheriff."

"And it ain't fair, neither."

A chorus of agreement rose from the men gathered outside the sheriff's office. Jared rested his thumbs on his gun belt eyeing this group of Stanford business owners in the growing darkness. Tom Keaton from the feed store, Rafe from the saloon, Marvin Ford who owned the Stanford Hotel, and of course, the sniveling Hayden Langston from the mercantile were in front, backed by about a half-dozen other men.

"Now, it ain't that we don't think it's a good idea," Tom said, "this community assistance program of yours."

"Yeah," Hayden agreed. "Free help from prisoners makes a lot of sense."

"Then what's the problem?" Jared demanded.

"Well, ain't nobody getting free help but the Cottonwood Café," Rafe said. "And that ain't right."

Another round of grumbled agreement rose from the men.

"We ought to all be getting free help," Hayden declared.

"Yeah, all of us," Marvin agreed.

Disgust roiled through Jared as he stared down at this group of able-bodied men, the owners of prosperous businesses. He didn't have that many prisoners, to start with—certainly not enough to accommodate them all. And the prisoners he did have, he wanted to use at Mattie's place so she wouldn't have to stand on her feet so long doing dishes.

Jared's first reaction was to call these men every name he could think of, tell them exactly what he thought of their whining and complaining, and run them off. Instead, he decided to handle it differently.

"Okay, boys, you've got a point," Jared said. "Fair is fair."

Jared went into his office, got a sheet of paper and the hammer and nails he used to tack up Wanted posters, and went outside again. He nailed the paper to the wall beside the door.

"Any of you men who can't manage your business and want me to send help to you instead of giving it to a pregnant widow, sign your name here." Jared gave the group a brisk nod, went inside his office and closed the door.

The next morning when he came outside, the first thing he did was look at the paper. Not one signature was scrawled there.

He smiled to himself, glad that little bit of bad news was behind him, anxious to get down to the Cottonwood for breakfast and to see Mattie. But something else needed his attention and he wanted to get it handled early.

Gray clouds hung low on the western horizon. Folks hurried along the boardwalk, unconcerned, it seemed, that a storm might be heading their way.

The Lady Luck Saloon was open for business when Jared arrived, though only two men sat at a table, playing cards. Rafe Duncan, a faded white apron tied around him, stood behind the bar polishing glasses.

"Drinking this early in the day, Sheriff?" Rafe joked. "Must be a lot of crime in Stanford."

Jared smiled and leaned against the bar. "No, but I could sure use a cup of coffee, if you've got one."

"Sure thing." Rafe disappeared into the rear of the saloon and brought out a mug of steaming coffee. "So what brings you over here?"

"Got a problem," he said, sipping from the mug. "Mrs. Pomeroy and her Ladies for the Betterment of Stanford Committee."

Rafe pulled on his long mustache and shook his head. "I figured you'd be over here sooner or later. Those ladies were always giving Sheriff Hickert hell about something. What do they want me to do this time?"

"Just about everything you can imagine, and then some."

"The way I look at it, Sheriff, nothing short of me

closing down my place will make Mrs. Pomeroy happy. But I can't do that. It's my livelihood. My customers need a place to go where they can blow off steam, relax a little, have a drink. And they don't cause that much trouble.''

"I agree with you, Rafe," Jared said. "Your saloon is a lot quieter than most."

"Listen, I'm willing to do everything I can to make Stanford a good place to live. I'm already opening later on Sundays, and I don't have no working girls in here, just to accommodate Mrs. Pomeroy and her committee. But I've got a business to run. I can't keep jumping through hoops for those ladies and still make a living," Rafe said.

Jared nodded. Everything the barkeep said made sense. Jared had made it a point to go by the Lady Luck several times a day since arriving in Stanford, to keep an eye on things, and so far, the problems were more a nuisance than real trouble.

"I appreciate that Mrs. Pomeroy is on your back, Sheriff," Rafe said. "I'll do what I can to keep things quiet."

"Thanks, Rafe."

Jared dropped coins on the bar and left, wondering if that would be enough to pacify Mrs. Pomeroy and get her to sell him Mattie's brooch.

He'd walked a short way, mulling it over in his mind, when a wagon pulled up and the driver shouted to him.

"Sheriff, there's something going on out by my

farm you might want to check on,'' the gray-haired man said.

Jared didn't recognize him. ''Where's that?''

''Name's Pitney. My place's west of here.'' He nodded back the way he'd come. ''Them folks across the road from me ain't sounding too good. I heard the missus screaming.''

''Which neighbors?''

''Them McCafferty folks.''

''Maybe she's having the baby?''

''No, sir. Ain't that kind of screaming.''

''Well? How do I look?''

Mattie spread out her arms and stood straight, waiting for Mrs. Nance's answer. The woman squinted, tapped her finger against her chin, looked her up and down, then pronounced, ''You look every bit the prosperous businesswoman you are.''

Smiling, Mattie touched her hand to the skirt of her gray dress. It wasn't her best. Her best dress was the dark blue one she'd worn to Del's funeral. But since that day, Mattie had been unable to put it on. This morning, more than ever, she didn't want to be reminded of her failures.

''Mr. Burrows can't say no,'' Mrs. Nance predicted.

''I don't see how he can,'' Mattie agreed, using the small mirror near the cupboards to pin her hat in place. ''I've already gotten the okay from the town council to host the supper. All I need now is the money to pay for everything. Surely Mr. Burrows will grant me a loan.''

The money she'd made from the sale of her mother's brooch had covered the expenses of the proposal, with a little left over. Her presentation, which had cost a pretty penny, was a necessary business expense, as Mattie saw it. Especially given the fact that the town council hadn't wanted her there in the first place. She couldn't have done anything less and been awarded the supper.

''Mr. Burrows has been running the bank for a long time,'' Mrs. Nance said. ''He knows a good business deal when he sees one.''

Mattie gave herself one final look in the mirror, slipped into her cloak, then picked up her satchel and handbag and turned once more to Mrs. Nance. ''I'm going over there right now and get this handled.''

Mrs. Nance smiled kindly. ''You'll do just fine.''

As Mattie left the kitchen of the Cottonwood, the wind whipped her cloak and skirts around her and a fat raindrop landed on her cheek. She hurried toward the bank, hoping this storm wasn't a premonition of things to come.

Despite the rain, which kept everyone else out of the bank, Mattie had to wait to see Mr. Burrows. She sat primly in the straight-backed chair outside his closed office door, mentally rehearsing the things she intended to tell him.

She'd never asked for a loan before, never even asked for credit at any of the stores in Stanford.

Maybe, for once, Del would have come in handy, since he obviously had no qualms about asking for such things.

Squeezing her eyes closed for a moment, Mattie envisioned the grand night at the Cottonwood that loomed ahead. The Eastern investors, prominent citizens, businessmen, ranchers, mine owners, town officials, all assembled in her restaurant. The supper would be glorious, sure to be talked about for years to come in Stanford.

But for Mattie, the best part was that with the profits she'd earn from hosting the supper, she could invest in her restaurant. She'd improve her menu, return it to its previous high standard. She'd rehire the Spencer girls, and Billy, of course. All her old customers would come back. Business would flourish.

And her baby's future would, too.

Mattie smiled to herself, imagining how grand it would be, how all her problems would be solved, once Mr. Burrows approved her loan.

Finally, after another half hour dragged by, the office door opened and the banker stepped out. He wore a cravat and a coat; the buttons strained across his belly

Mattie bounded out of her chair, her heart suddenly racing in her chest. "Mr. Burrows, thank you for seeing me."

He pulled his watch from his pocket and frowned at it. "I don't have much time, Mrs. Ingram."

She tightened her grip on her satchel. "It's important that I speak with you."

He grunted as if he doubted it, then motioned her inside his office.

Mattie sat on the edge of the chair in front of his big desk. One wall of his office was covered with books, another held cupboards and shelves of ledgers. A clock ticked ominously in the silence.

"All right, then, what is it?" Mr. Burrows asked, his leather chair groaning and creaking as he sat down.

Mattie gulped. This had seemed so much easier when she'd rehearsed earlier.

"I'm here to ask for a loan, Mr. Burrows."

He glanced at the papers on his desk. "Is that so?"

"Yes, sir. It's to cover the expenses of the supper I'm hosting."

His heavy brows drew together so deeply his eyelids all but disappeared. "You mean to tell me that you don't have the money to pay for the supper?"

"I have some of it."

"But not all of it?"

"Well, no. If you'll recall, Mr. Burrows, I'm decorating the restaurant extensively and cooking a grand meal." Mattie's hand shook as she drew a tablet from her satchel and presented it to him. "I've prepared this detailed list of requirements. I've noted the money I already have, and estimated how much more I'll need."

Mr. Burrows's cheeks puffed out as he looked down

his nose at her tablet. Mattie's throat went dry, but she had to say something. She couldn't stand the silence.

"The Cottonwood Café has been in business here in Stanford for a very long time, as you know."

Mr. Burrows didn't respond.

"I can repay the loan as soon as the supper's over. I'll bring the money to you right away."

He grunted, still studying the tablet of figures. Mattie's mind worked feverishly, trying to think of something else to say, something that would impress Mr. Burrows. She wished she could decipher the furrow of his brow, the way he chewed on his lip. Was that a good sign? Did it mean he understood the estimates she'd prepared? That he would approve her loan request?

"Very nicely done," Mr. Burrows said, passing the tablet back to her.

Mattie nearly fell out of her chair with relief. "Oh, thank you, Mr. Burrows. You won't regret this. I'll pay you back as soon—"

"Oh, no, Mrs. Ingram, you don't understand. I'm not approving your loan."

Her stomach lurched and her heart banged in her chest. Mattie opened her mouth, but no words came out.

"Good day, Mrs. Ingram," he said, rising from his chair.

"But—but wait." She shook her head frantically. "I don't understand. Why not grant my loan?"

"First of all, it isn't good business to go committing

yourself to a big supper, and have the whole town counting on you, when you haven't got the money to pay for it.''

"But businesses get loans all the time for this sort of thing. I know they do," Mattie said. "You'll get your money back, Mr. Burrows. I know the restaurant business inside and out. I've been running the Cotton-wood for—"

"Well, that's just not true," Mr. Burrows said. "Your parents ran the restaurant, and it wasn't long after they died that your husband took over."

A sick knot jerked in Mattie's stomach. "Del?"

"And since he died, your business has fallen off considerably, now isn't that true?"

"Well, yes, but—"

"Mrs. Ingram, it's no secret that you're paying debts all over town."

"Those aren't *my*—"

Mr. Burrows held up his thick hand. "My mind is made up. I cannot under any circumstances grant you that loan."

"But—" Mattie's throat closed off and tears pushed against the backs of her eyes.

"And I expect you to go to the council and let them know another restaurant will have to host the supper." Mr. Burrows opened his office door. "Good day, Mrs. Ingram."

Mattie managed to keep her head up and her back straight as she gathered her handbag, satchel and tablet. She managed to keep her tears at bay, and somehow managed not to punch Mr. Burrows square in the nose as she left the bank.

But when she reached the boardwalk and slipped into the solitude of the alley next door, in the shelter of the building that kept the last of the storm's raindrops at bay, she couldn't hold in her emotions another second.

"Oh!" That pompous old windbag! How dare he talk to her that way! What a fool he was, thinking Del had run the Cottonwood well, and that she was the one who'd handled it poorly. That the debts Del had piled up were hers. Mr. Burrows had blamed her—*her*—for everything that was wrong, everything Del had caused.

Mattie paced fitfully, tears springing to her eyes. Then anger overtook her. She wanted to go back into that bank and tell that awful Mr. Burrows how wrong he was. She wanted to make him listen to her explanations. She wanted to force him to give her that loan. She wanted…

Jared.

He sprang into her mind so unexpectedly, Mattie gasped. Jared? She wanted Jared? At this, one of the worst moments of her life, she wanted Jared?

Yes. Yes, she wanted him. She wanted to see him, talk to him, touch him. She wanted him to look at her in that reasonable way of his and tell her everything would be all right. She wanted to lean against him and feel his arms around her, hear him assure her everything would be fine.

Yes, she wanted Jared, and she wanted him now.

Chapter Eighteen

The worst of the rain had stopped, but a fine mist continued as Jared rode back into town. Beneath his poncho he was relatively dry, but that did nothing to improve his mood.

On days like this, he hated his job. And not because of the weather.

Despite the light rain and the low-hanging gray sky, a number of folks went about their business on the streets of Stanford. Jared was cold, damp and anxious to get a hot meal in his belly, but couldn't stop watching everything and everybody as he rode through town. That's when he saw Mr. Hopkins.

The old man sat huddled in the doorway at the side entrance of the Silver Bell Restaurant, trying to make himself as small as possible, trying to stay dry.

Jared pulled his horse to a stop. "You got someplace to get out of this weather, Mr. Hopkins?"

He shrugged as if it didn't matter and pulled his threadbare coat tighter around him.

"Are you drinking again?" Jared asked.

"No, sir, Sheriff," he answered clearly.

Jared scanned the sky, judging the possibility of more rain. "Yeah? Well, you look like you're drunk to me. Get on over to the jail. I'll be there in a bit."

Jared stayed until Mr. Hopkins got to his feet, then took his horse to the livery and walked back to the jail. The place was quiet when he arrived. Billy wasn't around, since they had no prisoners, except now for Mr. Hopkins. Jared lit a fire in the potbellied stove, then found the old man standing in a cell, staring at the wall.

"Go on into the office," Jared told him. "Warm yourself by the fire."

While Mr. Hopkins ambled into the office, Jared went into his room and changed into warm, dry clothes.

"Get out of those wet things," he said, joining Mr. Hopkins by the fire.

Jared held his hands out, warming them, as the old man shucked off two worn, tattered coats. Beneath them was a frayed, black leather sword belt, trimmed with two rows of embroidery, fastened with a U.S. Army regulation belt plate.

"Were you in the army?" Jared asked.

"Yes, sir, I was." Mr. Hopkins draped his coats on the back of the rocking chair near the stove. "It was my privilege to serve under Major Meade with the Army of the Potomac."

That was the most Jared had ever heard Mr. Hopkins say. "After you warm up, go on back to the cell. I'll get something to eat over here in a while."

Jared went outside then and watched the wagons and carriages make their way through the rain-softened dirt of Main Street. The wind had died down and the mist had dispelled. The air smelled fresh.

His heart sinking heavier in his chest, Jared tried not to think very much at that particular moment. If he studied the situation for the rest of his life, he still wouldn't figure it out.

Even after all these years of being a lawman, he didn't understand some of the things people did to one another. Especially people who claimed they loved each other. How? Why? He didn't know.

Billy came striding up the boardwalk, his face grim. "Heard you went out to the McCafferty place."

Jared's jaw tightened.

"This ain't good, is it?" Billy said, shaking his head. "I told you my aunt Frannie says there's something mighty peculiar about that Mr. McCafferty, and my aunt Frannie is almost always right."

"She surely is in this case." Jared pulled on the tight muscles of his neck. "I'll fill you in on everything in a while, Billy, but right now get over to the Cottonwood and pick up a meal. We've got a prisoner."

"Yes, sir." Billy turned to leave.

"And don't let Mattie come back with you. I don't want her out in this damp weather."

"Yes, sir."

"And find Mr. Pitney and have him come by the jail before he leaves town today, will you?"

"I'll do it, Sheriff. Quick as a bunny."

Jared watched Billy hustle down the boardwalk, then turn back to him and lift his shoulders helplessly, before hurrying on his way again. Jared had no idea what Billy was trying to get at until he saw Mattie barreling toward him.

Pink colored her cheeks. Her cloak billowed out behind her, and the little feather on her hat lay straight back.

At that moment, Jared didn't care that she might be mad at him. Nor did it matter that she was out in the damp weather, negotiating slippery surfaces, and he ought to fuss at her for being careless, in her condition.

What mattered to Jared at the moment was that Mattie was full of good health, running over with determination and drive. For all the aggravation and anguish her hardheadedness caused him, he took comfort in the fact that she could fend for herself, that she would stand up for herself. And always, no matter where he went or what he did, she would take care of his baby.

Jared's heart pounded harder as he watched her approach. How he loved her. How he wanted to hold her, take care of her, be at her side always. Darn, stubborn woman. Why wouldn't she let him?

It was something. What, he didn't know, exactly. But it was something.

Something more than her wanting her independence, wanting to run her own life. Something more, even, than the way Del had treated her.

And if Jared could figure out what it was, he'd stand a hell of a better chance at getting her to marry him.

He straightened, bracing himself, as Mattie charged up to him, her nose flared a little, her breath heaving. Lord, she was pretty when she was fired up. Just about the prettiest thing Jared had ever seen. Yet he dared not smile.

Mattie planted herself in front of him. "I want you to go arrest that Mr. Burrows!"

"Mr. Burrows? The bank—"

"No! Wait! Don't arrest him. Shoot him!" She pointed her finger at Jared. "And don't just wing him, either."

"Now, Mattie—"

"No! Shooting's too good for him. Hang him!"

Jared studied her for a few seconds, then rubbed his chin thoughtfully. "I really can't hang the man, Mattie."

She clenched her fists. "I am a citizen of this town, and you are the sheriff. I insist you do *something!* The man deserves to be punished!"

"Okay." Jared nodded toward the jail. "How about if I throw him in a cell and you can poke him with a stick?"

Mattie's eyes narrowed and she ground her lips together, apparently visualizing the possibility. Then she shook her head. "Not nearly bad enough. What else can we do?"

"Hold on, Mattie." He stepped closer and looked down at her. "What's got you so riled up?"

"Oh! That awful Mr. Burrows. You should be mad at him, too, Jared," she told him. "He's robbing your son of his future."

"Whoa. Stop." Jared waved his hand. "Back up. Start at the beginning. What's this all about?"

Mattie drew in a big breath, pushing away most of her anger, and told him that she'd been to see Mr. Burrows about a business loan.

"He turned you down, huh?"

"Yes. And don't you dare offer to loan me the money yourself, Jared, or give it to me, either. I'm going to manage this supper on my own."

Jared held up both palms in surrender. "I wouldn't dream of offering you the money."

"Well, good, because—"

Mattie stopped short as something on the boardwalk across the street caught her attention. Jared followed her line of vision but saw nothing unusual, just the townsfolk going about their business.

Whatever it was took the anger out of Mattie completely. She seemed to wither right before his eyes.

"What's wrong?" he asked, glancing from her to the folks on the other side of the street.

"Hannah Keaton." Mattie's gaze followed each step the woman took.

"Tom's wife? The fella who owns the feed store?" Jared had seen her in town before—one of the women he'd come to notice all the time now who, like Mattie, was expecting a baby. "What's she got you so upset for?"

"She's the one," Mattie whispered, still watching the woman. "The one Del followed here to Stanford. The one he was in love with...while he was married to me."

Jared glanced at Hannah Keaton, then back to Mattie. "You're sure?"

"He told me," Mattie said softly. "Sometimes I can't help but wonder..." She seemed lost in her thoughts for a moment.

"Wonder what, Mattie?"

"I wonder if that's Del's baby she's carrying."

Jared studied Mattie's face, the little wrinkle in her brow, her lips pressed together, and knew there was something more.

"What else, Mattie?"

After a moment, she looked up at him. "I wonder why Del loved her and not me. Why I was such a poor wife that he went elsewhere."

Even after that confession, she still looked troubled.

"And?" Jared asked.

Mattie shrugged and gazed across the street again. "I wonder why I didn't fight harder for Del after he started going out so much and stayed out all night. What kind of wife would just let her husband go like that?"

"Come with me." Jared took her hand and went into the jailhouse, into his bedroom. Across the hall, Mr. Hopkins snored softly in his cell bunk.

"Del Ingram was a fool, Mattie, and a terrible husband. It didn't have anything to do with the kind of wife you were."

"But it must have. It has to. Why else would he want Hannah and not me? Why else would he go out most every evening? Stay out all night, sometimes?" Mattie shook her head. "No, it had to have been me. I did something wrong. I wasn't a good wife."

"You were a fine wife."

"I tried. Really, I tried. I actually liked..." She waved her hand toward Jared's bunk. "You know."

"I can vouch for that."

"Nothing I did was right in his eyes. Nothing I did was good enough."

Jared caught her chin and turned her face to his. "Ingram wasn't man enough for you, Mattie."

"No." She turned away. "I did something wrong. Otherwise, he would have wanted me. He'd have come home at night. I didn't try hard enough. I just wasn't...desirable."

"The hell you aren't." Jared caught her arms and pulled her to him. She gasped and color flooded her cheeks as he ground himself against her intimately. "This is how desirable you are, Mattie. I don't *get* this way. I *stay* this way. Del Ingram was a fool to leave you in a cold bed. I'd never do that."

He brought his mouth down on hers in a demanding kiss, working their lips together until Mattie leaned her head back, welcoming him.

He lifted his head and splayed his palm across her cheek. Her hot breath panted against his lips.

"Maybe you didn't love him."

"Wh-what?" she asked, her eyes glassy with desire.

"If he didn't kiss you like this, if you didn't kiss him the way you're kissing me now, then your marriage was wrong from the start. It didn't stand a chance," Jared said. "And there was nothing you could have done to change it."

Mattie shook her head, clinging to Jared's shoulders. "But I did love Del. At first. I'm sure of it."

"No, you didn't. Del was a big talker—even as a kid. He could sell anything to anybody. He sold himself to you because it suited him. But don't—don't!—think that meant there's anything wrong with you."

Mattie eased away from him, but he didn't let her get far.

"You seem to know a lot about marriage," she whispered.

"I know I love you."

She stepped back. "You don't know that."

"Yes, I do." Jared took her arms and pulled her close again.

"No. I was married to Del all that time and I—"

"I love you, Mattie." Jared gazed deeply into her eyes.

"No…"

Whistling and shuffling feet in the hallway caught Jared's attention, as Billy appeared at Mr. Hopkins's cell with a food tray.

"Hi, Miss Mattie," he called, as if there was nothing unusual about seeing her in Jared's bedroom, as if he didn't notice the strained looks on both their flushed faces. "I found Mr. Pitney like you asked, Sheriff. He'll be by here directly."

"I'd better go," Mattie murmured, ducking her head.

"I'll walk you to the restaurant."

"No, I'll—"

"I'll walk you."

He did just that, but neither of them spoke. The damp wind was cool in their faces, yet did nothing to alleviate the heat between them. Jared didn't go into the Cottonwood with her; he figured he'd said enough already.

By the time he got back to the jail, Mr. Pitney was there. Jared told both him and Billy what he'd discovered at the McCafferty place that morning.

"But she claims he didn't hit her?" Billy asked, scratching his head. "A big bruise right on her face, and she wouldn't tell you her husband was the one who did it?"

"I think she was too scared," Jared said. "I told her I'd bring her into town, find her a place to live, someplace safe until she had the baby. But she wouldn't do it."

"Can't you arrest McCafferty?" Mr. Pitney asked.

"Not if his wife won't say he's the one who hit her," Jared said. "I'll ride out that way more often, keep an eye on things. Mr. Pitney, I'd appreciate it if you'd let me know if anything else goes on.''

He nodded. ''I'll do what I can.''

''I'd better get that tray back to the Cottonwood,'' Billy said.

Jared tossed him a coin. ''How about doing Mattie's dishes tonight, Billy?''

''Well, sure. But what about Mr. Hopkins?''

''He's doing something else.'' Jared turned to Mr. Pitney. ''Do you know Mr. Hopkins?''

''No, sir, I don't.''

Jared nodded toward the cells in the back of the jailhouse. ''Come on back and meet him. I think you two have a lot in common.''

Chapter Nineteen

"Lordy day, I never heard two old men talk so much in my life," Billy declared. "Fact is, I never heard Mr. Hopkins talk that much in the whole entire time I've known him, like he was talking to Mr. Pitney when they left here yesterday."

"Is that right?" Jared asked, rising from the desk in his office.

"And all over the two of them serving in the war together." Billy grinned as he swept the floor. "And then, Mr. Pitney offering Mr. Hopkins a place to stay out at his farm? My aunt Frannie, she was plumb surprised when I told her about it. That was downright smart of you, Sheriff, to put the two of them together like that."

Jared settled his hat on his head. "I'm going out for a while."

"Uh, Sheriff?" Billy paused in his sweeping. "You reckon you could do me a favor?"

"Depends on what it is."

"You remember how my aunt Frannie's got it in her head that I need to go back East and work for my uncle, 'cause I don't have no real job here in Stanford? Well, sir, I was wondering if'n you could go talk to my aunt Frannie and tell her all about how I'm doing with my temporary deputy duties, so's I won't have to go back East and work in that can factory."

"Sure, Billy. I'll talk to her."

He smiled broadly. "Thank you, Sheriff. Thank you kindly."

When Jared left the jail, the sun was out, warming the air and drying up the last of yesterday's rain. He walked to the Cottonwood; things were quiet, as usual, for midafternoon. Both Mattie and Mrs. Nance were at the worktable, bent over a tablet of figures.

"Afternoon, ladies," he called.

Mrs. Nance whispered something to Mattie. She shook her head frantically and turned the tablet over.

"Something wrong?" Jared asked. He took a closer look at Mattie, noting the dark circles beneath her eyes.

"Nothing," she said quickly.

"Everything's wrong," Mrs. Nance said. Mattie glared at her, but the woman went right on. "She hardly slept a wink last night, worrying about how she'll manage this supper with no bank loan, worrying that she'll have to tell the town council to give it to the Silver Bell."

"I'll find a way," Mattie insisted.

Mrs. Nance rolled her eyes. "She's so stubborn."

Jared resisted the urge to voice his agreement. Instead he said, "The supper is still a few days away. Mattie will figure out something."

She sat a little straighter. "Thank you, Jared."

"Will it be all right if I steal you away from here for a few minutes?" he asked. "I've got something I want to show you."

Mattie shook her head. "I shouldn't, really, there's so much to be done."

"Oh, go on," Mrs. Nance insisted, slipping from the stool. "I'll handle anything that comes up."

"Where are you taking me?" Mattie asked, as they left the restaurant.

He couldn't hide his smile. "You'll see."

They walked to Mattie's house, where Jared gestured grandly to a large object covered with a drape sitting on her front porch. He swept off the covering, revealing an oak cradle.

"What do you think?" he asked. "I had it made special for the baby and delivered here. Do you like it?"

Mattie ran her fingers over the fine finish and the elegant carvings at the hood and foot. "It's beautiful. I've never seen anything so lovely." She looked at Jared. "But you shouldn't have. You've already bought so much. It's not right."

He raised an eyebrow at her. "Do you think you're the only one who already loves this baby?"

Mattie gulped, taken completely by surprise. Emotion welled inside her, flooding her eyes with tears. "Oh, Jared, that's the sweetest thing I've ever heard."

He touched her upper arms, drawing her closer. "Would this be a good time to ask you to marry me?"

Mattie sniffled. "No."

"Well, I guess it never hurts to ask."

"I don't know why I'm crying," she said, fanning her face. "It's just—"

"The baby." Jared passed her his handkerchief. "I know."

"How can you be so nice to me?" Mattie asked, looking up at him as fresh tears spilled down her cheeks. "How can you want to marry me?"

"I told you, Mattie. I love you."

She swiped at her tears, trying to force down her emotions enough to talk to him. It wasn't just her financial worries that had kept her awake last night. Jared had been on her mind, too. In fact, he'd occupied even more of her thoughts than the possibility of losing the investors' supper. But she didn't understand how that could be. Keeping her restaurant was the most important thing in her life. Wasn't it?

"You were right about me not loving Del," Mattie said, gulping down tears. "I guess I was more lonely than anything. And he seemed so wonderful when he courted me."

"You didn't love Del, because he wasn't worth loving," Jared told her. "He didn't stick around. He didn't try to make a go of it. Not all husbands are like that, Mattie. I won't be that kind of husband."

Without giving it a second's thought, Mattie knew he was right. Jared would always be there. After their first night together, when he'd awakened and found her gone, he could have simply left town. He hadn't, though. He'd come after her. Marched right into the kitchen of her restaurant, and he hadn't left that day until she'd asked him to.

When he'd come back to Stanford to take the sheriff's job, and discovered she was pregnant, he could have hightailed it out of town. Turned his back and let her fend for herself. He could have claimed the baby wasn't his, washed his hands of the whole thing, and no one would have been the wiser.

Jared hadn't done any of those things. Instead, he'd worried over her, helped with her business, tried to make her life easier, bought clothes for her and lavished gifts on the baby, who wasn't even born yet.

"You've been wonderful, Jared. When you're around me, you're truly thoughtful and kind," Mattie said. "But—"

"But how do you know I won't turn into the same kind of husband Del was? Is that what you're wondering?"

Mattie looked away, wishing with all her heart she could tell him no, that wasn't what she wondered. What she feared. But in truth, it was.

He seemed to read her thoughts. "Who do you trust in this town? Billy? Mrs. Nance? Who?"

She dabbed at her eyes, not understanding what he

was getting at. "I trust lots of people. Certainly Billy and Mrs. Nance."

"You ask them. Ask anybody. Especially Billy, since he's spent so much time with me. Ask him what kind of man I am when I'm not around you. Ask him how I run my life, how I treat people. Ask him."

Mattie sniffed again. "But marriage is such a big step. And there's the baby to consider."

"A wife. A baby." Jared shook his head. "It doesn't scare me, Mattie."

"Oh! Would you please stop making so much sense? You know I hate it when you do that!"

Overwhelmed, Mattie sobbed into the handkerchief with one hand and reached out for Jared with the other. He snuggled her against him, smoothing his fingers through her hair.

She was tired, so tired. Worn out from thinking and worrying, planning and hoping. At that moment, Mattie wanted to let go of everything, melt into Jared's embrace and stay there forever.

He lifted her off her feet into his arms. "What are you doing?" she asked.

"I figured I'd better do this while I can. In a few more months, you'll be bigger than two heifers and a sow. I'll be lucky if I can pull you out of a chair, let alone pick you up."

Knowing he was teasing, she giggled through her tears. "Oh, hush," she said, and swatted him on the shoulder.

Jared settled into the porch swing and sat her beside

him, then snuggled her against his chest, with both arms around her. "You need to rest for a while."

Mattie sat up. "Good gracious, Jared, people can see us from the road. What will they say?"

"They'll probably say 'what a great husband Sheriff McQuaid would make' and 'what's wrong with Mattie that she won't marry him?'" He eased her against his shoulder again, only to have her straighten once more.

"But, Jared, out here in public like this—"

"We can go inside," he offered. "If you'll recall, I have other ways of making you relax. Several other ways."

She blushed a bright red. "Jared—"

"Mattie." He looked deep into her eyes. "Everything is going to be fine."

In that instant, she had no doubts that they would be, just as Jared had said. Mattie laid her head on his shoulder and closed her eyes.

"Would this be a good time to ask you to marry me?" he whispered.

"No."

He glided the swing back and forth, and she fell asleep.

While it wasn't as good as rolling around in bed with her, Jared had thoroughly enjoyed cuddling Mattie close while she slept. It hadn't lasted nearly long enough to suit him. Neither had it pleased him that she wanted to go back to the restaurant. But the nap had done her good, so he'd walked her over, hung around until he'd gotten underfoot, then left.

Jared wished he could say the rest of his day promised to be just as enjoyable. Impossible, considering what he had to do. With a resolute sigh, he hunted down Mrs. Pomeroy.

"Yes, Sheriff?" she said, when he approached her outside the mercantile.

"I wanted you to know, ma'am, that I did as we discussed. I talked to Rafe at the Lady Luck."

Her brows raised. "And?"

"And the truth is, Mrs. Pomeroy, he's already done quite a bit to accommodate you ladies, and what you're asking will make it tough for him to run his business."

"I see." She folded her hands in front of her.

"But I want you to know that I intend to stay close to the Lady Luck. I'll keep an eye on things, make sure they don't get out of hand. You and the ladies of your committee can rest assured I'll do everything in my power to keep a lid on any trouble at the saloon," Jared explained.

"Is that so?"

"Yes, ma'am. I guarantee it." Jared cleared his throat. "Like I said, I've done everything I can, so I'd appreciate it if you'd sell me that brooch we talked about."

Mrs. Pomeroy stared at him, her lips pinched together, her eyes narrowed. Finally, she drew in a great breath of air, stretching her neck upward and leveling her gaze at him.

"Never!" she declared. "You, Sheriff McQuaid, are woefully inadequate in the discharge of your duties. Sheriff Hickert was far, far superior. You are ineffective, uncouth and totally lacking in decorum. You don't deserve to hold the office of sheriff. I intend to make my feelings known to the town council at once, and I will see to it that—"

Gunfire from down the street interrupted Mrs. Pomeroy's tirade. They both swung around and saw men running out of the bat-wing doors of the Lady Luck Saloon.

As if that proved her point, Mrs. Pomeroy tossed her head and stormed away.

Jared cursed through gritted teeth, drew his pistol and headed for the Lady Luck.

Chapter Twenty

"This ain't good," Billy predicted mournfully as Jared wrestled his prisoner into the cell. "This ain't good a'tall."

Jared dropped Johnny Ballard onto the bunk, then closed and locked the cell door. The boy mumbled drunken curses as he flopped around like a fish on a riverbank.

"Big Jim's gonna be mad as a bear with a sore butt when he finds out you've arrested his son again," Billy said, shaking his head.

Jared gave a curse and stalked into the office. Johnny Ballard had gotten drunk again and, like before, started shooting up the saloon. Thankfully, nobody had gotten hurt. Except for Jared, when the kid had caught his chin with a lucky punch.

"I want you to ride out to the Three B Ranch." Jared yanked open his desk drawer.

Billy gulped. "You want me to go out to the Ballard place?"

Jared slammed the prisoner ledger down on his desk. "You tell Jim Ballard to get into town. I want this settled tonight."

"You want me to tell that to Big Jim?" Billy's eyes widened and he wiped his palms against his baggy trousers. "Well, sir, all right. If'n that's what you want me to do."

"Damn right it is. And don't come back without him."

Billy hurried out the door.

Grumbling and snarling, Jared entered Johnny Ballard's arrest in the ledger. Damn, this couldn't have happened at a worse time. That kid had made him look like a fool in front of Mrs. Pomeroy. There he'd stood, promising her there'd be no more trouble at the Lady Luck, and the Ballard boy had started shooting up the place.

"Damn it!" Jared slammed his drawer shut. Now the woman would never sell him Mattie's brooch.

He stalked out of the office, needing some air, trying to walk off some of his anger. He hadn't gone far when a tiny flash of blue darted toward him.

Chuckie Waldron. No way in hell was that kid going to kick him again. Jared spun around and made a grab for him.

A little squeal sounded. He froze. It wasn't Chuckie.

Standing on the boardwalk was a little girl no more than six years old. She had carrot-red pigtails and wore a blue dress.

"Are you the theriff?" She gazed up at him with fearful eyes.

"Huh?"

"The theriff?" Big tears pooled in her eyes as she pointed to the badge on his chest. "Mama thayth the theriff is thuppothed to help people. Are you the theriff?"

Jared had never felt so big and clumsy in his life, towering over this tiny girl who was on the verge of sobbing. He glanced around, feeling useless, looking for somebody to help him, but saw no one. Finally, he pushed his hat back on his head and knelt in front of her.

"I'm the sheriff. Is something wrong?"

"Yeth." She dug her knuckles into one eye, fighting back tears. "My mama'th lotht."

A little shower of spittle rained on Jared's chin, caused by the fact that the child's two front teeth were missing. Jared ran his sleeve over his face.

"She's lost, huh?" He gave her a little smile. "As it happens, finding lost mamas is what I do best."

She blinked back her tears. "Really?"

"Sure. Now, what's your name?"

"Thally."

Jared wiped his cheek. "Okay, Sally, come on up here and we'll find your mama."

He lifted her with one arm. "What's your mama's name?"

"Mama."

"All right." Jared turned in a slow circle. "Do you see her anywhere?"

"No, thir."

"What were you doing in town?"

"Thopping at the thtore."

Jared dried his cheek with his cuff. "Where do you live, Sally?"

"I don't know." Her bottom lip poked out. "Thuppose mama never comth back?"

"She'll come back. Mamas never stay lost for long."

Jared didn't have much to go on to find the little girl's mother. But, more than likely, the woman had already realized her child was missing and was frantically searching at this moment.

Turning, he saw Ben and Abel and their checkerboard at their usual spot in front of the mercantile.

"We seen her mama a little bit ago," Abel said, "with her other young-uns, looking at the toys in the window there."

"Didn't recognize her, though," Ben added. "Must be passing through or coming to town early for the big doings."

"Give a yell if you spot her, will you, boys?"

"Sure thing, Sheriff."

Jared carried Sally into the mercantile, thinking maybe her mama was there. Hayden didn't recognize the child, nor had he seen her mother. Jared bought her a peppermint stick and went outside again. They looked at the toys displayed in the window, and Sally licked her candy until a commotion broke out behind them.

Sally whipped around, poking Jared in the eye with her peppermint stick. "Mama!"

The young woman, surrounded by four redheaded children, rushed over, holding out her arms. She yanked Sally away, hugging and kissing her.

"Thank you, Sheriff, thank you for finding her! I didn't take my eye off her for a minute—I swear, not even a minute, and she was gone."

Jared nodded, looking at the other kids swarming around her. "Looks like you've got your hands full." He pulled coins from his pocket and handed them to the oldest boy. "Go inside the mercantile, son, get some peppermint for everybody."

A chorus of squeals and thank-yous rose from the children as they all rushed into the store. Their mother followed, but Sally pushed away, looping her arms around Jared's neck.

"Thankth, Therriff."

"You're welcome, Sally,"

She planted a sticky kiss on his cheek; Jared didn't wipe it off.

He watched them go, the young mother doing her best to corral her brood, the children racing toward the candy counter with bright faces. Jared couldn't help feeling pleased.

But as he turned to leave, he spotted Mrs. Pomeroy across the street, glaring at him. She looked as if she'd been standing there for a while. Probably plotting ways to get him fired, Jared figured.

He took a turn through town, as was his custom, looking things over, keeping an eye out for trouble. With the impending arrival of the Eastern investors and all that went with it, a lot of new faces were in Stanford, anxiously awaiting the festivities. The town council had given him the three deputies they'd promised; he considered putting them to work sooner than planned.

As was also Jared's custom when he made his rounds through town, he went by the Cottonwood Café. Mattie looked as if she felt better, despite the frown lines in her forehead; getting the money to pay for the investors' supper occupied most of her thoughts, it seemed.

He didn't stay long because it was so damn hard not to insist she take the money from him. But he managed to hold his tongue. Mattie wanted to work out her problems on her own. He was willing to let her—up to a point.

Leaving the restaurant, he spotted Billy riding back into town with Jim Ballard. When Jared got to the jail, Big Jim was outside his son's cell, chewing on him pretty good. For once Johnny looked as if he were glad to be locked up, out of his father's reach.

"Mr. Ballard?" Jared called.

The rancher gave his son a final scathing look, and walked into the office, fuming and shaking his head. "That boy. Damn! What's wrong with him?"

"Mr. Ballard, that boy of yours is on his way to being completely worthless," Jared told him. "Your wife is ruining him."

"That's for damn sure."

"And you're not doing much to help."

Ballard glared at Jared for a moment, then huffed. "I paid for the damages to the saloon. What'll it cost to get him out of jail?"

"I told you before, Mr. Ballard, if this happened again it was going to take more than you paying a fine to get the boy released." Jared sat down behind his desk and gestured to a chair on the other side. Ballard grumbled, then sat down.

Jared took out the prisoner ledger and showed Big Jim the page bearing his son's name and the list of offenses beneath it.

"Look, Sheriff, I'll give you my word he won't cause any more trouble."

"These are serious offenses."

"I know," Ballard said. "And I'll see to it he's properly punished. He'll not come back to Stanford unless I'm with him, I swear."

Jared shook his head.

"Sheriff, you've got to understand." Ballard shifted as if he didn't like having to explain. "I can't go home without that boy."

"Your wife, huh?"

"My wife. Now, there must be something we can work out."

Jared opened his mouth with the intention of telling

Ballard that his wife was his own problem. Johnny and his drunken behavior was Jared's problem.

But he didn't say anything. Instead, an idea came to him. He thought it over for a moment.

While Johnny had caused some damage to the Lady Luck, it wasn't too bad; not as bad, really, as some of the fistfights that occasionally broke out. The boy hadn't injured anyone, hadn't killed anyone. Jim was paying for the damages, and Jared believed he'd keep his promise not to allow the boy back in town. All things considered, Johnny's crimes weren't that bad.

"The Three B is a cattle ranch, isn't it?" Jared asked.

"Sure is."

"You've probably got other livestock out there, too, to feed your hands. Chickens and hogs?"

"Of course."

"I'll bet you've got a good-size vegetable garden."

"What are you getting at, Sheriff?"

Jared sat back in his chair. "Tell me, Mr. Ballard, are you familiar with the sheriff's office's community assistance program?"

"Oh, my goodness, I can hardly believe it!"

Mattie pressed her fingers against her lips to keep from squealing with delight. "This is really happening, isn't it?" she gasped. "I'm not dreaming, am I?"

"If it's a dream, I don't want to wake up," Mrs. Nance declared.

The women stepped out of the way as four men

from the Three B Ranch unloaded crates of supplies from wagons and carried them into the storage room of the Cottonwood Café.

Mattie turned to Billy as he directed the ranch hands. "Mr. Ballard is donating all this food for the investors' supper?"

Billy frowned. "Yes, ma'am."

"But why? I don't understand. What made him make such a generous donation?"

Billy dragged the back of his hand across his mouth. "Well, Miss Mattie, all I can say is that Big Jim just thought it was the right thing to do, him being so community minded and all."

"It's an excellent chance to show off the meat from his cattle," Mattie agreed. "Is that the sort of thing those investors will be interested in?"

Billy glanced away. "I reckon so."

"And all he wants in return is for me to make an announcement the night of the supper acknowledging the food was donated by the Three B Ranch?" Mattie shook her head in wonder. "Why, it's an answer to my prayer."

"Something like that," Billy mumbled. "Excuse me, Miss Mattie, I got to keep a close eye on where these men are putting the food."

Mattie's heart raced as she watched the ranch hands make trip after trip from the wagons to the storage room. She could hardly believe it! Yet here it was.

All her planning and scheming, all the wakeful nights and dark days she'd spent worrying about how she'd pay for the food, and now her problem was solved. Her restaurant was saved, her future secure. Hers and her baby's.

Jared. She had to tell Jared at once.

Mattie slipped past Billy, reaching for her shawl and handbag. "I've got to give this good news to Jared right away. Do you mind keeping an eye on things?"

"No, I reckon not."

Mattie glanced up at Billy, but he looked away. She realized then how odd his behavior had been since the Three B Ranch wagons had showed up.

"Billy, is something wrong?"

"No."

She'd known Billy for a long time. He'd worked alongside her at the restaurant, helping with every facet of its operation. Washing dishes was the least of his contribution. It certainly wasn't like him to be short with her, or to not be just as thrilled as she by this unexpected good fortune.

"Something's wrong, Billy, I can tell by looking at you," Mattie said, leaving her shawl and handbag where they were. "What is it?"

"It's not my place to say, Miss Mattie. The sheriff wouldn't like it."

"Jared?" A chill went up her spine. "What's he got to do with this?"

"Ain't none of my business, really, what he does. He's the sheriff and I'm a deputy. A temporary deputy, at that."

When Jared had challenged her to talk to anyone in

town—namely Billy—about him, Mattie had considered doing it. It seemed, as Jared suggested, the best way to learn what sort of man he truly was. But in the end it didn't feel right, asking about him behind his back.

Now, though, Mattie got a whole different idea about Jared. Billy was definitely upset about something Jared had done, and that something, it seemed now, had to do with her.

Mattie decided to take Jared up on his offer.

"Would you come with me, Billy?" She walked into the dining room, empty of diners, with him behind her. Quickly, she pulled the curtains closed.

"Has Jared done something he shouldn't have?"

Billy winced. "It's not proper for me to say nothing against him."

Her stomach tightened. So it was true. "I have a right to know the truth, don't you think?"

"Well..."

"We've been friends for a long time, you and I. You know how I count on you, how I value you."

"Sure thing, Miss Mattie. And I appreciate everything you've done for me, everything you've been through."

She stood a little straighter. "Then tell me what Jared has done wrong."

"Everything? All of it?"

For an instant, Mattie felt lightheaded. Jared had done a great number of things he shouldn't have?

She steeled herself. "Yes. I want to know every-thing."

"Well, if'n you're sure." Billy drew in a deep breath. "First off, it was helping them Bishop people. They'd gone an' run up a bill at the mercantile and hadn't been paying it. The sheriff and me went out to talk to them, and wouldn't you know it, he ended up paying for it himself."

Mattie blinked up at him. "Jared paid the Bishops' account out of his own pocket?"

"Yes, ma'am, he did. And I just don't think that's right. My aunt Frannie says that if'n you make a debt, you ought to pay it yourself," Billy told her. "And then, on top of that, the sheriff sent me out to the Bishop farm to work for a whole day, and paid that out of his own pocket, to boot."

Mattie just looked at Billy, not knowing what to say.

"Then," he continued, "the sheriff came up with this community assistance program of his, but really, it weren't nothing but an excuse to help you with your chores."

"Me? Only me?"

"Yes, ma'am. 'Course now, I ain't saying you didn't need the help, things being what they are and all. But when the other businessmen in town com-plained, the sheriff shamed them into shutting up about it, 'cause you needed the help worse. And most of those men the sheriff arrested weren't doing all that much wrong. He even arrested Mr. Hopkins one time, claiming he was drunk, when he wasn't.''

"You think Jared is abusing his authority as sheriff?''

"Well, yeah, sort of.'' Billy rubbed his chin. "'Course now, most of the prisoners he gathered up were down on their luck, needing a clean dry place to stay at night, sort of like Mr. Hopkins. Some of them, well, they didn't hardly want to leave the jail. And the sheriff did find Mr. Hopkins a friend in Mr. Pitney.''

"Jared did that?''

"Oh, yes, ma'am. So, to be fair, I reckon it wasn't all that bad a thing he did. And to be fair, Sheriff McQuaid don't cheat with his sheriffing funds. Sometimes old Sheriff Hickert would do that, you know—put a little of the fine money in his pocket that he shouldn't have. And Sheriff McQuaid has made up with everybody in town. Most everybody, that is, except for Mrs. Pomeroy, but he's still trying with her.''

"What about his…personal life?''

"Oh, the sheriff ain't one for carousing around, if you get my meaning, Miss Mattie. He tends to his sheriff duties. He goes down to the Lady Luck every once in a while, but it's mostly just to check on things.''

Mattie wanted to ask him specifically whether Jared had been to the parlor house, but couldn't find the words. She inclined her head toward the restaurant's kitchen. "What about this donation from the Ballard ranch? Did Jared have something to do with it?''

"That's how come he let Johnny out of jail the last time. He sort of traded Jim Ballard. Food for his boy."

Mattie sank into one of the dining room chairs.

"You okay, Miss Mattie? You don't look so good. You want me to get the doctor or something?"

"No, Billy, I'm fine. I just need a little time to think."

Mattie gazed out the window. She had a lot of things to think about.

Chapter Twenty-One

The crowd lined both sides of Main Street. Children sat on the edge of the boardwalk, some on their father's shoulders. Older boys had climbed onto roofs. A few waved miniature flags they'd bought for a penny, waiting for the parade to start.

Jared moved through the crowds, smiling politely and keeping an eye out for trouble. The Eastern investors had arrived on the morning train and were now seated with the mayor and town council at the grandstand erected just down the street.

So far, things had gone smoothly. The three deputies the council had assigned him had helped out in the past and knew what to do. Jared had given them a few instructions and sent them out to patrol. Billy wasn't among them; he had too much to do at the Cottonwood. The big supper was tonight.

With all the new people in town for the festivities, trouble was liable to come with them. Pickpockets, con men, thieves. Jared hadn't seen any problems yet, hadn't had reports of any, or complaints from citizens. Mostly all he'd done was give directions to the newcomers and answer their questions. Which suited him just fine.

Down the street, Jared saw Billy and the Spencer girls standing in front of the Cottonwood Café, shading their eyes from the sun, waiting to catch a glimpse of the parade when it started.

The Cottonwood had been open for breakfast, but was closed now to decorate the dining room and get ready for tonight's supper. Jared had gone by this morning and eaten in the kitchen. Thanks to all the visitors to Stanford, business had been brisk.

The restaurant's door opened and Mattie stepped outside. Jared made his way through the crowd toward her.

"Howdy, Sheriff," Billy called. He gestured with his hand. "Ain't this something?"

"It sure is." Jared smiled at Mattie. "How's everything going inside?"

She smiled back, and they walked a few feet away from the others. "All on schedule."

"Are you feeling all right? You're not overdoing it, are you?"

"I'm fine."

A few minutes passed while Mattie gazed up at him. She'd been doing that a lot in the last few days—just looking at him. He'd seen her on the street and in the mercantile once, and each time, he'd caught her watching, as if she were studying him, thinking hard about something. Jared didn't know what.

"You sure you're feeling all right?" he asked.

"Never better." Mattie smiled gently. "Never."

A cheer rose from the crowd. Because Jared was taller, he saw the parade heading their way.

"I've got to go." He escorted her to Billy's side, away from the press of people, so she wouldn't get jostled. "I'll be back later."

Having everyone's attention focused on the parade created a perfect opportunity for criminals to strike. Jared moved through the crowd, keeping an eye on the businesses and citizens rather than the brightly decorated wagons passing by.

When the parade ended, everyone gathered around the grandstand to hear Stanford's volunteer band play, listen to the speeches and get a closer look at the investors. Jared made a sweep of the nearly deserted businesses, then headed toward the grandstand.

A flash of blue darted in front of him, and Chuckie Waldron kicked him in the knee.

Jared squeezed his lips together to keep from cursing. He didn't have time to waste on this kid, not today of all days. But when he swung around, sure the boy would have darted away as he usually did, he found Chuckie glaring up at him.

"I ain't 'fraid of no lawman," the boy declared. He squinted his eyes at Jared and stuck out his chin.

A town full of strangers, and this was his biggest criminal.

Jared rubbed his knee. "Go home, Chuckie. I haven't got time for you."

Chuckie pushed his chin farther out. "I ain't going nowhere, and you can't make me."

Jared's irritation grew. "Look, Chuckie, you'd better go home before you get into serious trouble."

"You can take me to jail. I don't care."

"Look here, you'd—"

Chuckie stuck out his tongue and wiggled his butt back and forth.

"All right. That's it. Let's go."

Jared expected the boy to turn tail and run for home, but he didn't. Instead, he followed Jared down the boardwalk.

Darn kid. He needed to be taught a lesson. But Jared didn't have time today. Still, he couldn't just turn away and let a five-year-old get the upper hand.

Jared paused at the edge of the boardwalk, ready to cross the street. Tiny fingers curled against his palm, sending a rush up his arm. He looked down to find Chuckie holding his hand.

"I'm not 'posed to cross the street by myself," he explained.

Jared's heart softened. "That happens with a lot of the outlaws I know."

Hand in hand, they crossed the street and stepped up onto the boardwalk on the other side.

"Are you 'resting me, Sheriff?" Chuckie asked excitedly, bouncing on his toes, still clinging to Jared's hand.

No, he intended to take him to his parents down at the barbershop and let them figure out what to do with the boy. But Chuckie had other ideas. He broke free of Jared's hand and raced ahead, darting into the jailhouse.

"Is them the cells, Sheriff?" Chuckie's eyes were big as saucers as he pointed down the hallway. "Is that where you're putting me?"

"That's where prisoners go. Looks pretty scary, doesn't it."

"Shoot, no," Chuckie declared, hitching up his trousers. He dashed down the hallway and into one of the cells. "See? I ain't scared."

Hellfire, probably half the town was getting carried away by shoplifters at this moment, and here Jared was fooling around with this kid.

"Go home, Chuckie."

"Huh-uh." The boy folded his arms across his chest.

Jared blew out an exasperated sigh. "You want to be in jail? Fine, you'll be in jail." He swung the door closed and stalked away.

He hadn't gone halfway across his office when Chuckie let out a piercing scream that turned him around. The boy stood in the center of the cell, arms at his sides, face turned up, big tears cascading down his cheeks.

"I don't want to be no outlaw no more," Chuckie wailed. "I don't like this place!"

Jared opened the door, which had never been locked, and knelt in front of the boy.

"I want my mama!"

Surely Chuckie Waldron wasn't the first person locked in this cell to think that.

"Come on, son, we'll get your mama." Jared picked him up. Chuckie collapsed onto his shoulder, squeezing his neck and crying in his ear.

The Cottonwood Café surely rivaled the finest restaurant in the East, Jared decided as he took his seat along with everyone else. Mattie's decorating ideas had transformed the Café's cozy, homey atmosphere to one of refined elegance. White tablecloths gleamed in the candlelight, fresh roses added a touch of color, all highlighted by blue bunting draped artfully around the room.

The mayor and councilmen, Stanford's businessmen, their wives, and the Easterners had all turned out in their best attire. Jared had put on his Sunday shirt and tie.

But truthfully, he didn't want to be here, and had come only because the council insisted. Jared wanted to be back in the kitchen helping Mattie. This was a big day for her, and a lot was riding on her shoulders. He'd stopped by earlier, expecting total chaos in the kitchen, but instead had found it almost serene. Everyone knew their job and went about it efficiently. Jared was pleased to see that Billy handed out directions and answered questions, relieving Mattie of much of the responsibility.

Still, whether they needed him in the kitchen or not, it was where Jared wanted to be. He worried that Mattie was overdoing it, tiring herself too much, physically as well as emotionally.

When the mayor finally finished his remarks, Reverend Harris offered a prayer, and supper was announced.

The Spencer girls looked pretty in dark blue skirts, crisp white blouses and red aprons as they served. Conversation hummed softly; forks clicked against plates. When dessert and coffee were finished, Mayor Rayburn rose with his napkin tucked under his chin, calling Mattie's name. As she slipped through the curtain from the kitchen, the mayor thanked her for the fine meal, and everyone applauded. She beamed with delight. Jared had never been more proud of anyone in his life.

Afterward, when everyone finally left the restaurant, Jared went into the kitchen. Mrs. Nance, Billy and the Spencer girls were all busy cleaning, washing and scrubbing. Mattie, her sleeves rolled back, dried dishes.

When she saw Jared, she let out a whoop and threw her arms around his neck. It took all his strength not to whirl her around or squeeze too tightly.

"Everything went perfectly!" she declared, wide-eyed and smiling. She waved the dish towel in her hand around the kitchen. "Thanks to these wonderful people."

"You all did a great job," Jared declared. "The food was the best I ever tasted."

"Everyone else must have thought so, too," Mrs. Nance said. "We've hardly a crumb left over."

"Are you about finished up for the night?" Jared asked. Though he'd never seen Mattie happier, he could tell the day had been tough on her. She looked tired and a little pale. He wanted to get her home and off her feet.

"Just awhile longer," Mattie said.

"Can I borrow Billy?" When Mattie nodded, Jared whispered to him and sent him out the back door. "I'll give you a hand in the dining room."

By the time they'd collected the candles and flowers from each table, folded the cloths and put out the blue checkered ones, Mrs. Nance and the Spencer girls had finished everything in the kitchen.

"Good night," Mattie called as they all went out the back door together. "Get some rest. We'll surely have a busy day tomorrow."

Jared tucked Mattie's arm in his as they headed toward her house. To his pleasure, she didn't protest. In fact, she seemed to accept it as normal. But it concerned him that she walked a little slower than usual; the day had taken its toll.

Mattie couldn't remember when she'd been so tired. Everything ached. But she was filled with so much excitement she couldn't keep quiet. Jared didn't seem to mind as she told him every little thing that had happened at the Cottonwood today.

When they reached her house, Mattie stopped suddenly. Lantern light burned in the windows.

Jared patted her hand. "I sent Billy over to make things comfortable for you."

Please and surprised, Mattie smiled. "How thoughtful."

"Couldn't do any less for the owner of the most prosperous restaurant in Stanford."

When they got inside there was no sign of Billy. Flickering lanterns softly illuminated the kitchen, and steam rose from the bathtub in the corner.

Mattie's knees nearly gave out. "You had Billy make me a bath? Oh, Jared...that's just the sweetest thing."

"Now, don't cry." Jared waved his hand frantically. "Go get your nightclothes and get into the tub."

Mattie fetched her things, then closed the curtain around the tub, undressed and sank into the warm water.

Heavenly. Absolutely heavenly. She lay back, resting her head against the tub, and slid deeper into the water.

On the other side of the curtain, she heard Jared moving around the kitchen. Here she sat, naked, with only a thin piece of fabric and his honor separating them, and Mattie didn't feel uncomfortable at all. In fact, having him close at such an intimate moment seemed completely normal.

Mattie closed her eyes, comfortable and secure.

She stayed in the water until it started to cool and she could barely hold her eyes open. Her limbs seemed heavy and sluggish as she dried herself and slipped her yellow nightgown over her head. When she pulled back the curtain, Jared waited.

Her heart beat a little faster at the sight of him. Seemingly, it was the only part of her moving. Her feet stuck to the floor and her breathing nearly stopped.

Strong, sturdy Jared. Handsome. Thoughtful, kind, caring. It seemed he'd been in her life forever, he fit so well. He belonged there, with her.

The idea didn't scare Mattie. Instead, it pleased her.

Yet where had that notion come from? What did it mean? For so long she'd struggled to hold Jared at arm's length. Now she was comfortable with his closeness. How had that happened? When had it happened? Did it mean that she'd accepted him? That these deeper feelings for him meant she'd fallen in—

"Feeling better?" Jared asked, still standing across the room from her.

Mattie touched her hand to her nightgown, aware of how thin it was. "Much better. But tired."

"You should get into bed." He came forward, but instead of motioning her out of the room, he blocked her path. A long moment dragged by while he just looked at her, sending a charge through her.

"Would it be all right if I...?" he began.

She expected him to ask if he could kiss her, he had

such a look of love on his face. He'd never asked before, he'd just done it. But this time, the intensity of his expression seemed deeper.

"Would it be all right," he asked softly, "if I touched the baby?"

Mattie's heart melted, then swelled so suddenly she thought it might burst through her chest.

"Please?" he asked.

"It's not moving yet, or—"

"Please."

She nodded. "Of course."

Standing sideways next to her, Jared looped one arm around her shoulder and rested his head against hers. With exquisite care, he placed his palm low on her stomach.

The warmth of his hand spread through her. His breath puffed against her cheek.

"Makes me happy to know she's safe inside you," he whispered against Mattie's ear. "Growing strong. Protected. Where nothing can hurt her."

Jared stood there awhile longer, then moved his hand away and kissed her forehead. "You'd better get into bed."

In her bedroom, he turned down the coverlet. Mattie sank onto the feather mattress and curled onto her side, facing him.

"I didn't know I was so tired," she mumbled.

Jared blew out the lantern and disappeared. But then the bed behind her shifted and she felt his body snuggle against hers.

Mattie roused. "Jared, you can't—"

"I won't stay all night."

Satisfied, Mattie laid her head on the pillow. How comfortable he was against her. All those hard muscles, yet pleasing as an eiderdown quilt.

"Would this be a good time to ask you to marry me?" Jared asked.

"No."

He looped his arm over her and found her hand beneath the covers, then laced their fingers together. "I love you, Mattie."

She fell asleep.

Waking the next morning, Mattie couldn't help but feel a little disappointed that Jared wasn't there. He'd had to leave, of course. It certainly wouldn't do for him to be seen leaving her place in the morning. But the bed, the house, everything seemed a little empty without him.

Everything, including her life. Mattie couldn't imagine facing a day without him, now. Since she'd talked to Billy and he'd told her all he knew about Jared—the private Jared—she'd begun to think maybe, just maybe, he was truly a nice man. Maybe he was sincere in his feelings. Maybe, just maybe, he really loved her.

With a sigh, Mattie sat up. She wished she could be certain, somehow, that Jared wouldn't turn out like Del. With all her heart she wished it. If only there was some way to know for sure. Something Jared could tell her. Something she could learn that would dispel her fears.

But there was no way to be certain. The leap of faith she'd taken with her first marriage had been a disaster. Mattie wouldn't do that again. Especially now that she had a baby to consider.

Pushing back the covers, she rose, wondering when she'd see Jared today. Business would be brisk at the Cottonwood, and he had his hands full, with all the visitors in town.

She peered out her window. Seemed she wouldn't have to wait to see Jared, after all. He was out back.

But what she didn't understand was why he was digging a big hole in her yard.

Chapter Twenty-Two

When Mattie stepped onto her back porch, tieing her robe around her, Jared stopped digging. The morning sun edged over the horizon, coloring the gray dawn a bright orange.

He smiled broadly and waved, then planted the shovel in the loose dirt and walked over. "'Morning."

"Why are you digging a hole in my backyard?"

"For the baby." Jared pushed past her into the kitchen. "How about some coffee?"

"The baby?" Mattie followed him inside and closed the door.

Jared pumped water into the basin and washed his hands. "I'm planting a tree."

Mattie raised an eyebrow, wondering if the morning sun was hotter than she'd thought. "You're planting a tree for the baby?"

"For shade. She'll need a cool place to play." Jared dried his hands and tossed the linen towel on the sideboard, then pointed out the window. "I'm planting it in just the right spot where we can keep an eye on her from in here.''

''But, Jared, it will be years before she can play under a shade tree.''

''Meaning what?'' He looked hard at her. ''That you don't think I'll be around when it happens?''

Mattie's shoulders sagged under the weight of his accusation. How delightful it would be to imagine the two of them watching their baby through the window together in the years to come. To grow close, grow old.

With all her heart she wished she could tell him she believed all those things would happen. But Mattie couldn't.

He seemed to read her thoughts. ''You don't think I'll stick around, do you?''

Sorrowfully, Mattie shook her head. ''No, Jared, I don't. I'm sorry, but I don't.''

''Because of Del.''

She sighed heavily. ''Yes.''

''Don't you believe me when I say I love you?'' Jared took a step closer. ''Don't you trust me yet?''

He sounded hurt and she couldn't blame him. Still, she had to be truthful. ''I want to, Jared. Truly, I do. But I'm afraid things will turn out the way they did with Del.''

''He didn't love you. I do.''

''You don't understand,'' Mattie insisted. ''Marriage is a tremendous commitment. You don't know what you'd be getting yourself into.''

"I won't change after we're married."

"You don't know that."

"Yes, I do," Jared told her, a hint of anger in his voice.

"You make promises, but you can't know if you'll keep them. Things change after the wedding. People change."

"I won't change."

Mattie clenched her fist. "You can't know that!"

"Yes, I can!"

"No, you can't—"

"I know because I used to be married!"

She gasped, the fight, the anger, the very breath going out of her.

Jared looked stunned, as if he hadn't meant to blurt that out. He squeezed his eyes shut for an instant and rubbed his fingers hard against his forehead, then turned away.

"You...you were married?" Mattie asked.

"Yes, I was married," he said, hardly above a whisper. Another moment passed, and finally, he turned back to her. "A long time ago."

Mattie gaped at him, trying to understand. He'd been married? She'd had no idea, no inkling.

But maybe she had, Mattie realized, thinking back on how understanding and concerned he'd been over her and the baby she carried. How careful. How he seemed to know things that an unmarried man shouldn't know.

She took a step closer, but sensed he needed some

distance between them, so she didn't go any farther. The pain, though old, showed in his face.

"Do you want to tell me about it? If you don't, I'll understand."

He looked away once more, as if gathering strength, then straightened his shoulders and turned to her.

"Lucy and I met when we were just kids in school. The minute I laid eyes on her I knew I loved her. Such a pretty thing." Jared smiled faintly. "We still weren't much more than kids when we got married. Bought us a few acres, starting farming. Happy...we were so happy."

"What happened?" Mattie asked.

"She died." His smile disappeared. Jared drew in a deep breath as if fortifying himself against the memory. "Lucy died...calling out my name...trying to bring our baby into the world."

"Oh, Jared..." Tears sprang to Mattie's eyes and she wanted to run to him, hold him, but couldn't find the strength to move. "The...the baby?"

Jared shook his head. "He didn't make it, either."

Protectively, Mattie's hand went to her stomach. Jared followed her movement, and it seemed to rob him of all his strength. He sank into the kitchen chair. With his foot, he pushed out the chair next to him. Mattie sat down.

"After that, I couldn't bear living there," Jared said. "I sold the farm and took off. Ended up a marshal. Dealing with scum and criminals seemed a relief, in a way. I didn't have to be nice, didn't have to pretend I cared about anybody or anything. They were easy to hate—and I hated everybody.''

"But you changed, Jared. You're not that kind of man now."

"It finally wore off. Took a long time, but it did. Took a lot longer, still, to figure out what I wanted in life." He uttered a short laugh. "In a way, I have Del Ingram to thank for that."

"Because he died?"

"Probably the only good thing the bastard ever did," Jared said. "When I laid eyes on you at Del's funeral, Mattie, I knew what I wanted. I knew I was ready."

She smiled. "You wanted a family again."

"Yes." He reached across the table and took her hand. "So you see, I do know what it's like to love a woman. To have a wife. A home. To want a baby. You don't have to be afraid, Mattie. I won't change. I know what I'm getting into."

She covered his hand with hers. "I know it was painful for you to tell me about your wife and...baby."

"Is it enough to prove that you can trust me?"

"Jared, I—"

A fist pounded on the front door with such force that both Mattie and Jared jumped. She followed him through the house and, when Jared jerked open the door, saw Billy on her porch. His face was white.

"You've got to come, Sheriff. Right now. Trouble at the McCafferty place."

Jared took off without a backward look. Mattie clung to the door, watching him and Billy hurry away.

A pool of uneasiness welled inside her. She wanted to run after Jared, make him come back to her, back where he'd be safe.

He'd left without a word. She hadn't had time to say anything.

Not even to tell him that she'd fallen in love with him.

At the jail, Jared heard what had happened from Mr. Pitney, while Billy got the horses ready.

"I don't know what set McCafferty off," Pitney said. "Just before dawn, I heard him yelling. Heard his wife crying. Terrible things he accused her of. Terrible. That went on for a while. Then I heard gunshots."

"Did you go over there?" Jared asked.

"Sure. Me and Hopkins together. But McCafferty opened fire on us through the window. I came to fetch you, and Hopkins stayed to keep an eye on things."

"Did you see or hear anything of Mrs. McCafferty after the gunshots?"

Pitney shook his head.

"She had the baby yet?"

"Don't know."

Jared pulled two rifles from the rack and left the jail with Pitney as Billy rode up, leading another horse. Jared mounted and tossed one of the guns to Billy.

"The other deputies can keep an eye on things in town," Jared said. "I want you with me."

The three of them rode out of town.

When they reached Pitney's farm, Hopkins came out on the porch to meet them.

"I tried to go over there again, Sheriff," he said. "I worked my way through the trees and called out, but McCafferty opened fired like before."

Jared dismounted. "Could you see inside the house?"

"No, sir."

"Hear anything?"

"You mean like the wife?" Hopkins shook his head. "Not a sound."

"What about the baby? Did you hear it crying?"

"Didn't hear nothing."

Jared studied the lay of the land between Pitney's place and McCafferty's. Trees offered enough cover for him to get close, but the yard that surrounded the house was wide-open.

"What's your plan, Sheriff?" Pitney asked.

"With the woman in there and maybe a baby, I don't want any shooting. I'll try to talk him out first," Jared said. "If that doesn't work, Billy, you draw his fire and I'll go in through the back."

Billy straightened his shoulders. "Yes, sir."

"We'll cover your right flank," Pitney said. He ducked inside and came out with two rifles.

"No shooting into the McCafferty house," Jared told them.

Jared and Billy crossed the road and eased through the trees. Pitney and Hopkins worked their way to the opposite side of the McCafferty house, using Pitney's barns and outbuildings for cover. When Jared saw they were in position, he called out, identifying himself and telling McCafferty to come out with his hands up.

Gunfire shattered a side window and a bullet dug into the tree just above Jared's head.

At the next tree over, Billy gulped. "Guess that's your answer, Sheriff."

"I guess it is." Still, Jared tried again. A hail of bullets peppered the trees. Bark splintered. Limbs and leaves ripped away. Jared and Billy dived to the ground.

"I'll work my way around back," Jared said. "You cover me."

Billy nodded. "Yes, sir."

"And don't fire into the house."

"No, sir, I won't."

Jared looked at him for a moment. Billy seemed to know what he was thinking.

"Don't worry, Sheriff. I got you covered."

Billy squeezed off a couple of shots as Jared made his way toward the rear of the house. In the distance, he heard Pitney and Hopkins firing, too. When he reached the back door, Jared kicked it open. He sprang inside, rifle at his shoulder, finger on the trigger.

He only had a second to see Mrs. McCafferty on the floor before a shot exploded in the room.

* * *

"Come, sit down," Mrs. Nance said.

Mattie pressed closer to the front window of the Cottonwood, her gaze trained on the street, and shook her head. "No, I can't."

Most of the breakfast crowd had left the café already, yet those remaining talked about the same thing. Word had spread quickly through town this morning about the shooting at the McCafferty place.

Rumors and speculation had hopped like wildfire from table to table since the restaurant opened. McCafferty was unstable. He'd had problems before he'd moved to Stanford. People talked about his wife, whom almost no one knew. The baby.

And Jared was there now.

Mattie pressed her fingers to her lips, trying to keep calm. That he'd spent ten years as a marshal dealing with criminals far worse than McCafferty should have relieved her concern for Jared. It didn't. He knew what he was doing, she knew. Still, she worried.

"It's not good for you to be standing here like this," Mrs. Nance said. "You or the baby."

Mattie touched her hand protectively to her stomach. The baby. Jared's baby. What if—

Mrs. Nance took her arm. "Come into the kitchen and get off your feet."

Mattie shook her head. "No. I want to stay here. I want—"

"He'll be fine," Mrs. Nance said. "The sheriff knows his business. He'll come back to you."

"And if he doesn't?" The horror of that possibility sent a wave of panic through Mattie. What if Jared didn't return? If she never saw him again? If she lost him—forever? How could she go on without him when she loved him so much?

And, yes, she did love him. She'd loved him for a long time—probably right from the beginning—but had been afraid to face her own feelings.

Mattie wasn't afraid anymore. Except for Jared's safety.

"Now, don't get yourself all upset," Mrs. Nance said, leading her across the dining room. "You don't even know for sure what's going on out there. Come into the kitchen."

A rumble rose from the diners. Mattie spun around as several clattered to the windows. She tore away from Mrs. Nance and pushed through the crowd.

A wagon rolled down Main Street. Billy sat up top. Pitney and Hopkins rode beside him. A single horse was tethered to the tailgate. Inside lay two shrouded bodies.

Mattie gasped and plastered her palm to the glass, her gaze sweeping the street. Jared. Where was Jared?

She shoved her way through the diners. Mrs. Nance grabbed her arm, but Mattie shook her off and charged outside, running after the wagon.

People gawked from the boardwalk. Traffic slowed, the drivers looking.

"Billy!"

The wagon stopped. There were two bodies in the

back, Mattie saw. One small. One big. Big enough to be Jared?

Mattie bit back tears. No, no, it couldn't be. It just couldn't.

Breathless, frantic, she gazed up at Billy. He seemed to have aged ten years. No expression showed on his face, just a blank, haunted look, as if he'd seen too much.

"Jared?" she asked, barely able to choke out the word.

Billy seemed lost for a moment. "At the jail. The reverend's on his way."

Chapter Twenty-Three

Mattie hurried toward the jailhouse, a hundred thoughts exploding in her mind. Would Jared be there? Was he injured? Why had Billy sent for Reverend Harris?

As long as Jared was alive, Mattie silently swore, she could deal with anything else. *Please, God, make him be alive.*

Steeling herself, Mattie burst through the door to his office. Her knees nearly gave out.

Jared. There he sat, calm and composed, gently swaying in the rocking chair beside the stove.

Tears sprang to her eyes. Thank God. Thank God everything was all right.

Mattie rushed to him, but stopped abruptly halfway across the room at the sight of the odd little bundle cradled in Jared's arms.

A sickening knot rose in her throat. No, everything was not all right.

A few seconds passed before Jared's gaze came up

to meet hers. His face was drawn, haggard, as if, like Billy, he, too, had seen too much.

"The...bodies in the wagon?" she asked.

"The McCaffertys." Jared's voice sounded hollow, empty.

Another moment passed while Mattie pulled together enough courage to question him further. She gestured to the bundle in his arms.

"Is that—" Her voice broke. She tried again. "Is that...their baby?"

Tears welled in Jared's eyes. He nodded slowly.

Mattie blinked hard, trying to hold back her own tears. "Is it...?"

"Sleeping." Jared gulped.

Her knees nearly gave out. "It's all right?"

Jared glanced down. "He slept through everything. As if, somehow, he knows what's waiting for him when he wakes up."

She sank to her knees beside the rocker, tears trickling down her cheeks.

"The little fella's got nothing," Jared said hoarsely. "No mama. No papa. Not even a name."

Gently, Mattie pulled the blanket away from the baby's face. Tiny, fragile, the newborn had his eyes closed in peaceful slumber. She glided her thumb across his cheek, the softness skimming up her arm, straight to her heart.

She sniffed back her tears. "What happened?"

"From the looks of things, Mrs. McCafferty gave

birth during the night. Her husband shot her, killed her, this morning.''

"But why?''

"Damned if I know…. Pitney said he heard Mc-Cafferty screaming at her, saying she wasn't pure anymore, the baby wasn't his. Crazy things like that.'' Jared shook his head. "McCafferty turned the gun on himself, took his own life.''

"Now we'll never know the why of it.'' Mattie stroked her fingers through the baby's dark hair. "What will happen to the little one?''

"Billy's sending Reverend Harris over here to get him. They'll take care of him, find him a home.'' Jared snuggled the baby a little closer. "I…I just wanted to hold him for a while.''

Mattie wanted to hold them both. She pressed her palm against the baby and settled her head on Jared's shoulder.

Sometime later, when the reverend and his wife arrived, Jared reluctantly turned the baby over to them.

"Oh, you poor little dear,'' Mrs. Harris murmured, folding the child in her arms. "Don't worry, we're going to take good care of you. Find you a new home, and a mama and papa who'll raise you proper.''

"Did the McCaffertys have any family?'' Jared asked.

Reverend Harris shook his head. "None I know of. I'll send a telegram, see what I can uncover.''

"Do you know any families around here willing to take a newborn?" Jared asked.

"We'll find someone," Mrs. Harris promised.

"But what if you don't?" Mattie asked.

"There's always the orphans' asylum over in Carson City," the reverend said. "Hopefully, it won't come to that."

When the minister and his wife left with the baby, Mattie felt a little part of herself going with them. She glanced up at Jared. He took a step toward the door, and for a moment Mattie thought he intended to take the baby back, but he didn't.

He shook his head wearily. "Let's get out of here."

They headed to the Cottonwood. Jared seemed to walk a little slower, hold her arm a little tighter. Mattie stepped carefully. The life growing inside her suddenly seemed more fragile and precious.

Billy sat on the restaurant's back steps when they arrived, still looking as if most of the spirit had drained out of him.

"You did yourself proud out there today," Jared said. "I was glad to have you as my deputy."

Billy shook his head. "You can forget about talking to Aunt Frannie about me being a lawman. I don't want to be no deputy anymore. Not after today."

Mattie couldn't blame him. Jared didn't object, either. "What will you do?" she asked.

"Reckon I'll head back East and work in my uncle's can factory." Billy rose from the steps. "I'll help you out here at the restaurant, Miss Mattie, until I go. If'n that's all right with you.''

"Of course, Billy," she said. "But you don't have to work today. If you need time off, it's understandable.''

"No, ma'am. I'd rather stay busy."

He ambled into the Cottonwood. Mattie hated to see him leave Stanford, but couldn't really blame him. Even Jared, hardened by years as a lawman, had been affected by what he'd seen today. It was all the more difficult for Billy.

"Hungry?" Mattie asked.

Jared shrugged, as if it didn't matter. "I have to take care of some…things."

He'd have to write the official report, answer questions of everyone he'd encounter, relive this morning over and over. Mattie wanted to shelter him from that, even if it was just for a short while.

"You need to eat something first," she said, overcome by the need to feed him, take care of him.

Inside the Cottonwood, Mattie made sure Mrs. Nance, Billy and the Spencer girls had everything under control, then packed a basket. She and Jared went to her house.

"Do you think Reverend Harris will find a home for the McCafferty baby?" Mattie asked, as she emptied the basket on her kitchen table.

Jared hung his hat by the door and took plates from the cupboard. "Sure."

"But a good home? One where he'll be loved?"

Jared shook his head wearily. "I don't know, Mattie. I just wish..."

"Wish what?"

"I don't know." He turned away.

What he needed at the moment wasn't the food she'd brought. Mattie looped her arms around his waist and pressed herself against his back. He was tense, rigid.

"You don't feel guilty about what happened, do you?" she asked. "Thinking that if you'd done things differently, or gotten there sooner, it would have changed things?"

"No." Jared covered her hands with his and seemed to relax a little. "No matter what I might have done differently, it wouldn't have changed anything. Mc-Cafferty being the kind of man he was, things would have ended the same, sooner or later."

He turned in the circle of her arms. "It's just such a waste," he said.

Mattie snuggled closer, resting her head on his chest, anxious to comfort him, to give him what strength she had. They held each other for a long while, content with the silence.

Finally, Mattie spoke. "Would this be a good time to tell you that I love you?"

She felt him grow tense again. Mattie looked up and smiled. "I love you, Jared."

He frowned. "You do?"

"Yes," she said, smiling wider.

His frown deepened. "What made you decide that?"

"Your considerable charms just won me over."

"Finally?" He snorted. "I sure as hell worked hard enough at it."

"You're not done yet." Mattie looped her arms around his neck. "I don't want to think about death anymore. Or husbands hurting wives. Or babies being orphaned."

Jared leaned his head down. "I can make you forget."

"I seem to recall that you're quite good at that," Mattie said, rubbing her cheek against his.

He captured her lips with a deep kiss. "You're sure?"

"Very sure," she whispered.

Once more he kissed her, blending their mouths together until he moaned. Mattie rose on tiptoes, welcoming him, twining her fingers through his hair. He stopped, took her hand and led her to the bedroom.

A cool afternoon breeze floated through the windows as Mattie stood with Jared at the side of the bed. When they'd done this before, it was in the dark, and in a frantic rush. Now, neither of them hurried.

Slowly, Jared undressed her, stripping away the layers of her clothing, tossing them aside until she was naked. She returned the favor, pulling off his clothes, revealing his hard, muscular body. They gazed at each other, smiling, enjoying the sight.

Mattie had never felt so at ease before, yet never so

excited. And never so sure that this was exactly where she belonged in life. Here, with Jared.

She stepped into his embrace and he welcomed her with hot kisses that trailed down her neck. His hands cupped her bottom, pressing her against him, then rose to capture her breasts.

Her hands wandered over his wide shoulders, through the curly hair of his chest, then lower. Jared groaned, kissing her more deeply, then scooped her up and onto the bed.

He couldn't get enough of her. The taste. The feel. The scent that was her. Jared kissed her, touched her, explored until she writhed beneath his hand. She returned his favors, teasing, caressing, until he couldn't tolerate the wait.

Mattie slid her leg along his, urging him closer. He eased between her thighs, fighting the need to drive himself into her, remembering that inside her, along with the supreme delight only she could provide, was also his baby.

Instead, he rocked gently against her—cautiously, carefully, straining to hold back.

Mattie didn't make it easy for him. She pulled at his hair, pushing her hips up to meet his until she exploded around him. He held on for a few seconds, then followed. Sweet relief overtook him, and he collapsed on the bed beside her.

"I have a confession," Mattie whispered.

"Hmm..."

Beside her, Jared lay with his eyes closed as evening shadows stretched across the bedroom. His chest rose and fell evenly; his features were relaxed.

"I asked Billy about you, about what kind of person you are."

"Uh-huh."

Mattie pushed herself up on her elbow. "Jared, are you listening?"

"Hmm?" His eyes opened, then fluttered closed again. "Yeah...sure..."

"I wanted to ask him if you'd been to the parlor house since you'd arrived in Stanford, but I was too embarrassed." She stroked her fingers across his chest. "But I have my answer now. You've been saving up, all right."

Something resembling a grin pulled at his lips. "Just for you..."

"Jared?"

"Hmm...?"

"This would be a good time for you to ask me to marry you."

"Okay..." A moment passed, then Jared opened one eye. "Huh?"

Mattie smiled. "I said, this would be a good time to ask me to marry you."

"*Huh?*" Jared launched himself upright in the bed, sending pillow and coverlet flying. "What? Huh? What did you say?"

Mattie fell back on her pillow. "You heard me."

"You'll marry me?"

She traced her finger down his chest. "If you ask me."

Jared caught her hand, kissed her palm, then pressed it against his cheek. "Mattie, will you marry me?"

"Yes, Jared, I'll marry you." Mattie opened her arms, expecting a hug, a deep kiss to seal their commitment. Instead, Jared jumped out of bed.

"Come on. Get up. Let's go," he ordered, scrambling around the room, gathering their clothes.

"Go? Go where?"

"To the church. Right now." He stopped and pointed his finger at her. "I'm not taking any chances that you'll change your mind."

"I won't change my mind."

Jared jerked his thumb. "Out of bed. Now."

Mattie rolled her eyes. "Reverend Harris is going to love this."

"Reverend Harris?" Jared called, striding through the church door, pulling Mattie along with him.

The minister, seated in the first pew, head bowed in prayer, got to his feet. "Is something wrong, Sheriff? Did something happen?"

"No, sir. Everything's fine. Fine and dandy."

"I was just praying for the McCafferty baby," Reverend Harris said. "Praying for a good home."

Jared nodded toward the door. "Your wife told us you were here. She's on her way over."

"What for?" The reverend looked back and forth between the two of them.

Taking Mattie's hand firmly in his, Jared said, "I want you to marry us. Right now."

"No, no, no." Reverend Harris wagged his head so hard his shoulders shook. "I'm not marrying you two. Not after last time."

"She wants to marry me. Just ask her." Jared nudged Mattie with his elbow. "Tell him, honey."

"It's true, Reverend. I love Jared very much."

"See? She loves me."

"And I want to marry him."

"Right now," Jared added.

Mattie smiled. "Yes. Right now."

"I don't know..." Reverend Harris stroked his chin, shaking his head.

The church door opened and Mrs. Harris bustled down the aisle, carrying a bundle of daisies. "The baby's sound asleep, like a little angel." She pressed flowers to her heart and smiled warmly at Mattie. "Oh, a wedding! I love weddings."

"There's not going to be a wedding," Reverend Harris said.

"Sure there is." Jared grabbed the daisies from Mrs. Harris and thrust them at Mattie. "See? We've got flowers. It's a wedding. Come on. Let's get this show on the road."

"Jared, please." Mattie patted his arm. "Reverend, I know I wasn't sure the last time we were here, but I'm sure now. I love Jared. I want to be his wife. Please, marry us."

Reverend Harris's gaze swept between the two of them. "You truly love this man?" he asked.

Mattie snuggled closer to Jared. "Truly."

"And you love this woman?"

"Oh, hell, yes—excuse me, Reverend. Yes, sir, I love her."

Another moment passed while Reverend Harris contemplated their future, then he finally nodded. "All right. I'll marry you."

"Great." Jared waved his hand. "Get on with it."

"Jared," Mattie admonished.

"Sorry," he mumbled. "You just take your time, Reverend. Handle this ceremony as you see fit."

The minister fetched his Bible from the altar and opened it solemnly. "Dearly beloved, we are gathered together—"

"Wait." Mattie looked up at Jared. "I can keep the restaurant, can't I?"

"Sure," he said, then he spoke to the reverend. "Go ahead."

Reverend Harris adjusted his spectacles. "Let's see, oh yes. We are gathered together to join this—"

"Reverend? Hold up a minute." Jared turned to Mattie. "But we'll get you extra help when you're further along with the baby. I don't want you wearing yourself out."

Mattie nodded. "That's fine."

"Get on with it, Reverend."

The minister cleared his throat. "Do you, Jared

McQuaid, take this woman to be your lawfully wedded wife—''

"Excuse me, Reverend," Mattie said. "Jared, I'd like to continue living in my house. You don't mind, do you? Considering…everything?''

"Your house is perfect," Jared declared.

Reverend Harris drummed his fingers on the pages of his Bible. "May I continue?''

"Sure thing," Jared told him.

He grunted, then lifted his Bible higher. "Do you promise to—''

"Jared, I just can't stand the thought of the McCafferty baby going to strangers," Mattie said. "I know I should have mentioned it sooner, but you should know how I feel before we're married. Do you think that we, I mean, would it be all right if you and I—''

"I was hoping you'd say that." He smiled down at her and gave her hand a squeeze. "We'll talk about it when we're finished here. See what the reverend thinks.''

"Oh, of course." Mattie smiled at Reverend Harris. "Sorry. Please go on with the ceremony.''

"There's nothing else you two need to discuss?'' he asked, his lips pinched together.

Mattie and Jared considered each other for a moment.

"Nope. Not me," Jared said.

"I'm fine with everything," Mattie agreed.

"Good." Reverend Harris drew in a deep breath.

"Do you, Mattie Ingram, take this man to be your lawfully wedded husband? To love, honor and obey—"

"Stop!" Mattie rolled her eyes at Jared. "You don't expect me to *obey* you, do you?"

He just grinned. "Mattie, honey, it never occurred to me for a minute that you would."

"Then, yes," Mattie told the reverend. "Yes, to everything."

"I now pronounce you man and wife." Reverend Harris closed his Bible with a snap. "And praise the Lord."

Epilogue

Mattie woke to the same sound she'd fallen asleep to, the gentle creaking of the rocking chair at her bedside. Cold winter winds buffeted the house, but tucked beneath the covers, she was warm and secure.

And tired. Bringing a new baby into the world caused that.

Seated in the rocker, Jared looked just as tired. He'd clucked over her relentlessly the last few months of her pregnancy, then paced and fretted, not sleeping a wink last night or this morning during her labor. He'd burst through the bedroom door at the baby's first cry, haggard and sick with worry.

But Mattie had been fine, the baby healthy and strong, well on the way to being spoiled rotten, because Jared refused to put the little thing down.

"Have you been here all this time?" Mattie asked.

"And where else should I be, besides with my wife and new daughter?" Jared smiled down at the baby in his arms. "The streets of Stanford will be safe without me for a while."

The town council had long ago appointed a deputy, not counting Chuckie Waldron, whom Jared had deputized in a ceremony at the jailhouse and presented with a toy gun and a silver star from the Bloomingdale Brothers catalog.

"Are things going all right at the Cottonwood?" Mattie asked.

"Billy's handling things just fine," Jared assured her.

They'd hired Billy to manage the restaurant full-time, since Mattie had had little time or energy in the last few months to run it herself.

"Did you think about a name?" Mattie asked.

"Ann Elizabeth McQuaid sounds fine to me," Jared told her. "Is it all right if we call her Annie?"

"Sounds perfect."

"If you're feeling up to it we'll introduce her to her brother tonight."

A week after they were married, the McCafferty baby had become John Jared McQuaid, and right now was being cared for by Mrs. Harris.

Jared rose from the rocker, carefully holding the pink-bundled baby, and dug a small package from the dresser drawer. He knelt beside the bed and handed it to Mattie.

"It's for our daughter," he said.

Mattie smiled, remembering the evening in the restaurant when Jared had insisted on ordering a doll from the catalog to present to the baby the day she was born.

"A little small for a doll, isn't it?" Mattie asked, peeling away the wrapping.

"I decided to give her something different."

"Goodness, you're full of surprises." Mattie pried the top off of the box and gasped. "Oh, Jared, what— when—how did you manage?"

He smiled as Mattie lifted her mother's brooch from the box. "I bought it from Mrs. Pomeroy."

"Mrs. Pomeroy did something nice—for *you?*"

"Yeah, well, I've been working my charm on her for a lot of months now. I finally wore her down."

"Oh, Jared, thank you."

He put one arm around Mattie. "Would this be a good time to tell you that I love you?"

She smiled. "It would be a perfect time."

"I love you, Mattie."

"I love you, too."

* * * * *

MONTANA MAVERICKS

MONTANA MAVERICKS HISTORICALS

Discover the origins
of Montana's most popular family...

On sale September 2001
THE GUNSLINGER'S BRIDE
by **Cheryl St.John**
Outlaw Brock Kincaid returns home to make peace with his brothers
and finds love in the arms of an old flame with a secret.

On sale October 2001
WHITEFEATHER'S WOMAN
by **Deborah Hale**
Kincaid Ranch foreman John Whitefeather breaks all the rules when
the Native American dares to fall in love with nanny Jane Harris.

On sale November 2001
A CONVENIENT WIFE
by **Carolyn Davidson**
Whitehorn doctor Winston Gray enters into a marriage of
convenience with a pregnant rancher's daughter, only to
discover he's found his heart's desire!

MONTANA MAVERICKS

**RETURN TO WHITEHORN—WHERE LEGENDS ARE BEGUN
AND LOVE LASTS FOREVER BENEATH THE BIG SKY...**

 Harlequin Historicals°
Historical Romantic Adventure!

TRAVEL TO A LAND LONG AGO
AND FAR AWAY WHEN YOU READ
A HARLEQUIN HISTORICAL NOVEL

ON SALE SEPTEMBER 2001
THE MACKINTOSH BRIDE
by **Debra Lee Brown**
A young clan leader must choose between duty and desire
when he falls in love with a woman from a rival clan.

THE SLEEPING BEAUTY
by **Jacqueline Navin**
A fortune hunter enters into a marriage of convenience
to a beautiful heiress with a mysterious secret.

ON SALE OCTOBER 2001
IRONHEART
by **Emily French**
A brave knight returns from the Holy Land and
is mistaken for a noble lady's betrothed.

AUTUMN'S BRIDE
by **Catherine Archer**
FINAL BOOK IN THE SEASONS' BRIDES SERIES.
When a nobleman is wounded by brigands, a young
woman loses her heart while nursing him back to health.

Visit us at www.eHarlequin.com   HHMED20

Harlequin invites you to walk down the aisle...

To honor our year long celebration of weddings, we are offering an exciting opportunity for you to own the Harlequin Bride Doll. Handcrafted in fine bisque porcelain, the wedding doll is dressed for her wedding day in a cream satin gown accented by lace trim. She carries an exquisite traditional bridal bouquet and wears a cathedral-length dotted Swiss veil. Embroidered flowers cascade down her lace overskirt to the scalloped hemline; underneath all is a multi-layered crinoline.

Join us in our celebration of weddings by sending away for your own Harlequin Bride Doll. This doll regularly retails for $74.95 U.S./approx. $108.68 CDN. One doll per household. Requests must be received no later than December 31, 2001. Offer good while quantities of gifts last. Please allow 6-8 weeks for delivery. Offer good in the U.S. and Canada only. Become part of this exciting offer!

Simply complete the order form and mail to:
"A Walk Down the Aisle"

IN U.S.A	IN CANADA
P.O. Box 9057	P.O. Box 622
3010 Walden Ave.	Fort Erie, Ontario
Buffalo, NY 14269-9057	L2A 5X3

Enclosed are eight (8) proofs of purchase found in the last pages of every specially marked Harlequin series book and $3.75 check or money order (for postage and handling). Please send my Harlequin Bride Doll to:

_____

Name (PLEASE PRINT)

_____

Address   Apt. #

_____

City   State/Prov.   Zip/Postal Code

_____

Account # (if applicable)   **097 KIK DAEW**

HARLEQUIN®
Makes any time special ®

Visit us at www.eHarlequin.com

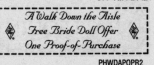

A Walk Down the Aisle
Free Bride Doll Offer
One Proof-of-Purchase

PHWDAPOPR2

COMING SOON...

AN EXCITING
OPPORTUNITY TO SAVE
ON THE PURCHASE OF
HARLEQUIN AND
SILHOUETTE BOOKS!

*DETAILS TO FOLLOW
IN OCTOBER 2001!*

YOU WON'T WANT TO MISS IT!

PHQ401